F

The Good Karm

Michie brings the Buddha s teachings to life through an engaging and enjoyable story showing the power that loving kindness and community have in creating the ideal conditions for awakening.

Sharon Salzberg, author of *Lovingkindness and Real Change*

David's writing is compelling and beautiful, urging the reader onwards to the next page of wisdom and adventure. Wonderfully crafted around very real issues within Zimbabwe, the descriptions of people and places are impossible not to recognise. Magical!

Roxy Danckwerts, Founder, Wild is Life/Zimbabwe Elephant Nursery

This book, like the jewels Rinpoche speaks of, is to be treasured. I read it with delight at the evocative details of the enchanting Zimbabwean sanctuary David has created with the power of his words, and then I read again to absorb the life lessons and the teachings explained so eloquently, as is always the case with his writing. I found myself experiencing a gamut of profound emotions as I read, feeling that I had finally found a story that perfectly explains the infinite connections between humans, animals and nature, a connection that is so central to my own life here in Zimbabwe.

Sarah Carter, Co-Founder, The Twala Trust Animal Sanctuary

The Good Karma Refuge for Elephants is a charming story of belonging and purpose, illuminated by the transformative practice of guru yoga. Michie offers a clear and insightful exploration of how the dharma, guided by the wisdom of a teacher, can infuse an ordinary life with meaning, fulfillment, and enduring connection.

Kimberly Brown, author of *Happy Relationships and Steady, Calm, and Brave*

From the first page to the last, readers will be immersed in this peaceful vista of stunning beauty, long-held customs, and a deep symbiosis between people, land, and animals ... Tenets of Buddhism thread throughout Robbie's journey, as he takes part in constructing a temple, learns the power of reflections like "I am because we are," and grasps that Africa "is a state of being as much as a place."

Publishers Weekly (Booklife Review)

The Good Karma Refuge

for Elephants

Also by David Michie

Fiction
The Dalai Lama's Cat Series

The Dalai Lama's Cat

The Dalai Lama's Cat and The Art of Purring

The Dalai Lama's Cat and The Power of Meow

The Dalai Lama's Cat and The Four Paws of Spiritual Success

The Dalai Lama's Cat: Awaken the Kitten Within

The Dalai Lama's Cat and The Claw of Attraction

Matt Lester Spiritual Thrillers

The Magician of Lhasa

The Secret Mantra

Other Fiction

Instant Karma: The day it happened

The Queen's Corgi

The Astral Traveler's Handbook & Other Tales

Nonfiction

Buddhism for Busy People: Finding Happiness in an Uncertain World

Hurry Up and Meditate: Your Starter Kit for Inner Peace and Better Health

Enlightenment to Go: Shantideva

and the Power of Compassion to Transform Your Life

Mindfulness is Better than Chocolate

Buddhism for Pet Lovers: Supporting our Closest Companions

through Life and Death

The Good Karma Refuge

for Elephants

David Michie

CONCH

CONCH BOOKS

Cover design: Margot Hutton

Editor: Margaret Devere

Author photo: Janmarie Michie

Book design/layout: Jami Carpenter

Cataloguing-in-Publication details are available from the National Library of Australia

www.trove.nla.gov.au

ISBN: 978-0-6458531-3-1

Homage

With heartfelt gratitude to my precious gurus:

Les Sheehy, extraordinary source of inspiration and wisdom;

Geshe Acharya Thubten Loden, peerless master
and embodiment of the Dharma; and

Zasep Tulku Rinpoche, precious Vajra Acharya and yogi.

Guru is Buddha, Guru is Dharma, Guru is Sangha,
Guru is the source of all happiness.
To all gurus I prostrate, make offerings and go for refuge.

May this book carry waves of inspiration from my own gurus
to the hearts and minds of countless living beings.

May all beings have happiness and the true causes of happiness.

May all beings be free from suffering and the true causes of suffering;

May all beings never be parted from the happiness that is without suffering,
the great joy of nirvana liberation; and

May all beings abide in peace and equanimity,
their minds free from attachment and aversion, and free from ignorance.

THE RUWA BUDDHIST SOCIETY

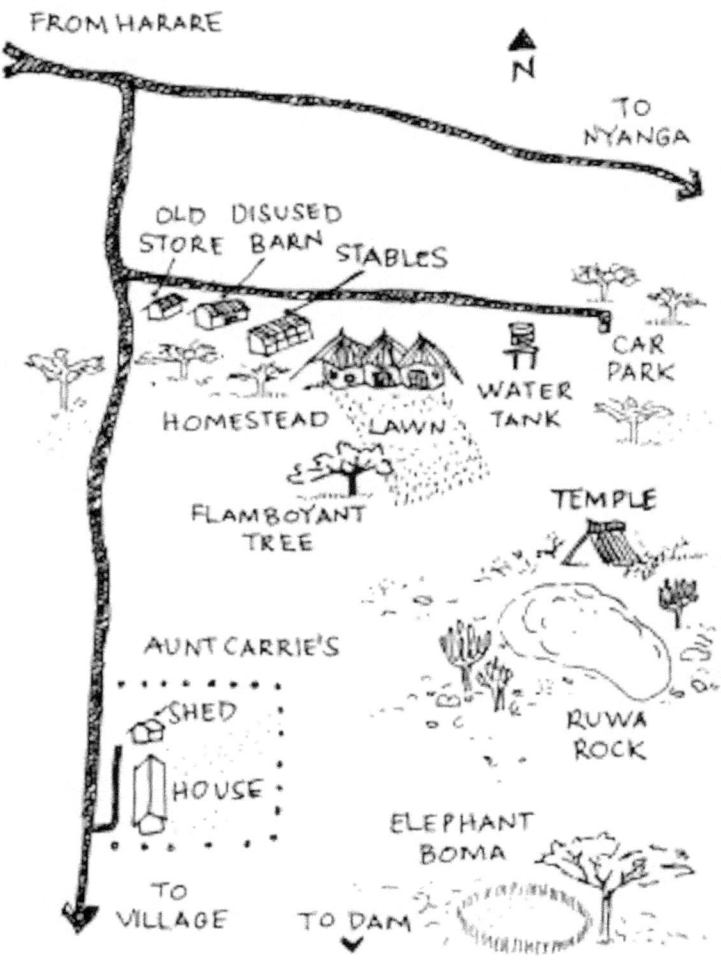

Glossary

Amarula: a creamy, marula-based South African liqueur like Baileys

bakkie: southern African term for a pickup truck

boykie: southern African slang word for a boy or man who is a whiz-kid, leader

dassie: a rock hyrax found in Southern African kopjes

doek: southern African term for headscarf

gogo: an affectionately respectful Zimbabwean term for an elderly woman, literally "grandmother"

gompa: a secluded place of meditation

guti: Shona word for light rain/drizzle or mist

'Jerusalema': an upbeat, Zulu song that became famous through fundraising dance performances in southern Africa during Covid

katundu: Chewa word commonly used in Zimbabwe to mean stuff, possessions

kopje: a small hill, usually formed from granite boulders

Kumusha Pinotage: made by Zimbabwean winemaker Tinashe Nyamudoka, featured in the documentary *Blind Ambition*

maningi: Zimbabwean slang for "lots of"

marimba: an African xylophone

mbira: a Shona musical instrument of a wooden sounding board and attached metal tines

mbudzi: Shona for goat

msasa: a tree of central Africa (especially Zimbabwe), with fragrant white flowers and compound leaves that are crimson and bronze in spring.

mealies: corn/maize

melk terte: milk tart, a traditional southern African treat

muti: derived from African word for "tree," meaning any kind of medicine/treatment more generally

oke: southern African slang for a man

rondavel: southern African word for a circular house, based on traditional African dwellings

sem chen: Tibetan for "mind haver" — one who possesses consciousness and therefore Buddha nature

shamwari: Shona for "my friend"

shupa: Zimbabwe slang for 'annoy'

skellum: southern African slang for "rascal"

stupa: a monument symbolising enlightenment that is often also a reliquary for sacred texts, or the remains of a revered teacher

tanganda: popular Zimbabwean tea

thangka: a scroll painting or wall hanging depicting Buddhist deities, mandalas, etc.

ubuntu: African term emphasizing interconnectedness, meaning "I am because we are".

Prologue

London, UK

NICK BERKELEY chose to make the offer in the timeless elegance of his London club. At an immaculately set table in a discreet corner of the dining room, my mentor and good friend invited me to set up my own fund management business within the investment firm he chaired. I would be independent but would have a constant inflow of money to manage. I could set my own strategies yet be part of a global blue-chip brand. At the age of fifty-six, the opportunity promised to be the most lucrative of my career.

As our meal ended, we agreed that a few details needed to be resolved. Of these, my non-compete period seemed so unimportant that we hardly discussed it.

'Landers will put me on "gardening leave",' I said, referring to the firm where I'd made my name over the past decade. It was standard practice for investment directors who left for competitors to be placed on a period of paid leave during which all contact with clients was barred. Gardening leave was a hiatus during which you were forced to disappear.

'Six months?' he confirmed.

I nodded.

'Devon?' Nick and his wife had stayed at my country home in the past.

'Who knows?' I remembered the email I'd received from Aunt Carrie. 'Maybe a chance for that long-delayed visit to Zimbabwe.'

'Ah. Robbie Forbes goes back to his roots.' He regarded me with a perceptive gaze before prodding me in the chest with his forefinger. 'Maybe Africa is what makes you different.'

We exchanged a smile. It was a recurring theme of his — how I wasn't like so many of my fund manager contemporaries. How I was attuned to the longer game.

When the deal went official, several friends whom I told of my unfolding plans were sceptical.

'Isn't violent crime really awful there?' asked some.

'That's Jo'burg,' I answered. 'Not Zim.'

'No water or electricity?' Others looked dubious.

'Aunt Carrie lives off-grid. She has a borehole and solar panels. Zimbabweans "make a plan".' I quoted the unofficial national motto.

I was so settled in my London life and so busy preparing for my time away that the real threat posed by Africa never occurred to me. Even if it had, I would have dismissed it. Perhaps a form of protective amnesia made me oblivious to it. Having been abruptly removed from my childhood world at the end of school, I was heedless about what I would feel when I returned — the forceful, heartfelt jolt of homecoming.

It's an experience that affects many people, even those with no previous link to Africa. Anthropologists offer a plausible explanation. This place, they tell us, is the cradle of humanity. It's where our earliest ancestors lived. We emerged into the world from the womb of Africa. She is our mother and her blood courses through our veins. It was she who first held us in her arms, whose soft breath blew on our faces. We may have long forgotten the warmth of her sun on our skin, the caress of her satin dust on the soles of our feet. But when we return, we *feel* the belonging and we know that we have come home. Whatever we may be used to calling ourselves — British, American, European — much to our own surprise, we discover an earlier identity, for we are all children of Africa too.

In my own case, this revelation was accompanied by one of an even greater order. I could have met my guru Rinpoche anywhere in the world, but it so happened that I encountered him in Zimbabwe. Had I needed to arrive at a particular moment in life for the wisdom he imparted?

When the student is ready, the great inner traditions tell us, the teacher will appear. This process is less mystical than it may seem, suggesting only that whatever wisdom may exist in our lives, until our mind is open to its transformative power we are blind to it.

Before going on gardening leave, I had been a regular meditator for years, encouraged by my godmother Kay to spend twenty minutes each morning focusing on the breath. I benefited in ways hard to describe, but I wouldn't make any great claims about my practice. However, some subtle but important shift must have occurred, because it seems I was at a place that I was ready for what Rinpoche had to show me.

If I have learned anything from him it is that, far from living in an objective world, *how* we see, hear, and experience things arises, first and foremost, in our minds. This reversal of assumptions has the most extraordinary significance. Not least that if we wish to experience reality in its most exquisite form, we don't need to change the world around us or wait to go to heaven. By cultivating the mental causes, transcendent states are available to us here and now.

Africa nudges us towards a different way of being. She re-awakens us to a long-forgotten past when we lived with the immediacy of children, the innocence of young lovers, an openness we may believe was irretrievably lost.

When we can find simple joy in the dawn fragrance of African violets or the babble of bulbuls in the shrubs, in sweet wisps of mopane wood smoke from a village fire or in soulful gospel choruses rising from beneath a distant winter thorn tree, when no matter what streams through our senses we are filled with an unaccountable wonder, we know how it may be possible to leave our jaded selves behind. To let go of whatever notions we cling to and live with the same easy spontaneity as Rinpoche himself — a way of being where the heart is more benevolent and outward focused.

All of which brought me to a dilemma: Having tasted this exalted reality, at what point was I ready to return to my London life of long hours, relentless pressure, and untold riches? When should I tear myself away from Africa to apply what I had learned from my guru to the 'real' world?

It is a dilemma faced by each of us who has the immense good fortune to sit in the presence of a realised being and to feel the awe of connection ripple through eternity.

Chapter One

Ruwa, Zimbabwe

'THEY'RE HERE!'

On Ruwa Rock, three villagers exuberantly waved their arms. From the top of the *kopje*, the huge, eggplant-shaped granite boulder that balanced dramatically at the bottom of the garden — they could see the whole district below: a sun-baked sprawl of brown scrub and brittle trees. On this clear November morning, any vehicle turning off the main road would send up a trail of dust at the moment it turned onto the dirt track.

Down at the car park, the band struck up. Organising today's events with her usual joyful exuberance, Diva Derembwe had persuaded two marimba players and three drummers to accompany the welcoming committee who burst into Shona chorus. The sudden outbreak sent a troop of vervet monkeys scrambling through the msasa trees. The monkeys, in turn, set off Sonny and Cher, peacock and peahen, occupying their usual perches at either end of the thatched roof above us. As they brayed loudly, Mampara the wildebeest glanced up from the lush-green lawn before shaking his horned head with a dismissive snort.

Along with others lining the hallway of the former homestead, I took the white scarf out of my pocket, preparing for our visitor. Yogi Tarchin was the very first Tibetan teacher to visit the Ruwa Buddhist Society, and one of only a handful of lamas ever to visit Africa. Standing beside the large, snowy-haired Harris Gould, who along with Diva comprised the Ruwa Buddhist Society, I felt I was here under false pretences. Not only was my understanding of Buddhism shaky to say the least, I wasn't even a local. Not really.

I caught a glimpse of my reflection in a clouded, gilt-framed mirror and brushed a grey lock off my forehead before straightening my jacket. As I caught the tang of creosote from the tarred poles above merging with the equally long-held memory of Cobra Floor Polish, I thought how unlikely all this was. True, I was a willing participant in today's cheerful if quirky event, but it didn't seem to have much to do with me.

The singing and clapping rose to a crescendo as a battered Land Rover pulled up under the *msasas*. All of us in the hall turned to peer into the distance as the passenger door of the vehicle opened and a slight figure in a yellow shirt and ochre pants emerged. Diva greeted him with a deep bow and a proffered white scarf. Accepting the scarf, he raised it in his hands and, in the traditional Tibetan custom, placed it around her neck in blessing. Several more such offerings were being made by other greeters. As Himalayan etiquette was observed with impeccable formality, yards away the band whooped and jived with unrestrained vigour.

Diva ushered the lama towards the house. But Yogi Tarchin had other ideas. There was a lightness about him apparent even from here. An irrepressible spontaneity.

Turning to the musicians, he smiled broadly, clapping in rhythm. They responded with an appreciative lurch in volume. Several greeters needed no further encouragement and were soon dancing next to their VIP visitor. Village children materialised from nowhere, stamping their feet joyfully in the dust. The rising music level sparked a renewed frenzy among the vervet monkeys, who swooped dangerously low through the canopy, barking with excitement. For a moment it seemed that Yogi Tarchin's welcome might go chaotically off-course.

But then he turned to Diva, who was waiting in a fawn-coloured dress and high heels, perfectly tailored, as for every occasion. Dark hair falling in elaborately coiled braids, woven through for today's visitor with threads of red and gold, she guided the lama through the trees onto the emerald-green lawn that formed a luxuriant runner up to the house.

~

Forty-something Diva was a force of nature, compelling your attention with a combination of girlish frivolity and commanding power. Large, emotion-filled eyes decorated with startlingly brilliant eyeshadow would turn from deeply imploring to ecstatically grateful in an instant. Within moments of meeting, you'd feel connected to her seemingly boundless warmth. It was only because of Diva that I was here.

When Diva was a young woman two decades ago, experimenting with organic skin care products in the kitchen of her Chisipite home, Aunt Carrie had been her business mentor. Since then, Diva's Treasure Trees Apothecary business had grown from a cottage industry to a national brand, Diva becoming a local business celebrity. Fervent about the power of Zimbabwe's indigenous trees as a source of healing

7

and beauty, Diva was on a mission to popularise her unique range of baobab, kigelia, and other products.

When I'd travelled from London six weeks ago to help Aunt Carrie through cancer treatment, I'd soon met Diva, who was a regular visitor. When Carrie's health, instead of responding positively to treatment, took a grave turn for the worse, it had been Diva who'd arranged hospital admission at short notice. Diva who knew exactly how to access the best medical specialists. Diva who had helped Carrie and me as we found ourselves approaching the precipitous end.

Instead of supporting my mother's sister, the last of her generation in my family, through what was nothing more than a bothersome bump in her return to full health, I had ended up moving her from hospital to hospice and, days later, holding her hand as she passed away.

Carrie had made me the executor and a beneficiary of her will. She didn't own much — the house, a car, a modest amount in savings. There were a few items she wanted given to friends. It was a simple estate to dispose of. But what to do about her gardener with the dazzlingly optimistic name of Marvellous? He had worked here for well over a decade, and in a country where nine out of ten people were unemployed, his chances of finding a new job were non-existent.

What of Thor and Tiki, Carrie's wolfhound and Jack Russell respectively, who had only ever known life in this Ruwa house and who, in Carrie's absence, were increasingly bonding to me? What of the birds in the garden that Aunt Carrie fed every morning — a practice I continued? The village man who visited to sell her vegetables every Thursday morning? Mr Buba, a not-so-regular but no less important visitor, who made sure her inverter and generator worked smoothly when there was no electricity available — which was most days. A vulnerable ecosystem was coming to an abrupt end.

For the time being I stayed in the guest bedroom as I began wrapping up things. It wasn't how I envisaged spending my gardening leave, but having applied for probate, it would be at least two weeks until I could finalise the estate and depart.

~

I was emptying cupboards early one afternoon when I heard a car coming up the dust driveway. Thor and Tiki launched into a frenzy of barking. They settled when they recognised the car. It was Diva's Land Cruiser, the vehicle of choice for navigating Harare's dangerously potholed streets.

'It's not a social visit,' she explained, emerging from the cab wearing a bright floral top and white pants. Her eyes searched mine, and mine hers, with the intimacy that comes from shared grief.

'We have a Tibetan lama coming to the Ruwa Buddhist Society on Saturday. You'll be his neighbour, so I thought you might like to come *as* well,' she said, placing the emphasis, in that curious way of some Zimbabweans, on the "as".

'John Elliott's place, right?' I pointed across the garden.

She nodded. 'He left us the property.'

I remembered Carrie telling me how her neighbour of over thirty years had set up a charity to make sure that his cheetah was looked after when he died. He had stumbled across Bodhi in the bush as an abandoned cub just weeks old. Unable to find her mother, and with the cub's life in danger, he had reluctantly taken her home to raise, with the mothering of his domestic tabby cat, Football. Bodhi had grown quickly from mewing cub to lithe and muscular big cat. All efforts to rewild her ended in failure. No matter how suitable a release site they took her to, she always returned to John, Football, and the place she regarded as home.

John came to accept her as his constant if unlikely companion. When people went to visit him, they'd find Bodhi sprawled on a sofa beside him or lying in a patch of sunshine nearby. John became known locally as "the cheetah guy", the two of them even finding fame in a small way. There had been a few magazine articles and an appearance on a National Geographic documentary.

What neither John nor anyone else predicted was how Bodhi would react when John's time came to pass. He had died in his sleep one night at home, three years ago. By the following afternoon the cheetah had vanished, never to be seen again. The irony escaped no one: The whole reason John had set up the Ruwa Buddhist Society walked out the door the day he passed.

'Will the lama stay long?' I asked Diva.

'A few days,' she shrugged. 'Week or two at the most. It's up to him. When we heard about this Rinpoche visiting his brother up at Hwange, we got in touch and asked if he'd be willing to offer us a teaching.'

'On Saturday?' I confirmed.

'I know you meditate,' she responded to my hesitancy.

'Just basic breathing stuff.'

'Come along!' she beamed, her dangly bead earrings glinting in the light as she hooked me with her most persuasive appeal. 'Carrie would.'

It was true. Carrie's sense of community would take her next door, and she would probably also have been curious to meet a Tibetan lama. Although she wasn't religious in any formal way, in her last days at the hospice we had spoken freely of her imminent death and I'd been struck by how accepting, even positive she was about it — which made it easier for me to be accepting also. A near-death experience over a decade before had changed the way she felt about transitioning, as she called it. Her equanimity had been authentic. 'Don't waste any tears over me, Robbie,' she'd smiled on her pillow. 'I'm looking forward to what comes next.'

Diva and Yogi Tarchin were halfway up the lawn. John's former homestead comprised three large rondavels linked by broad passages in a sprawling crescent-shaped structure, all beneath a magnificent sweep of silver-grey thatch. Under the eaves, a string of vividly coloured Tibetan prayer flags fluttered in the breeze.

I wondered what the lama made of this oasis in the veldt. Shielding his eyes from the sun, he took in the immensity of Ruwa Rock, and somewhat closer, the long necks of Debbie and Kim, John Elliott's giraffes, who stood motionless in the distance observing the ruckus at the house. The lama chuckled on catching sight of a family of warthogs, affronted by the continuing din in the car park, sprinting across the lawn, tails aloft like radio aerials — Mum, Dad, and three piglets. An elegant pair of crowned cranes paused hesitantly in the shade of a gigantic flamboyant tree, observing the arrivals with their fine golden plumes raised on full alert.

Suddenly Rinpoche and Diva were out of the blazing sunshine and inside with us. In the flurry, dust motes shimmered in a mid-morning glow. One by one, we indoor greeters offered the lama our white scarves.

Other than bringing a scarf, I had not prepared for this encounter, nor did I expect anything in particular. But now that it was happening, I felt the strangest sensation. Not on account of Yogi Tarchin's appearance, although his warm brown eyes, ageless face, grey moustache, and goatee gave him the look of an archetypal eastern sage. Rather, it was a radiant sense of lightness, of joy, that seemed to emanate from him. The ineffable sensation that even though you could see and touch him, his presence was somehow more energetic than physical. As if his body were hardly there at all.

As I bent in offering, our eyes met. In that instant, it was as if Rinpoche gazed through the person I usually took myself to be and saw something more panoramic. Not a 56-year-old businessman who had returned to the country of his birth to take care of an ailing aunt and now found himself in limbo. Instead, a boundless reality beyond that, one from which I had been for so long disconnected that, incredibly, I had forgotten it was even there. So benevolent was Rinpoche's expression, however, so wholehearted his acceptance, that I felt a surge of the most powerful emotion. In his gaze was all the reassurance I could hope for, that however things appeared to be beneath the surface, all was well.

This entire experience happened in an instant — then he was moving on. I could tell it was the same for the others who encountered him. The briefest pause. The meeting of eyes and hearts. The upwelling of emotion. Next to me, Harris Gould brushed at his cheek.

We followed Diva and Rinpoche from the hall into the silent shadows of the sitting room, where mats and cushions had been laid out in preparation for a guided meditation. The lama glanced into the room before looking out the window to the sunshine.

'I think out is better,' he said, gesturing to the shade cast by the massive canopy of the flamboyant tree.

'Certainly, Rinpoche,' replied Diva. Then evidently feeling the need to explain, 'We thought that traditionally these things are done inside.'

He nodded, chuckling. 'Good to mix it up a bit, yes?'

Harris looked at me, his expression bright with significance.

As Diva guided the lama through the house to the guest rondavel, Harris and I began carrying meditation mats onto the lawn.

'You see?' he grunted.

I nodded.

~

When I'd met Harris earlier that week, he couldn't have been more fervent about what the visit by Yogi Tarchin meant. At Diva's request, I had brought over the hot water urn and tea service that Carrie had loaned Ruwa Buddhist Society on the handful of previous occasions they'd had gatherings. In the homestead kitchen, the large man with a white crop of hair, ruddy cheeks, and crystal blue eyes, who looked for all the world like an Old Testament prophet, if not Jove himself, had been bent over the sink replacing a tap washer.

'Rob Forbes,' I'd introduced myself when he'd helped me lift the urn onto the bench.

'Diva said you'd be coming,' he'd nodded. 'Kind of you to continue your aunt's tradition.'

'No problem.'

'You grew up near here?'

'Marondera,' I said. 'My dad taught at Peterhouse.'

'Where *I* went to school.' He studied me closely,

then his eyes gleamed in recognition. 'Euan Forbes? Head of Art?'

I nodded, reproaching myself, not for the first time, for oversharing.

'I can see the resemblance, now. Nice *oke*, your old man. Charismatic.'

It was the word people always used about my father the entertainer, who, given an audience, would be transformed into a swashbuckling raconteur. I watched him carefully as he remembered Dad, searching his eyes for the subtlest shift in expression, the tiniest clue that he had come upon a less than creditable memory. But if he recalled something negative, he didn't reveal it.

It had all been a very long time ago, I supposed. Not many people ever knew what happened, and most of those who did would have left the country or died. Our family's abrupt departure for Scotland — "Home", as my mother always referred to it — had not only been deeply upsetting but also mystifying. I was eighteen, and things in my own life had never seemed so promising — my first-ever girlfriend Mandy and I planned on going to university together. Why was Mum tearing the family away?

In the kitchen, Harris nodded towards the hot water urn. 'You've come back for the big day,' he noted. Before I could respond he continued, 'Not by coincidence.'

'My being here?' I asked, surprised.

'Your being here. Or any of us,' he said. 'When a highly realised Buddhist guru visits a place, it isn't by chance. Diva will tell you that she heard he was visiting his brother, Norbu, and she invited him to visit. Which is true, conventionally speaking. But he wouldn't be coming if we didn't have the karma for him to come.'

I pondered this for a moment, picking up on his use of the word "guru". 'My godmother,' I said, thinking of Kay, 'tells me that the guru is the foundation of all realisations.'

'That's what the texts say,' he nodded, 'as will those who've had the privilege of being with one.'

'He's only here for a few days,' Diva said. 'A week or two, tops.'

'I wouldn't get hung up about that.' The conviction in Harris's blue eyes was mesmerising. 'Lama time is quite different from our own.'

'Lama time?' I grinned.

'Days, weeks, months,' he shrugged his shoulders. 'He'll be here for as long as it takes.'

'To do what?'

'To change everything!' he said, an eager glow on his face. 'Don't you see?'

~

As Harris and I ferried mats outside, it wasn't long before we were joined by other helpers. More people were arriving, parking their cars under the msasas and walking across the lawn to sit in the shade. Diva had been concerned that there would be an embarrassingly low turnout — a lama's visit of this kind was unprecedented and she had no idea if people would be interested.

She needn't have worried. Plenty of people seemed drawn by a visiting Tibetan yogi. My niece, Riley, and her yoga class students were among them. We waved to one another as a dozen or so thirty-somethings, mostly women but a few men, arranged themselves before the slightly raised wooden platform which had been brought out to serve as a teaching throne. It was heartening to see the next generation mixing freely, friends since infancy, indifferent to skin colour, as during my childhood years, social attitudes in this country had been defined by race, the dynamics decidedly colonial.

Prosperous-looking couples emerged from sleek SUVs, alongside many from the battered Toyotas and Honda Fits that shared the ragged roads of nearby Harare. People of all ages and ethnicities took their places unselfconsciously under the tree, as purple-crested louries drank from the nearby bird bath, revealing flashes of dazzling red wing feathers when they took flight.

Mr Nzou, gardener and caretaker of the property, was also present, not just observing from the background but sitting in the front row of cushions and dressed with unusual formality. The lean man with the wizened face and curiously bowed posture was the only one here wearing a suit and tie. Next to him, I noticed, was a much younger Shona man sitting in perfect meditation pose, smooth as soapstone.

The cushions were soon occupied. The yoga class had to double up on their mats as more people kept arriving. It wasn't long before the entire area under shade was occupied, including two semi-circle rows of camping chairs at the back.

There was an informal festive atmosphere as we settled. Below a buzz of chatting and laughter was an undercurrent of expectation as we reached the start time — and still, people were drifting across the lawn to join us.

Looking at all those gathered, I wondered what Yogi Tarchin could possibly say that would resonate with such a diverse group. For so many Zimbabweans, life was a daily struggle just for the basics — food, water, electricity. But there were others who lived in substantial mansions with swimming pools, servants, and all life's luxuries. Would they not, each one of them, be seeking something different? All this in a country where Christianity rubs along uneasily with traditional ancestral spirit practices, the more fundamentalist groups shunning any view other than their own as "devil worship". In the midst of such conflicting notions, what might a Tibetan Buddhist lama do or say that could in any way be helpful?

From time to time, I glanced to the guest rondavel where sheer fabric billowed hazily through the open French doors. It was only after the last comers had arrived and settled that the curtains were drawn aside. A hush descended. Diva Derembwe was stepping into view and, moments later, Yogi Tarchin.

~

There was a cheerfulness about him as he walked. Also, a humility. Looking towards the group, he brought palms to his heart, eyes bright with welcome. As he drew closer, everyone rose to their feet. Diva ushered him to the cushion on the teaching dais. Rinpoche gestured that we should sit.

For the longest while after we settled, he remained in silence. Relaxed on his cushion, he looked from person to person in the group, his expression benevolent, even playful, and with the same inexpressible sense of knowing I'd felt earlier. That heartfelt connection that caught you completely unawares.

After some time, he looked farther out to where a small herd of kudu, drawn to the lush grass, stood poised in their extraordinary stillness. To where vervet monkeys, back in the tree canopy, grunted softly in the branches. To where African caper white butterflies fluttered in the breeze and the morning was vibrant with bird calls. He seemed to be inviting the background to become the foreground and, without a word being said, encouraged us to do the same.

It is a most unusual person who can appear in front of a group of strangers and feel comfortable saying nothing. In Yogi Tarchin's case, he wasn't simply comfortable, but radiant as the morning. Even in the short time he had been with us, it was as if we were no longer strangers. The dynamics had enigmatically but palpably shifted so that we were now a group who, through some unspoken agreement, were bound together on the same journey, hearts and minds drawn to his.

Sitting on the edge of the group, I looked across the short stretch of lawn to the flowerbeds lined with shrubs and the open veldt beyond. Into the tranquil morning came an inelegant thud as Sonny the peacock fluttered from the roof of the house to the ground, before unfolding his tail to its full, iridescent glory. There was a ripple of laughter as he shimmied towards the group, swaying his plumage. From inside the house, Football, the plush tabby cat, came to investigate, and sent Sonny backtracking. Taking in the group, Football made her way across the grass to a patch of dappled sunshine in the flowerbed, where she found a leafy spot to settle.

~

'This moment, here and now, is the only time that exists.' When Yogi Tarchin spoke, his voice was warm as honey, and although the observation came from the teaching throne, it resonated within.

'The past is gone. We will never again experience it.' He paused. 'The future has yet to arise, and who knows how it may unfold?'

As I took in his tranquil features, there was nothing for me to do but rest in the self-evident truth.

'If we are to find happiness,' he continued after a

while, 'and it is happiness that each of us seeks, then we can't find it in the past or the future. Neither of those times even exists, except as mere ideas. There is only one time when we can be happy, and that is this moment, here and now.'

There was fresh power in each word he spoke. Even though he said nothing I hadn't heard before, under the great, flowering branches of the flamboyant tree, I felt the meaning of his words with unusual significance.

'The time to be happy is now. The place to be happy is here. And the way to be happy is to make others so.'

~

He raised himself on his cushion to sit upright, rolling back his shoulders and tilting his head gently, assuming a meditation posture. Without being asked, everyone followed. 'Sit like a mountain!' was how Kay had described the pose.

'We begin,' he proposed, 'with gratitude. Gratitude for being together on a warm morning in this pristine place. Gratitude to John Elliott for creating the Ruwa Buddhist Society, which enables us to be here. Gratitude,' there was a special warmth in his voice, 'to a cheetah called Bodhi, who was the cause for him to create it.'

Diva had evidently told him the story. I wondered what Rinpoche made of it. Was it the case that Bodhi had served a particular purpose in having John set up the Ruwa Buddhist Society for the future benefit of others? Had her ultimate destiny always been to return to the wild?

From a state of gratitude, Rinpoche invited us to visualise, at our hearts, the radiant, golden bud of a lotus flower, its petals closed. The gold light filling the bud, he told us, was an energy that flowed naturally from our hearts. It symbolised our own loving kindness, an energy not to be underestimated.

He told us to imagine the lotus bud unfolding with delicate deliberation, light flooding from between the unfurling petals, suffusing our bodies and minds with the power of loving kindness. Had it been someone other than Yogi Tarchin guiding us through this visualisation, someone without the power to have us suspend our disbelief, who knows how this might have evolved. But such was his effortless authority, we did exactly as he asked. And just as he described, I felt waves of energy pass through my body, touching my crown, throat, and heart. Like pleasant shivers, subtle but tangible, they suggested the presence of ethereal but perceptible qualities I hadn't even known that I could summon.

He described light intensifying, the continued, ever-increasing wellspring at our heart being too great to be contained within our body. Gold light bursting from within us to include every other being sitting on the lawn that day — we were now aglow in the focus of one another's compassionate attention. Allow ourselves to feel it, he told us, as vividly as possible.

The gold light spilled farther, from our group under the tree out into the bush, north, south, west, and east, all the people and beings who lived there — including Bodhi. There being no limits to consciousness, nowhere that mind cannot travel, Rinpoche told us, we were to recollect friends, family, and especially those who might be suffering, wherever in the world they might be. We were to imagine the transformative power of light radiating through them too, freeing them from pain, removing all suffering. And not only that, but imbuing them with energy, healing, purpose, an abundance of love and compassion.

As his directions surged through me, I was aware

that the here and now was somehow subtly changing gears. In a way that was quite novel, each moment felt simultaneously more intense and yet more evanescent than before. Reality was simultaneously shifting both slowly and quickly. It was the most curious double-time, experienced with the fleeting hyper-reality of a dream.

After a while, he led us out of the meditation, the gold light withdrawing to our hearts, leaving behind only love and light, healing and coherence, in more dimensions than we had hitherto imagined. And having guided us through the most extraordinary evocation of happiness on behalf of others, he ended with the wish: 'May love, compassion, joy, and equanimity pervade the hearts and minds of all limitless beings throughout universal space.'

~

I can't remember what struck me first as I opened my eyes — the recognition that the sun had shifted by quite some way since I had closed them, or the presence, only a few yards away. Resplendent on the lawn, gazing directly towards Yogi Tarchin, the embodiment of his heartfelt invocation was a magnificent cheetah.

Power and grace personified, conjured as if out of the air, she lay on the lush carpet of green, her sleek gold fur marked with exquisite black spots. The dark tear streaks on her face drew my gaze to those piercing, amber eyes currently focused on Rinpoche. I sensed movement around me as others realised what was happening. Yogi Tarchin acknowledged Bodhi without looking directly at her. A sideways glance, a bowing of his upper body — his understanding was intuitive.

Finding ourselves in an unbelievable situation, it was hard not to focus on Bodhi, whether directly or indirectly. Untamed and yet so elegant. Such poise, such delicacy about her face and whiskers, illuminated like translucent wires in the morning sun. Had Rinpoche envisioned that this was going to happen? Had he designed the meditation for this purpose? Did he possess the power to summon, at will, living beings — even those who had been missing in the veldt for years?

We sat in wordless, exultant silence, knowing that we were experiencing an unprecedented marvel, soaking in the silent rapture. There was movement in the flowerbed. On the other side of the lama, Football was rousing herself. Getting to her feet, she performed a luxuriant sun salutation, before ambling over the grass behind the teaching throne. In no great hurry, she paused momentarily on the way to stretch first her left hind leg, then her right.

Several meditators were taking out their phones to record Football's progress, the deliberate, steady movement of her round fluffy form. She took not the least notice of Rinpoche nor the assembled group as she headed to Bodhi. Bodhi lowered her face as Football neared, the two of them gently head-butting. For a while I caught the sounds of deep-throated purring emerging from Bodhi. Then Football was licking the cheetah's forehead as if Bodhi were still a small cub, lavishing her daughter with a mother's love. After some while Bodhi reciprocated with several long strokes of her tongue around Football's face and neck. Then she rose and, in a few flowing motions, leaped effortlessly from the lawn through the flowerbed and vanished into the bush, Football following.

Spellbound, we sat together, trying to believe what we had just seen. It was hard not to wish that things didn't have to come to an end. Was what we had just witnessed really possible? On the teaching throne, Yogi Tarchin remained as unassuming and curiously tenuous as a dappled patch of sunlight.

~

From inside the homestead came a roar of indignation. Moments later, a three-legged vervet monkey scampered out the door, a strawberry tart in its only front paw, leaped onto the roof and on to a nearby tree. Gogo Margaret, the housekeeper, who had lived and worked here since John Elliott's time, cut a matronly, uniformed figure as she hurried from the veranda in pursuit of the miscreant, one hand shielding her eyes against the sunlight, the other brandishing a rolling pin.

'Skellum is stealing the lunch!' she announced portentously across the lawn.

Rinpoche dissolved into laughter, before bringing his palms together at his heart.

'Then, may Skellum and all living beings quickly, quickly attain enlightenment!' he declared before getting up from his seat, still chuckling.

Chapter Two

AFRICA DRAWS US IN. That is her magic. We arrive believing ourselves to be visitors from a different world, but so open are her people, so enchanting her animals, so heartfelt — if unexpected — our sense of connection, that soon we feel we belong.

Far from coming as a surprise to locals, our kinship is assumed. Spontaneously we are included in group invitations, asked favours of, given things we never requested but that turn out to be curiously gratifying. We become aware that we are the possessor of awe-inspiring powers derived from our access to even quite modest amounts of hard currency. The cost of a meal in a mid-market London restaurant is enough in Africa to remove someone's cataracts and restore their sight. For the cost of a meal for six, a fistula can be repaired, enabling a lame person to walk out of the wretched darkness of a hut in which they would otherwise have been condemned to live out their lives.

At the same time, we discover an unsuspected poverty about ourselves. Living on the edge of adversity intensifies people's gratitude for the things most of us take for granted. Every nourishing meal truly is a blessing. Each act of kindness is genuinely cherished. Free of any idea of being separate from one another, people place the highest value on the wider community. Joy is to be shared each day in simple acts of reconnection. How is it that we have moved so far away from this to our bleak, atomised bubbles of privilege?

On the first morning after I'd arrived, before I got out of bed or even so much as opened my eyes, it all came flooding back. Marvellous was watering pot plants while at the same time calling to a friend walking along the road. Yelling effusive Shona above the spray of the garden hose, he was utterly unconcerned about the presence of his employer's houseguest behind drawn bedroom curtain just yards away.

There was much joking and laughing that summer morning. I caught the cadences of words I hadn't heard for decades. The theatrical astonishment of *maiwe* (my-weh)! The indignant refusal of *aikona* (I-con-uh)! There was much talk of a *bhasikoro* (bicycle), and even a snatch of song before the conversation ended, as seemingly randomly as it had begun.

Marvellous edged farther away. Eyes still closed, I heard the contented clucking of bantam hens scrabbling in the flowerbed outside my window. The rhythmic cooing of Cape turtle doves in the lucky bean tree. The sound of the hot water boiler from around the back of the house. Those few reminders were all it took to feel an unanticipated strong tug of homecoming, the reassurance of a place I had known and loved — and to feel that I was back in the warm embrace of the Motherland.

~

That feeling returned four days later as I sat drinking Tanganda tea on Aunt Carrie's veranda, waiting for my niece, Riley, to arrive. During the wait for probate to be granted, I had been making inquiries about finding a new job for Marvellous, about re-homing the dogs, and about how best property could be sold or transferred. As I'd messaged Nick Berkeley, I expected to be leaving Zim by late November.

For reasons I found hard to fathom, I felt curiously settled in Ruwa. Carrie's house might be a run-down bungalow, with worn furniture, haphazard plumbing, and bric-a-brac dating back well over half a century, but the feel of the place was deeply familiar — the smell flicking through mildewing pages of Rhodesiana Reprint Library volumes on her bookshelves, and the gleam of copper wall plaques of kudu and sable so popular in the 1970s. Her home felt like a time warp. And looking into the garden that she'd created with Marvellous and his predecessors, the love that had given form to this vibrant Arcadia was palpable.

Nevertheless, the day was approaching that I'd be leaving, and there were two things I wanted to do before then. One was to visit Kay in Nyanga. Recently, her days had been taken up looking after an ailing friend, so we had yet to work out a time for me to travel. The other was what Riley and I were about to do right now. For reasons of pure nostalgia, we were going to admire sunset from the top of Ruwa Rock.

It was an adventure I had last enjoyed as a teenager, when my time had been filled with similarly innocent pursuits: school and cricket, trips into town to watch a movie or play Putt Putt in Eastlea. If I had pocket money, I'd buy an LP from Martin Locke's Spinalong. My parents protected me from the worst horrors of the bush war which had ended when I was sixteen, so that my school days were, in many ways, like those of kids in other countries.

In my last year I'd dated Mandy Ellis, a vivacious blonde senior at Roosevelt Girls who was active in amateur dramatics. How sophisticated we felt meeting at Chez Roger, under the 7 Arts Theatre, for a swift interval drink when she was in the chorus line of *My Fair Lady*, or ordering that favourite Southern African nightcap, Don Pedro — vanilla ice cream and whisky — at Mokador on the way home.

It was a thrilling time to be young with the world around us changing so dramatically. The *ancien régime* had been swept away, and gone with it, temporarily, the country's pariah status. From having been like a provincial British town run by a dour Presbyterian farmer, the place was awash with visitors from exotic and previously taboo countries. Waiting for a drink at Sandros, you were just as likely to come across partying Swedish aid workers with their beguiling Scandi accents as you were a squad of bearded Cubans in military fatigues. Having known nothing but sanctions and a narrow range of staples, shops were suddenly selling incomprehensible luxuries, the kinds of which I had seen only in magazines from overseas.

Our family couldn't afford them. But it was amazing to see people drinking real Moët & Chandon here in Zimbabwe! Or buying actual Côte d'or chocolate! Town was suddenly glamorously cosmopolitan. Mandy and I thrived on it.

Which made Mum and Dad's announcement all the more devastating. It was the end of the year and Kate had recently finished her O level exams. That afternoon I wrote the last of my A level papers. We were summoned to the dining room where supper was laid on one of the 'good' tablecloths and a bottle of white wine was frosty on the sideboard. All this was part of Mum's strong sense of doing things properly.

Dad, at home a muted version of his public persona, looked strangely nervous.

'We have something to celebrate!' Mum was determinedly cheerful as she nodded to Dad, bidding him to take over.

Kate and I exchanged glances.

Dad said he and Mum had waited until we finished our exams before breaking the important news. We probably knew that he and Mum had been 'going through' things. After much soul-searching they'd decided that it would be best for the family to migrate back to Scotland, specifically, to Inverness. In two months.

Kate hadn't waited to hear more. She leapt from the table, thundered down the corridor to her bedroom, and slammed the door behind her. Mum delivered a reproachful glance towards Dad. I saw his hand tremble as he raised the glass of wine to his lips. I, too, was poured a glass, whether to mark the end of exams or to commiserate, I couldn't be sure.

Over a meal I could barely eat, I offered to stay behind after they left. I could go to university in Cape Town, I said. I would put myself through my degree. Mandy and I already had the whole thing planned. I hadn't shared any details before, but I expect they guessed enough. They firmly resisted all suggestions other than their own. The plane tickets were already booked, Dad told me.

I knew there was no point arguing. What Dad meant by 'going through' things was that he and Mum had been having heated, furtive rows for weeks. About what I had no idea, except that he seemed to have done something to upset Mum, and she had issued an ultimatum.

She had never really been comfortable in Africa. Since the new government had taken over, with all their ministers referred to as Comrade This and Comrade

That, she was even less comfortable. Dad's unknown transgression was evidently the last straw. She had decided that the time had come to turn the page, for her and the children to begin a new chapter at Home. With or without him.

Days after the momentous announcement, Dad drove the two of us children to say goodbye to godmother Kay in Nyanga and to return a few borrowed yoga mats, blocks, and bolsters. Those at least were the purported reasons. Later I realised that my parents had probably been desperate for time apart.

Dad had thrown in his lot with Mum, no doubt for the sake of us kids. But the decision to leave had been devastating. The night of the announcement, after Mum had gone to bed. I tiptoed out to the studio at the back of the garage to speak to him. I had visited Dad late at night in the past, so it would be just the two of us. He always seemed more approachable at those times. But that night, unlike any time before, the door to his studio was shut. The garage was in darkness except for a narrow line of orange light showing under the door. From inside I heard a sound that shook me so much that for a while I stood unable to move: Dad was sobbing.

~

It was a long time since I'd thought about that ancient family trauma, I realised, as I lifted binoculars off the table. No doubt being at Aunt Carrie's, whom we used to visit so often, had caused the dormant memories to float to the surface.

Carrie's home overlooked the strip of veldt stretching from John Elliott's old homestead to a dam. On the other side of the bushland, the rock towered like an ancient sentinel from among a cluster of granite boulders and candelabra trees, so named because their large, fleshy branches looked exactly as if they should be topped by giant pillar candles.

Directly ahead, Debbie and Kim, sister giraffes, sauntered towards the acacias on the other side of Carrie's garden. I watched them through the binoculars, fascinated as they browsed and regurgitated cuds that travelled, golf ball size, from their stomachs all the way up their very long necks, before chewing ruminatively and staring for the longest time, blinking at me sultry eyed from under their extraordinarily long and beautiful lashes.

~

A car approached on the driveway. Thor and Tiki looked up from where they were dozing. It was the sound of Aunt Carrie's car, but they knew that Carrie was no longer with us. Bewildered, they rose to their feet and trotted around the side of the house, returning with Riley.

'Debbie and Kim?' she confirmed, following my gaze as she stepped onto the veranda.

'Uh-huh.'

She bent for a quick hug.

'Something's bothering me about Kim. You know, the taller one?' I handed her the binoculars. 'I'm worried she's hurt a back leg.'

Riley stared through the lenses.

She was an attractive girl, my niece — twenty-five years old with a strong, yoga teacher's physique, long blonde hair, and hazel eyes. She was also very Zimbabwean: straightforward and, without being bitter, unwaveringly free of illusions about other people's motives. Resilient and willing to turn her hand to whatever needed doing. Open. Curious.

After a while she lowered the binoculars. 'Can't see much.'

'It shows up when she's walking,' I said.

Six years ago Riley had come to stay with me in London for a gap break at the end of her schooling. I had a comfortable flat in central London which suited her, just as home-cooked meals or a congenial dining companion to visit local restaurants suited me when I got home from my work — often late. We'd shared a few adventures and a lot of laughs. Both of us new to the roles of uncle and niece, we'd enjoyed the closeness of being family without any special expectations.

Riley was one of Kate's two kids, the other being her son Sean. After the family move to Scotland, Kate had returned to Zimbabwe as soon as she could. The two of us kept in touch over the years but my sister and I had never been close. Not because of any falling out; we simply lived in different worlds. We'd seen a fair bit of one another with Carrie's funeral, but as always, when there wasn't something specific to talk about, it was as though an invisible ocean lay between us.

Sometimes I yearned for the closeness I saw other siblings enjoying, but for Kate and me that wasn't to be. With Riley, however, things were different. She and I clicked.

'You've been busy,' she observed, glancing about.

When Aunt Carrie was alive, the veranda table had been stacked with orderly piles of Bundu Bush guides, gardening books, and invariably a tea tray. Now it was empty, the sweeping teak surface highlighting the breadth and length of this outdoor room.

'Getting ready to head back to London.'

'So soon?' she pulled a face.

'With no Aunt Carrie,' I shrugged.

'Ja, hey,' Riley glanced pensively out at the bush. 'I know.'

Standing, I pointed to a box of Treasure Trees Apothecary products I'd gathered when tidying up the house. 'These are for you.'

'Lobster!' she protested, taking in the sizeable collection. 'You can't give me *everything*!'

My family nickname had come about when Kate, aged three, had failed to imitate a friend of my father's who used to call me "Robbie Robster". "Lobster" was so delightfully silly it had stuck.

'Yes, I can. I *am* Aunt Carrie's executor and an heir,' I reminded her.

This was exactly why, a week after Carrie died, I gave her car to Riley — Riley's own banger having long lost its suspension and its tyres being practically bald. On a yoga teacher's earnings there was little likelihood she could afford to replace it. Apart from the car and the house, Carrie's only asset was a bank account with its balance of $7,400.

We walked to Riley's car — the two of us sitting up front sporting our sunglasses, Thor and Tiki on their familiar backseat. I'd packed a cooler bag with drinks and snacks which I put in the footwell. As we headed up the dirt road behind Aunt Carrie's property, we lowered our windows, late afternoon warmth rushing against our faces, bringing with it the camphor-like tang of eucalyptus trees growing in the distance. It felt so free, so invigorating, gunning down an open road through the bush with nothing but blue sky above.

Both rear windows were lowered, and in the side mirror I could see that behind me wolfhound Thor had his whole woolly head out of the car relishing the wind in his face. On the other side, Jack Russell Tiki had both her front paws on the arm rest, thrusting her snout out appreciatively.

Riley and I exchanged a smile.

We pulled up in the Ruwa Buddhist Society car park. As soon as we had stepped from the vehicle and opened the back doors, the dogs were out, racing through the undergrowth in search of fresh scents, their paws flicking up bursts of tangerine dust. Riley and I headed along the side of the property to the rock. It was a gentle walk, late afternoon sunshine slanting across the scorched scrub.

The land sloped up, forming a hill about the size of a football pitch studded with granite boulders. Ruwa Rock, like a gigantic aubergine, lolled on its side. The fingers of candelabra trees stretched around it, as if balancing it on the heels of unseen hands.

A zigzag path and ascending boulders offered a natural staircase to the rock. I let Riley take the lead, given her familiarity. She occasionally brought her yoga group to practice here. Once she'd sent me a photo of them in warrior pose on the top, silhouetted against a dazzling red sunset.

As always in the African bush, there came constant reminders that you weren't alone. Reaching to lean against a boulder, there'd be a sudden skirmish, and you'd realise that a lizard had been sunning itself just inches away from your hand, perfectly camouflaged with the green-grey lichen. When there was a louder crash, we looked up to the inquiring face of a *dassie*. They loved kopjes, and rabbit-size droppings revealed their presence, but they were the shyest of creatures and it was rare to catch more than a glimpse.

After a brief scramble on hands and knees, we emerged at the lower end of the boulder and clambered towards the summit. Halfway along a limb stretched above the rock from a massive umbrella tree growing up the side. Parallel to the boulder, the branch was long and straight as a ceiling joist beneath the tree's soaring canopy.

We climbed the final few steps to the top, and I felt as heady as the very first time I'd come here as a boy. Suddenly I was at the top and could survey everything from horizon to horizon, not so much king of the castle as a more exalted observer. It was impossible not to be enthralled. Every other kopje in the district was so much smaller. All signs of human activity looked of little consequence — in the far northwest, the town of Ruwa was nothing more than a small grey smudge on the horizon.

I felt a sudden sense of insignificance, all the more powerful because that was exactly my experience as a ten-year-old boy when I'd first climbed up here on my own and gazed out to the far yonder. How tiny and ineffectual I had felt! Of what little consequence! However important my life and my work usually seemed, up here, on top of Ruwa Rock, without a word having been said, I was emphatically reminded of my place.

This close to the equator, it doesn't take long for day to turn into night. The sun was already dipping to the horizon, and the sky was deepening to a golden glow. As I put down the cooler bag, Riley shrugged off a small rucksack and took out a blanket that she flicked across the rock. The boulder was surprisingly flat at the top, and spacious as a farmhouse veranda. Thor and Tiki watched, tongues lolling and panting from their exertions, as I poured water into a bowl for them.

We hadn't even sat down yet when I noticed movement beneath the msasas.

'Is that Harris?' I asked, surprised by the tall, white-maned figure.

'With Tinashe,' confirmed Riley.

Tinashe was the young Shona man who had sat next to Mr Nzou on the day of Rinpoche's arrival. I had met him briefly over lunch that day and quickly

34

recognised an exceptional intellect.

The two were heading directly towards the rock, followed by two others. 'Luke and Bruno,' said Riley.

'Did you know they were coming?'

'No idea.' Riley was astonished. 'I mean, Luke said he might swing by. He had a meeting at Marondera.'

Riley's boyfriend, Luke, was a game ranger who looked as if he'd been sent by casting central, with his darkly rugged good looks, khaki hiking vests, and sunglasses. We'd spoken a few times and I'd been struck by his blend of Zim colloquialisms and wide-ranging global connections: International funding for conservation in this country spanned the world.

We exchanged waves with the approaching group.

Riley shot me a questioning glance. Not quite the sunset drink together we had envisaged.

I shrugged. 'More the merrier.'

Observing the big event, we watched the sun first touch the horizon, then start to sink below. Disappearing slowly to begin with, then sliding away much faster, it left behind a burnt orange sky turning to red, a vivid, impossibly scarlet sweep where it descended from view that was deepening in tone, moment by mesmerising moment.

'That image you sent me of your yoga class,' I told Riley. 'I used it as a screensaver.'

'Did you really?' she smiled.

'For months. I used to come here in my imagination.'

She put her arm around my shoulders and squeezed.

'Your ears must have been burning earlier,' she told me. 'Lakshmi was asking about you.'

'Lakshmi?'

'One of the girls in that photo. She saw you at

Rinpoche's session and thought you looked familiar. Quite the coincidence. It turns out that she worked at Landers for two months.'

'Really?'

'July and August, a few years ago. Ring any bells?'

I shook my head. 'Landers has so many staff.'

'That's what I said. But you're one of the *boykies*, so she would have noticed you.'

I pulled a droll expression.

'Still. A small world, hey?'

I nodded, taking in her freckled-faced enthusiasm. Right at this moment, Landers and London had never seemed so far away.

~

We heard the others scrambling between the boulders. Thor and Tiki growled half-heartedly. We shushed them as first Harris appeared, then Tinashe.

'Hurry or you'll miss the best bit!' called Riley.

'*A* highlight, my dear,' Harris countered her. 'Not *the* highlight.'

Tinashe greeted us softly, and I was again struck by the quality of stillness about him.

'I don't know what tops this.' I turned back to where the afterglow was deepening. A band of deep crimson, stretching improbably across the horizon, blurred upwards into sienna, which in turn faded to yellow, and that too lightened to the pale clarity of twilight.

'It *is* very special,' Harris murmured behind us after a while. 'And it is followed by another wonder from the opposite direction.'

'Oh!' Riley turned suddenly. 'Are you the full moon club?'

Harris nodded.

'And we thought *you* were the gate crashers!' she exclaimed.

Luke and Bruno appeared at the bottom of the rock.

'Every twenty-eight nights,' confirmed Harris, turning towards them. 'Best seats in the whole district.'

Luke and I were already friends, but I had heard of Bruno only from the others. As we exchanged greetings, I took in the tall, craggy-faced Italian who was pioneering organic teas in the country's eastern highlands. Entrepreneurial and enigmatic, he was said to come from aristocratic stock.

'I see our VIP guest is on his way,' observed Harris.

We followed his gaze. Yogi Tarchin was walking down the lawn from the Ruwa Buddhist Society homestead, accompanied by Diva.

'And is that ...?' asked Riley, prodding Luke with excitement.

Grinning, he nodded.

'*Incredibile!*' Bruno exclaimed on behalf of us all.

Following, just a short distance behind the lama and Diva, was Bodhi.

'I wondered if she was still around,' said Riley.

'She's been sleeping on the veranda of the guest bungalow,' reported Harris. 'Diva tells me she is quite taken with Yogi Tarchin.'

'Mush, hey?' Luke used Zimbo slang for "excellent". 'But as he's from Tibet, I'm surprised he's so chilled about a big cat.'

There was a pause while we watched the three of them in procession through the bush.

Tinashe spoke for the first time. 'The lama is no ordinary man.'

I glanced over, meeting his eyes. 'That's for sure.'

Thor was scratching himself, his hind leg rasping his side vigorously, when I was struck by a horrifying thought.

'The dogs! With Bodhi ...'

Luke glanced from the two of them to Riley. 'Have they met?' He gestured towards the cheetah.

'Carrie used to visit John with them often,' she told him. 'Bodhi was always there.'

'Ja, no, they'll be fine,' Luke turned to me. '*Shamwaris.*' He looked down again to where Bodhi's prowling form merged into the bush as the others got closer to the kopje. 'All the same,' he said drily, 'I hope they're feeding her.'

'Only the best,' confirmed Harris. 'Yogi Tarchin insists on it.'

~

A short while later the sunset display ended, and the vivid spectrum of colours drained to leave only deep blue. There was a sound from the other end of the rock: Yogi Tarchin and Diva had arrived. Rinpoche was leading the way, a lamp in the twilight. He closed his palms at his heart in greeting and we did the same. It wasn't a gesture I had made before, but as I reciprocated it felt entirely natural. A few footsteps behind him came Diva, bright with zeal.

'Thank you for letting me join your full moon club,' the lama said to Harris, chuckling.

'If I may let you into a secret, Rinpoche,' replied Harris, 'I *am* the full moon club. It's just me and whoever I can persuade to join me.'

'On that subject,' Riley looked behind Diva, 'did Bodhi follow you?'

'Not up the rock.' Diva shook her head.

There was a pause as we stared into the darkness,

then Luke said, 'She'll come if she wants. You can't make a cat do anything it doesn't want to.'

His words seemed to underline the rarity of what we had all witnessed last weekend on the lawn with Yogi Tarchin.

We settled on the rock amid a patchwork of throws, Yogi Tarchin sitting nearest the face of the rock, the rest of us forming a circle — Thor and Tiki toasting their tummies on the still-warm boulder behind Riley and me.

'It is starting,' observed Rinpoche.

Looking to the horizon opposite where the sun had descended, we took in the pearly haze where the sky was beginning to lighten.

The rising of the moon was as swift as the sun's setting. First, a large and lustrous rim appeared, and over a period of only a few minutes, the horizon birthed a huge orb of silver. On this night it appeared much bigger than usual and its rays were immeasurably brighter. Moonlight began streaming across the veldt, washing the arid landscape with luminosity, transforming barren soil and desiccated scrub into a still ocean. Grey boulders were burnished to gleaming silver. Stark trees and their leafless branches rose as mysterious silhouettes in the surreal moonscape.

'So peaceful!' said Diva.

Beside her, Yogi Tarchin nodded. As the moon tugged free of the horizon, I knew that no matter where I could be in the world right now, I wouldn't want to be anywhere else. Here with Yogi Tarchin on Ruwa Rock suddenly felt like the most extraordinary place. Evidently, others were sensing the same thing. But for

Tinashe, the rarity of the experience was a poignant reminder of a very different reality.

'I also feel this peace, Rinpoche. Here, with you.' The heartfelt sincerity of his words was palpable. 'And the meditation you shared with us was so special!'

The others were nodding.

'But most people, they are suffering. In this country there are no jobs. No money. The schools and hospitals are broken. With such hardship ...' his expression was anguished, 'is there any point in trying Buddhist practices? Should we even tell people to hope for a peaceful heart?'

'Tinashe,' responded Yogi Tarchin, infusing the three syllables of his name with such deep compassion that the young man was visibly moved, 'this is an important question. I understand why you ask.'

Tinashe's gaze was fixed to him as Yogi Tarchin leaned forward.

'But the suffering you speak of makes Africa a *better* place for Buddhism.'

Tinashe was startled.

'There is no power greater than suffering to put us on a journey of inner growth. It is when we suffer that we most wish to find an escape. To turn away from the true causes of our pain.'

Africa as a seedbed for Buddhism came as the most extraordinary notion.

Rinpoche paused, looking about our faces.

'I have many students in developed countries. Compared to people in Africa, materially speaking they have far more wealth and easier lives. Much leisure and many enjoyments. But having money doesn't make a person more mindful or benevolent or wise. A beautiful home and lifestyle don't offer purpose.

They may even be hindrances if they make us comfortably numb. How can we wish with all our hearts to free ourselves from our delusions, if they don't seem to cause us any great trouble?'

Tinashe regarded Yogi Tarchin, transfixed.

'I'd go even further,' the lama told him. 'You Zimbabweans, of all colours, are more naturally Buddhist than many other people.'

Beside him on the rock, Diva chortled quietly, a hand to her mouth.

'It's true!' he smiled. 'Do you not spend much of your time helping one another? Giving, sharing, taking care of those who need?'

In an instant I was taken back to my first morning here — Marvellous outside my window, shouting to a friend. Later in the day, that same friend wobbling along the dirt track on Marvellous's *bhasikoro*. How Aunt Carrie's circle of friends had included me in invitations and put me on their WhatsApp group that alerted members to where they could get fuel and groceries that were in short supply. How Diva had called in personal favours to get Aunt Carrie a bed, first in hospital, then in a hospice.

'In Africa,' said Tinashe, 'we call this *ubuntu*.'

'*Ubuntu?*' confirmed Rinpoche.

'It means, "I am because we are".'

His face lit up. 'You see! This is like Dharma teachings on interdependence. Many know the idea — but here in Africa you already practice it.'

'Because we have to!' joked Diva.

Everyone chuckled, knowing how difficult it would be trying to get the simplest things done without the advice, connections, or support of others. At the same time came the intriguing recognition that in our remote pocket of Africa, one of the core precepts of Buddhism was already the norm.

'Not only ubuntu,' Rinpoche continued. 'You also have strong minds. You are resilient. When things go wrong, you don't fall in a heap, or get angry at others, or waste time complaining. You "make a plan".'

When he said the phrase there was more merriment. For it was true!

'You Zimbabweans are patient,' he continued. 'You persevere. You don't expect instant results. These qualities, born from challenge, are precious beyond measure and,' he looked directly at Tinashe, '*you already possess them!*

'Africa and India,' he held up two entwined fingers, 'are much closer than most people believe.'

~

The moon was rising higher, and although smaller than when it had first loomed on the horizon, its light was even more dazzling. The bush was almost bright as day but bestowed with a lunar enchantment that rendered everything somehow magical.

'You've been here for a few days, Rinpoche,' Harris spoke after a while. 'Is there any advice you'd like to give us before you leave?'

The moment he asked the question I thought it an excellent one. If you have the good fortune to be in the presence of a person with such evident insight, why would you not seek whatever advice he cared to offer? Although I detected that Harris seemed to have taken himself by surprise with the query.

Yogi Tarchin looked at him approvingly. 'My only suggestion,' he said lightly, 'is that you should build a temple.'

His idea was met with astonished silence. Nobody

on the rock had ever contemplated such a thing! A Buddhist organisation with a temple wasn't, perhaps, a strange notion, but Yogi Tarchin proposed a level of commitment that seemed daunting. Being only a visitor, I didn't take his suggestion to include me.

The lama explained how a temple need not replicate a Himalayan *gompa* built for mountainous conditions. It could have a thatched African roof, made from local materials. He had discussed the idea with Mr Nzou, the groundsman who knew something about such structures. According to Mr Nzou, the build time could be as short as a few weeks. As for Buddha statues and *thangkas*, or wall-hangings, these were items that Rinpoche could arrange through contacts in Nepal.

As the lama spoke, it became clear that this was no casual suggestion. Harris's question hadn't been random. Nor was it by chance that we had found our way to the top of Ruwa Rock that evening. We might have believed that we were climbing here for reasons of nostalgia, or to admire the full moon, but in reality, the same inexplicable magnetism that had conjured Bodhi out of the bush after three years had also drawn us to this place.

Someone would be needed to supervise the builder and expedite the orders of construction materials, said Rinpoche, looking at Diva. Transport would be required to bring materials from Harare, he nodded towards Tinashe. The precise location of the temple and its orientation would have to be meticulously calculated, he observed, meeting Harris's gleaming eyes. A Bobcat machine would have to come in to prepare the ground.

'I have one,' Bruno murmured.

Social media was important to get the word out, he told Riley. And the animal enclosures might need to be reviewed, he addressed Luke. As for money, he said — I was the only one yet to been given a job — a small loan would be needed. I was relieved when he didn't fix on me. He wasn't looking at anyone.

'Rinpoche, we are a not-for-profit with no income,' Diva reminded him.

'Yes, yes. It can be a private loan to be paid off.'

'But how, if we have no funds?'

'The place you have, right here,' he said. 'It's very special. And with the right development there will come a time, soon, when people will visit from all over. Not just Harare. Not just Zimbabwe. From all of southern Africa,' Yogi Tarchin nodded. 'Even Europe too.'

We were following him with astonishment.

'The money will come back many times over.'

'Do you have a budget estimate?' I heard myself asking, perhaps out of professional habit.

He met my eyes directly. 'Just over $7,000,' he said.

~

We sat, each of us dumbfounded.

'If you don't want to build a temple, that's okay.' He spoke with his ineffable lightness. 'Take time to consider. But if you want to go ahead, I am here to serve you. To help. And ...' he chuckled, 'there is a sem chen I think would like me to stay for a while.' (Sem chen — Tibetan for "mind-haver", one who possesses consciousness and is therefore capable of enlightenment.)

He glanced up in a way that made us turn to follow his gaze. Sprawled on the long, straight branch of the umbrella tree, watching over us all, was Bodhi. She had climbed the tree soundlessly, heading to her paramount vantage point. From behind I heard the thump of Thor's tail against the rock. He was also looking at the cheetah. I was relieved by his welcoming response.

Moonlight filtered through the canopy of the

umbrella tree, creating a spectral haze around Bodhi, at supreme ease where she rested. By the time we had turned back to Yogi Tarchin, he was sitting more upright, in meditation posture, and as we followed suit, he directed us to turn around so that we were sitting looking out from the rock into the moonlit night.

Ahead of us was a vast, clear expanse of light beneath the astral sweep of the Milky Way. The night was serene but not silent — the sound of crickets in high-pitched descant, the breeze snagging stray lines of "Neria", the popular Shona song, from a village radio. In the warm night, the lama had us focus simply on breathing for a while to settle, before inviting us, simply but unusually, to rest our mind in its natural state.

'Mind is not something to be seen visually,' he said. 'Allow your gaze to relax unfocused or close your eyes if you prefer. When a thought arises, don't engage with it. Simply acknowledge. Accept. Let go of the thought and return your attention to mind itself. Seek merely to observe mind when it is free of agitation or dullness. To abide with the mind at rest.'

I had tried this exercise before briefly, during a seminar in London. Back then I had decided that my mind was too unmanageably busy — it was too great a struggle even to try. But here on the rock it felt quite different. Was it the extraordinary vista of moonlit clarity stretching from one horizon to the other? Or the sense of bathing in the expansive serenity of the lama? Somehow, here and now, it was so much easier to let go of thinking and just be.

'From high up it is easy to think of yourself as small. Insignificant.' I knew Rinpoche was addressing me directly — and I sensed the same recognition as the first time he had looked me in the eyes, as if everything about me was evident to him. But far from feeling intimidated, I felt the opposite.

'If we think of ourselves as merely physical beings, then yes, we are of little consequence. We are born, we live, we die, and whatever impact we make in the material world is soon forgotten.

'But does this view accord with reality? Mind is not matter, but energy. Formless. Its natural state is lucid, enabling any thought or sensation to arise. Mind has no size. It is certainly not as tiny as our heads. It is boundless, without beginning or end.

'Look out from here as if you are gazing into your own mind for yourself. Imagine that the clarity directly in front of you extends behind you too. And below you as much as above. Where are you, the observer, in all this, you may ask?'

After a pause he confirmed emphatically, 'You are all of it! Not observing it but being it. Consciousness without limits. Consciousness with a quality of profound peace. A tranquillity that deepens the longer you abide in it. When you can do this — even if for only a few moments — you catch a glimpse of your own Buddha nature.'

~

I can't say how long we sat there. Like the first time Yogi Tarchin guided us in meditation, I had the strangest sensation of double time. Until that night I had always considered my mind to be all that I thought about — my collected cognitions, feelings, convictions, and personal history. But the lama had revealed that mind was instead merely spacious awareness, a boundless sphere in which all cognitive activity could arise, abide, and pass. So utterly absorbing was this revelation that by the time he dedicated the session, the moon was high and the stars had shifted. Sweet perfume of night-jasmine floated to us from the Ruwa Buddhist Society

Garden above the dusty dryness of the bush.

We rose to our feet, too wonder-struck to speak. Even the dogs were becalmed. Bodhi was still with us, poised and watchful as a sentry, and for a while we gazed from the starscape to the monochrome veldt below. During our meditation session the giraffes had drawn closer — they were browsing on a thorn tree not far away. Riley sidled up to Luke, murmuring something. He lifted the binoculars fastened to his belt and studied the two of them. Then he turned with a smile. 'Ja, hey, you're right,' he nodded towards me. 'Kim *is* moving differently. I think she's pregnant. In the dry season, you know, other giraffes come here.'

'Our first baby at the Ruwa Buddhist Society!' Diva clapped her hands together.

'From the vast, spaciousness of mind itself,' Yogi Tarchin opened his arms wide, 'all arises.'

'Including baby giraffes?' confirmed Bruno.

'And thatched temples?' queried Diva.

'Sky-like wisdom is called "the mother" because it gives birth to all things!' Yogi Tarchin's eyes were bright. 'And with ubuntu,' he turned back to Diva, 'with "I am because we are", everything is possible!'

~

Later that night I sat for a while with Thor and Tiki on Aunt Carrie's moonlit veranda, sipping Amarula on ice and feeling grateful for time to absorb all that was happening. I had come to Zimbabwe for a particular purpose. That purpose had changed, regrettably, from carer to executor, a job that wouldn't take me long. Soon I would be rescheduling my flight home to London.

What I hadn't counted on was Yogi Tarchin. I had never met anyone like him and the way he effortlessly made things happen. The appearance of Bodhi from the bush last weekend after an absence of three years. The gathering of us all to the top of Ruwa Rock as if summoned to a meeting. How in his presence I had the sense that nothing about me was hidden to him — and yet I felt so comfortable that all I wanted was to immerse myself in his presence. It felt as if something extraordinary was happening here in Ruwa amid a flux of unlikely possibilities. In particular, Rinpoche's mention of $7,000 felt teasing, even mischievous, in reflecting almost the precise amount in Aunt Carrie's bank account.

If Rinpoche was staying perhaps for a month to oversee the building of a temple, where did that leave me? Instead of returning in late November, what if I pushed my plans back a few weeks? Might there be other epiphanies before it was time to go?

Chapter Three

TREASURE TREES CAFÉ was abuzz with activity that Saturday morning. Diva had converted the suburban home in Chisipite into a chic café as well as a retail outlet for her apothecary products and a wing of aromatherapy treatment rooms. In Harare it was on trend to turn former colonial-era bungalows and their gardens into verdant oases of restaurants, boutiques, or gymnasia. Locals termed it "island hopping", as they drove along the wrecked roads and through dishevelled suburbs from one such sanctuary to another.

For a moment I thought how distraught Mum would have been by the degradation of the once-trim capital. But I supposed she had been an island hopper, in her own way, on a wider scale. The bush, for her, had been as forbidding as any potholed road or decrepit former secondary school. It was a place you had to get through, eyes shut if necessary, until you reached the next outpost of civilisation. A woman with orthodox expectations, her only wish was for the same quiet, ordered family life she would have enjoyed back in Scotland. It was Dad, the adventurer, who had lured her here with an aplomb she'd found impossible to resist when they were both young. With so few jobs to be had in 1950s Scotland, what was there to lose?

Diva's emporium was just off Shortheath Road, down a driveway bordered by birds of paradise in extravagant bloom. Even before reaching reception you were enveloped in a bouquet of fragrances. The calming lavender and citrusy lemongrass I recognised, but along with them were other, more intriguing, indigenous scents. The sweet fruitiness of marula, or 'marriage tree' as it was known among the Shona people, which grew in both male and female genders, the fresh zing of anti-ageing moringa, the earthy, healing wafts of the legendary baobab — some of the 'treasure trees' after which Diva had named her business.

It was my first visit to the café. The tone was contemporary and stylish without being showy. Walking through a shop lined with shelves of beautifully merchandised creams, sprays, and diffusers, I stepped into an expansive space with ochre-coloured walls lit by warm lamps with clay bases. Sumptuous sofas were scattered with cushions in zebra, giraffe and leopard prints. Moody black-and-white photographs of wildlife decorated the walls, and Shona sculptures occupied soft-lit alcoves. Farther out was a veranda and lawn with dining tables and *mbira* music playing gently in the background.

Diva waved from across the room. She and Harris were sitting on a sofa, Tinashe facing them across a coffee table. I drew up a tub chair next to Tinashe. Diva was mid-way through a story about a client's miraculous response to baobab treatment for rheumatoid arthritis. Her bead earrings glinted as she gestured effusively. I guessed that from this corner table she'd miss nothing that was going on. Next to her, Harris, with his swept-back silver hair and indigo shirt, regarded her with benign affection. Tinashe, smooth and somewhat formal in a cream linen jacket, was very, very still as he listened to her tale.

After we'd ordered coffees, Diva came directly to the reason why she'd invited us.

'We've had a few days to consider Yogi Tarchin's advice,' she said, looking around. 'What do you think?'

Harris shot her a droll look before turning to Tinashe and me. 'As Diva knows, I've always thought that Ruwa Buddhist Society could be much more than a retirement home for John Elliot's animals, much as we love them.'

I remembered how, on our very first meeting, Harris had seemed almost oracular in his expectations of Yogi Tarchin's visit.

'Rinpoche asked you to help with the siting of the temple,' said Tinashe. 'Is that something you could do?'

'It would be the commission of a lifetime,' he replied. 'A privilege rarely accorded.'

'A Buddhist temple in Africa?' I mused. 'Couldn't be many of those.'

Harris assumed a momentous expression. '31 degrees East,' he said. 'Have you heard of it?'

We shook our heads.

'Centre of the earth's landmasses. A line of longitude that touches more land than any other. The opposite side of the planet is nearly all ocean. So, it's a very special meridian — you might say a sacred one. Thousands of years ago the pyramid of Giza was constructed on 31 East. And most people are aware of the significance of the Great Pyramid's location.'

I wondered where he was going with this when he asked, 'What would you say is the most important ancient monument in Africa *south* of the equator?'

'Great Zimbabwe,' Tinashe and I chimed together. The mysterious fortress with its looming conical tower had been the capital of a medieval kingdom in Zimbabwe's southeast. "House of stone" was the literal translation of the word "Zimbabwe". And along with the ancient, patterned walls, archaeologists had also discovered at Great Zimbabwe a repository of other arcane artefacts, including the country's best-known emblem, the enigmatic Zimbabwe bird.

Leaning towards us he said, 'Great Zimbabwe is also built on 31 degrees East.'

'First I've heard of it.' I was startled.

'Most Zimbabweans don't know, let alone anyone else. The meridian was vital to earlier civilisations. Somewhere along the way we've forgotten its significance.'

'Isn't the meridian aligned with Orion's belt?' I asked.

'There are many correlations between 31 East and the stars,' he nodded. 'But there's a reason, much closer to home, that makes it special.' As he looked from one to the other of us, his blue eyes were bright with significance. '31 degrees East,' he intoned, 'runs straight through Ruwa.'

Tinashe and I shared a look of amazement — with each other and with Diva, who evidently had heard Harris speak of this before.

'Ruwa Rock is slap bang in the middle of it.'

'When we were on Ruwa Rock a few nights ago, we were sitting in the same line as the pyramid of Giza and Great Zimbabwe?' confirmed Tinashe.

'Exactly,' said Harris with a smile, before leaning back into the sofa. 'Why would I *not* want to bring out my GPS unit to help align a temple in the right place?

How few other people have ever had that honour?'

~

During the awe-struck lull that followed, a waiter arrived with our coffee.

Diva fixed her attention on Tinashe. 'What about you, Tina?' She evidently didn't want to get side-tracked with talk of ancient symbols and mystic meridians. 'Is a temple project something you'd be willing to help with?'

'I've got a vehicle I could use,' he nodded. 'But I'd need money for fuel.'

'Of course.'

Riley had told me that Tinashe was a science teacher with two university degrees. In Zimbabwe, where most people didn't have formal jobs, the monthly wages received even by those who did seldom covered more than a few days' living expenses, which was why many people had second or third jobs to scrape by. I was wondering where Tinashe worked that involved driving a truck when he turned to tell me, 'I collect garbage every morning. 4.30 am.'

'Okay.' Privatised garbage collectors had sprung up in the wealthier northern suburbs after the collapse of waste collection by local municipalities.

'Tinashe is a man of many parts,' Diva said approvingly. 'Very mechanically minded. He can bring an old car back to life like no one I've seen.'

'Useful skill in a place like Zim,' I said. 'Tell me, Tinashe, how did you come to Buddhism?'

'Because of a girl called Pema,' his face lit up. 'From Bhutan. I met her when working for a cruise company in the Mediterranean.'

In moments I'd had to reframe my idea of Tinashe from teacher to garbage collector to cruise liner employee with a Bhutanese girlfriend. A man of many parts, Diva had said. I glanced over at her. 'I see what you mean!'

'Pema is finishing her studies in Britain,' Tinashe continued. 'I am hoping that after that she'll want to be with me.'

Diva reached to squeeze his hand supportively. 'I am quite sure she will.' She turned to focus on me. 'And you, Rob? Are you with us on the temple project?'

'I'm here only briefly,' I replied, appreciating her candour. 'I'm happy to help if there's something I can do. It seems that you are the one who'd have the main burden of managing contractors.'

'A time burden,' she nodded. 'If we use suppliers whom I already know, it's something I can manage. But the loan is not something I'd want to ask Herbert for.'

Herbert Derembwe, Diva's husband, was a well-regarded Harare lawyer and general fixer.

'I can do the loan,' I said.

I hadn't expected any money from Aunt Carrie, nor did I need it. I was happy to let them have it — but I held back from saying it was a donation just yet.

Diva looked relieved. 'That would be more than wonderful!'

~

Talk turned to next steps. Diva had thoughts on suppliers and said she'd set up a meeting with Rinpoche. There was discussion about the ideas he had developed with Mr Nzou. In passing, Diva explained how, ahead of his visit, Yogi Tarchin had asked to meet the local chief. Elderly and bedridden, the chief had nominated Mr Nzou as his representative — which was how the groundsman had come in unusually formal attire to occupy the front row at Rinpoche's first appearance.

As for Rinpoche himself, Diva said she needed to confirm that he was willing to stay on until the build was complete.

'Perhaps,' Tinashe suggested, 'we could ask him to be our Spiritual Director? That is what other Buddhist centres do for continuity. Not only for the next few months, but far beyond.'

'Good idea!' agreed Diva.

Tinashe's smooth exterior evidently concealed great depths.

'So, Rob,' Diva looked at me with that irrepressible verve. 'You might be staying to see the temple built?'

All three of them studied me intently. I looked at their expectant faces. 'I've never met anyone like Yogi Tarchin,' I said simply.

From their expressions it was clear I needn't say more.

'When I'm with him,' Diva agreed, 'it's like he can read my mind. I have this feeling of peace. Like everything makes sense.'

'He's a catalyst.' Harris's blue eyes were glistening. 'The way that Bodhi just appeared from the bush! The way he got us all together on top of the rock ...'

'Glad I wasn't the only one who noticed!' I chuckled.

'How often ...' continued Harris, 'does that happen?'

'From the first time I saw him,' agreed Tinashe, 'I felt this connection. I was so excited I couldn't wait to tell Pema. You know the Bhutanese understand more about these things. It's their culture. They are the only Tibetan Buddhist country in the world.'

'And what did she say?' Diva was eager.

'She said I had met my guru,' he replied, seeming to bow slightly as he touched the jacket pocket carrying his phone. 'She wrote me the most beautiful email.'

As he spoke the words I felt a powerful and contradictory response — part of me resonating strongly with what he said, while some other force held me back.

Harris looked at the young man, fascinated. 'Are you willing to share what she said?'

Tinashe nodded in that cool, somehow removed manner, taking his phone out and searching for the email. He glanced at our expectant faces before beginning to read:

'"When you meet your guru, dear Tinashe, you have met a very precious being who will be your lifelong companion. He is no ordinary friend, and is even closer than family, because ..."' he looked up at us, '"he is the companion of your heart".'

Moved by the power of the sentiment, Diva raised a hand to her throat.

'"Your guru",' continued Tinashe, '"opens the door to a secret world you never knew existed but that has always been as available as the one that you imagine to be real. You will find it so beautiful, such a joyful place to visit that, once you have seen it you will yearn to stay".'

I remembered how I'd felt during the meditation sessions with Yogi Tarchin, first on the lawn, then later on Ruwa Rock. Unlike anyone else I spent time with, when I was sitting with him I felt as if we were in an immaculate place. Was this Pema's secret world?

'"You will want to make this divine mandala your own. And you will! For there's a blessing a guru can give you that cannot be found in books or by watching videos. A blessing that comes only from being by his side and learning from him as a potter gazes at the hands of his master, not wishing to miss out on a single moment as he turns a lump of clay into an exquisite vase. It doesn't matter so much what the master teaches as how he is when you are with him. This is *transmission* as it has passed from great masters to students since the time of the Buddha".'

Pema expressed a learning that went beyond words. An apprenticeship deeper than the simple transfer of information. She was pointing to embodiment of a more subtle, energetic kind.

"'Be humble, dear Tinashe. We all have failings, sometimes flaws that the whole world sees except for ourselves. It is our guru's job to reveal them to us. To be a mirror. We may not always like what he shows. We may have to endure painful corrections. It is challenging when our master pushes us beyond the limits we would accept if we were trying to find the way on our own".

"'But with our guru's help we go beyond. We can settle the mind and attain special insight. If we can sit downwind of divinity and experience the clear light directly for ourselves, not just as an idea or a teaching but as a vivid reality, if we are able to do this even for a few precious moments",' Tinashe swallowed, before concluding somewhat shakily, "'it will eclipse anything else we can do in our whole life".'

For a while he sat, staring at his phone as we all absorbed the enormity of what he'd said.

~

'Wow!' Harris exclaimed after a while.

Diva's eyes brimmed with tears.

Pema's words were among the most insightful I had encountered. They came from a place of knowing. And they intensified the conflict I had felt a short time earlier. I knew exactly why.

Yogi Tarchin had already taken me to unknown states where I yearned to stay, just as Pema had described. I had no doubt that he was an extraordinary person. But my visit to Zimbabwe was temporary. I had a new business to set up in London. Nick Berkeley and many other people were counting on me to do it. However evocative the notion of sitting at the elbow of the perfect guru on a journey of transcendence might be, the timing just wasn't right.

'That's a beautiful message,' Diva murmured finally.

Tinashe nodded.

'Pema is quite exceptional,' I observed.

'She is,' agreed Tinashe.

'Hopefully she will come to visit,' said Diva, 'so that we can walk the journey together.'

There was a pause before I said, 'Ubuntu.'

Remembering Yogi Tarchin on the moonlit rock, we shared a smile.

~

Harris looked at his watch and said he was meeting a bookseller friend, Peter, at Old Stables Market in Borrowdale for lunch. Diva said that she'd get in touch with Yogi Tarchin later to talk about the temple. As we rose from our chairs, Tinashe bade farewell. Diva led me to the shop where she handed me two of her premium baobab gift boxes — one to pass onto Yogi Tarchin and one for me.

She waxed enthusiastic about the exceptional properties of baobab seeds for moisturising and stimulating the collagen that keeps skin elastic and youthful. Eyes bright, she told me how Zimbabwe's own tree of life had potent anti-inflammatory effects, not to mention antioxidant qualities that slowed cellular damage. Mid-stream, she caught sight of someone across the shop.

'Lakshmi!'

A striking young Indian woman, in her late thirties, with the poise of a maharani, came towards us.

'Lovely to see you.' She and Diva embraced before Diva introduced us.

'Riley, my niece, mentioned you to me,' I told her, as we shook hands.

'Such a coincidence!' she exclaimed. There was a vibrancy about her face as she told Diva how she'd worked for Landers a few years ago. Her eyes were so familiar that I recognised them instantly. Which meetings had we sat in, I wondered? What projects had she been involved with?

'I'm here on the off chance we can get a reflexology session for Dad,' she told Diva. 'The last one gave him such a boost.'

'Let's make a plan.' Diva led her to the reception counter.

Lakshmi glanced over her shoulder. An elderly Indian man with a walking stick was hobbling over the pavers. 'I asked him to wait in the car,' she said anxiously.

'Don't worry, I'll help,' I offered, 'while you sort out an appointment.'

Moments later, I was at the old man's side. 'May I offer you a hand?'

'No need for fuss,' he replied, his eyes focused on the ground.

'Lakshmi's seeing if she can get you an appointment.'

He grunted, progressing to the entrance in a slow but steady shuffle. 'You work here?' he asked.

'No. Just a friend. You know Riley?'

He nodded. 'The yoga girl?'

'Yes,' I replied. 'I'm her uncle. Rob Forbes.'

The old man's gaze shot up, meeting my face with an expression of such intensity that I was shaken to the core. Not only the force of it, but the emotion: he stared at me with sudden wide-eyed dread.

'We've got you in, Mr Kumar!' Diva breezed towards us with Lakshmi. 'An appointment in ten minutes.'

Disconcerted, I said my goodbyes and stepped away.

What had triggered the old man, I wondered; walking to the car? Or was his reaction nothing personal? Perhaps he was a troubled soul? All the same, it was a disturbing encounter that left me unsettled. I didn't know what to make of it.

~

Back in the car heading past Chisipite Senior School, I opened the window, resting my elbow on the door and enjoying the warm summer breeze. My thoughts returned to our meeting and in particular to the message about guru yoga so movingly expressed by Pema. Her words reminded me of a conversation I'd once had with Kay. My godmother divided her time between Nyanga, in Zimbabwe's eastern highlands, and a home in Italy. In her eighties she was still an inveterate traveller, both literally and through the books she read. She had become a Buddhist midway through life and it had been on one of her annual visits through London that she'd explained something about how Buddhists thought of their teachers as being like Buddhas.

'Isn't that sacrilege?' I'd asked, surprised. In the Presbyterian church of my upbringing, it would have been heresy to suggest that Padre Nisbet was in any way comparable to Jesus.

'Completely different approach,' Kay had shaken her head. 'When we see someone admirable, we can worship them or we can seek to *be* like them. Buddhists choose the second approach. Our guru shows us how.'

'A lot of pressure for the guru,' I remarked.

'The qualities of the guru arise mainly from our minds. We're encouraged to focus on the positive and find antidotes for whatever negatives we perceive.'

'Even if they're corrupt?'

'Using common sense, naturally.' She'd rolled her eyes at my contrariness. 'Any therapist will tell you that the way that people seem to us is as much about our own minds as it is about the people.'

I was reflecting on this when Kay startled me more. 'It's said that your guru is even kinder to you than the historical Shakyamuni Buddha.'

'How's that possible?'

'Does Shakyamuni Buddha turn up to offer you regular classes? Does he listen to your problems and give you encouragement and support?'

'Sounds quite radical,' I observed.

'Oh, it is!' Kay's hazel eyes glinted behind her spectacles. 'Buddha turned the way we see things upside down.'

The following morning, I called Thor and Tiki and we set out to deliver Yogi Tarchin's gift. Following the same dirt road we'd used on our drive with Riley, I relished walking through the open veldt, the sun warm on my skin as the two dogs scrambled through the bush from one irresistible scent to another.

We came to a stretch where at the side of the track was a scattering of small, fine, funnel-shaped holes in the sand. Remembering them from my childhood, I paused, getting down on my haunches to study them more closely. Ant lion traps. Tiny cone-shaped pits, they were designed to catch unwary ants and other insects who would come too close to their edge. Loose grains of sand would send an unwary insect tumbling to the bottom where the creator of the trap, a so-called "ant-lion", was awaiting with its sharp mandibles. It had been a boyhood game to tickle the side of a cone with a small twig, simulating a falling ant, before placing the twig at the bottom of the cone to see if an ant-lion — a small, squirming larvae not much bigger than an ant itself — was clamped onto the end.

Getting up, I continued walking, taking in another day's cloudless blue sky. In the distance, a group of villagers in the white robes of the Apostolic church had gathered under the green boughs of a winter thorn tree. Fragments of a voice raised in impassioned prayer carried to where I was walking, *mvura* being frequently invoked: rain. In these parts, where most people were subsistence farmers, rain was of overwhelming importance, especially at this time of the year. With last year's harvest nearly exhausted, every day without rain was another day closer to starvation.

Pretty soon the congregants were singing hymns, voices raised in heartfelt, a capella gospel as they swayed from side to side, hands clapping. Rhythm and music pervaded Africa as instinctively as crickets heralded nightfall or birds chorused at dawn. As music was never far below the surface, no celebration or entreaty continued very long without a spontaneous outbreak. And when you sing — as my choirmaster father used to say — you are happy.

The lawn of the Ruwa Buddhist Society was an oasis after the biscuit brown outside, the lush smell as striking as its shimmering green. Sonny and Cher were book-ending the chevron-styled thatch ridge. Mampara the wildebeest grazed contentedly. On the other side of the flower bed, Debbie and Kim were browsing on acacia leaves.

I approached the homestead, planning to leave Diva's gift for Rinpoche on the hall table with a note.

But as I reached the veranda, I found him sitting on a sofa — legs and torso in the sun, face in the shade. He rose to greet me.

'No — please, sit!' I felt awkward disturbing him.

'Good, good,' he was shaking my hand, meeting my eyes with a twinkle.

'From Diva with love,' I said, handing him the box with both hands.

Diva's Baobab Box was elegantly presented in olive green tones, the calligraphy and Treasure Trees Apothecary logo embossed in gold. Containing shower soap, body lotion, and other skincare products, it was her premium range — and looked it.

Yogi Tarchin accepted the box. 'This is good for skin, yes?'

'I've been using it for years,' I told him.

Kay had brought me Diva's baobab skin cream once when passing through London. My pale Scottish skin got dry during winter. The lotion made all the difference. And I relished the fragrant reminder of home.

Rinpoche placed the gift with some ceremony on the hall table before offering me coffee. A short while later he was pouring a cup, which somehow felt wrong after all the reverential statements on the subject of the guru that I'd absorbed yesterday. But given the lama's casual lightness, it also seemed quite normal.

'I am very happy that the group decided to build the temple,' he beamed, handing me my coffee. He had resumed his place on the sofa. I faced him in a cane chair.

'We're only doing it out of selfishness, Rinpoche,' I replied. 'We all want to keep you here a bit longer!'

He chuckled. 'And thank *you*, personally, for your generous offer of the loan.'

'Aunt Carrie died and left some money.' I gestured

towards her house, maintaining the fiction that he didn't know exactly what had happened. 'I'm a beneficiary, and I really don't need the money. I want to offer it as a gift.'

His eyes met mine. 'Diva says you return to London soon?'

'I'm starting a new job,' I confirmed. 'Right now, I'm waiting for legal permission to sort out Carrie's estate. After that happens, I'll be going.'

'You know about business,' he looked at me evenly. 'And I have a favour to ask. Would you help manage things here until you leave?'

'You mean, building the temple?' His request caught me unawares.

He shook his head. 'Diva is doing that. But we need help with digital arrangements for the society.'

'A website, you mean' I queried. 'Member database?'

He nodded. Then, almost casually, 'And perhaps help with the animals.'

From what I could tell, the animals had done very well since John Elliott had died.

Noting my surprise, he said. 'There may be more coming. As Ruwa Buddhist Society gets more active and people hear about us, there may be newcomers. We may need enclosures. Luke knows about these things.'

'Sure,' I nodded. Neither the help with a website nor the less obvious request about new animals seemed especially burdensome.

'You can set up an office in here,' he gestured to the room inside overlooking the lawn. 'Two or three mornings a week.'

Would it take that long, I wondered?

'And we can meditate.'

I didn't know if his suggestion applied to the days

when I was to help manage things or to this particular moment. But he was looking into the morning with an unfocused gaze and I found myself drawn to the experience as if willingly slipping into an absorbing vortex of peace. I also found my gaze softening as I watched a pair of kudu emerge from the bush with their elaborate, corkscrew horns, to join Mampara, the wildebeest, in grazing. A lilac-breasted roller, a favourite bird of my childhood, swooped from the trees in a flash of purple, turquoise, yellow, and green, and began sipping from the birdbath under the orange-lit flamboyant tree.

Like the Buddhist pure land that Kay had once described, in Yogi Tarchin's presence the garden seemed to shift to a rare and elevated aspect, transformed into a place of exalted beauty, and all the creatures in it, in some mysterious and indescribable way, revealing themselves as divine. For the longest time I was lost to it. And when Rinpoche spoke, it felt like he was revealing, in this first personal audience I'd ever had with him, particular insights from another realm.

'You are different from others.' He spoke in that light, ethereal voice that almost wasn't there. 'You always have been different. Not satisfied with conventional views.'

This was true. All through school I'd felt like an outsider. When my parents had moved overseas and I'd started work, I'd had more space to be myself, but the contrarian streak was always there. Even Nick Berkeley used to tease me about it, and how it had led to my passive funds management approach.

'You have an inclination to the Dharma. This is not cultural. It's from lifetimes ago — many of them — when you followed the path.'

From the way he spoke, this felt less a deduction and more a singular glimpse through time.

'The Buddha once said that to be born as a human being with an inclination to the Dharma and the time to pursue that inclination is as rare as a turtle that comes to the top of the ocean once every hundred years just happening to stick its neck through a golden yoke floating on the surface. In other words, almost impossible.'

It was a striking metaphor — one that underlined the spectacular improbability of my life.

'When you consider all the billions of people with consciousness, who, just like us, wish only to be happy and to avoid suffering. Who wish for lives with privilege and wisdom, just like ours. But they have no idea about the nature of reality. No prospect of avoiding suffering and death. They continue unknowingly to perpetuate their own pain.

'You are different. You are inexpressibly special, Rob.' I felt a shiver pass through me. What I would have felt immodest to analyse too deeply, Yogi Tarchin had just spelt out unambiguously. A statement that was awesome in the truest sense.

'You are so close,' he continued. 'On the edge. After lifetimes on the path you are almost there. This human life, here and now, you are living on an island of jewels. Compared to the lives of most other beings, it is so easy for you to collect treasures of extraordinary value.'

I could see the tropical island, right there, its golden beaches strewn with emeralds, rubies, and diamonds the size of grapes or even nectarines.

'Whatever you do,' he implored, 'don't leave the island empty-handed!'

As he said this, his eyes met mine — and the hairs of my neck stood on end. There was an urgency about his plea, his call to action. Everything he said led to this conclusion. The incomprehensible good fortune of my circumstances and my specialness — underlined by the fleeting rarity of this opportunity.

~

There was something else too. The skimming of fur against my shoulder and right cheek, a sliding sensation along with the awareness of sinuous muscularity. Bodhi the cheetah was gliding past, deliberately rubbing against me all the way from her shoulders to her haunches, before sweeping my neck with her whip-strong tail, artfully flicking its tip against my cheek as she went. She hopped onto the sofa next to the lama and turned to gaze impassively at the lawn. Yogi Tarchin glanced at me as if having a cheetah sit next to him was the most natural thing in the world.

'She likes you,' he observed, brushing his shoulder with his hand to indicate the significance of her closeness.

'You think?' I felt flattered if this was so.

'Don't look at her eyes directly,' he cautioned.

I remembered this advice from my childhood — cats took such eye contact from strangers as a bid for dominance.

'Not until she is ready.'

I pondered this for a moment. 'How will I know she is ready?' I asked.

He tilted his head mysteriously. 'It happens naturally.'

We were looking out again, marvelling at what we saw. The island of jewels, I pondered. This was it! I was here! By an unaccountable stroke of good fortune I had somehow found myself on it, and here I sat with the lama and his cheetah on a dazzling November day. Spellbound, I remained in that serene awareness until the black goat Mbudzi appeared from the garden, crossing the lawn just in front of where we sat. Lounging on its back was Skellum, the three-legged vervet monkey, his small charcoal face bright with impudence — until he caught sight of Bodhi. With a screech of terror, he leapt off the goat and raced up the side of the house. Yogi Tarchin and I looked at each other and chuckled. On the sofa Bodhi flicked her ears dismissively, all the while gazing into the summer morning.

I was soon saying goodbye, summoning the dogs who were as relaxed in Bodhi's presence as she was uninterested in them. About to leave, Rinpoche said, almost as an aside, 'You are the executor, right?'

I was intrigued how easily he moved from the mundane to the divine and back again. To him, they were two sides of the same coin.

'You have been through every room of her house?'

I nodded. I had been methodical. From top to bottom including the attic. 'There's only the shed left,' I remembered.

That had been the domain of Carrie's long-late husband Adrian. I'd been in it only briefly, concluding that its contents would have to be transferred wholesale to the nearest garbage tip.

'Check everything in it. All the parts. Every drawer. Perhaps there is something helpful for you and others.'

I touched my palm to my chest. 'Thank you, Rinpoche.'

~

Intrigued by Yogi Tarchin's advice, as soon as I got home, I collected the keys and walked to the shed. On one side there was a single door and a roller entrance leading to a driveway — the latter for Uncle Adrian to move the old cars he used to rebuild, restoration being his hobby. I had opened the door only to peek inside, discovering that Aunt Carrie had used the shed as a dumping ground for old paperwork, electrical appliances, suitcases, and a miscellany of household items.

This time I unlocked the roller door and hauled it juddering upwards. It felt as if it hadn't been opened for a very long time. I stood for a while surveying what was there. I already knew about the towers of boxes, but further inside were tarpaulins acting as dust sheets — beneath them, a variety of benches laden with car parts. I discovered that the largest sheet concealed not more household junk, but the chassis of an old Jaguar motor car. The shed walls, I noticed, were mounted with tool panels — dusty but arranged in methodical order. Not so much a shed, as Aunt Carrie used to call it, as a workshop. Suddenly I recalled what Diva had said about Tinashe: 'He can bring an old car back to life like no one I've seen.' Could he use these tools, I wondered? Maybe even salvage some of the car parts?

Check every drawer, Rinpoche had directed. Under the benchtops there were a few storage drawers containing lubricants, paints, and car-related items. Poking about behind an upended trunk, I came across half a dozen wide and shallow drawers from what looked like a battered map cabinet. When I scraped open the first few drawers, I found layout plans of unknown houses. Large black and white portrait photographs, curling at the edges. Many assembly diagrams for vehicles.

In the fourth drawer down was an old-fashioned sketch pad. I remembered others exactly like it from Dad's painting studio. Just like those, this one was labelled 'E. Forbes' on the front cover in his distinctive hand. He used to explain how he liked to paint a subject only after working on a variety of sketches, perhaps from different angles. The sketches were drafts

— preparation, in a way — for the final thing. As I took the pad out of the drawer and turned through its pages, I understood why he had left this particular sketch pad in Africa.

There were portraits of a woman, and even though she was dressed in a blouse, the sketches were much more than a simple record of someone's appearance. They conveyed attraction, desire that was evident at a glance — and quite unlike any other work I'd ever seen of his. The woman evidently held an allure for him, although it seemed more than only erotic. A mystique, holding some kind of promise represented by what she held in the open palm of her left hand: a miniature of the Zodiac bowl — one of the arcane treasures retrieved from the ruins of Great Zimbabwe.

For a long while I stood in the heat of the afternoon, lifting my eyes from the sketch pad to the bush beyond, reflecting how Yogi Tarchin seemed to throw open doors effortlessly, not so much to a single secret world as to a multiplicity of them.

"Guru yoga", Kay once told me, was what happened when you wished to yoke your mind to that of the lama. When you recognised the extraordinary benefits of so doing. The idea had seemed obscure and somewhat far-fetched when she explained it to me. Since Rinpoche's arrival, however, it had begun to make sense. To use Pema's evocative image, not for a single moment did I wish to take my eyes off the hands of the potter as he transformed the clay of my mundane reality into an unknown wonder.

Chapter Four

LIFE SOON DANCED to a different rhythm. Every morning I'd wake, shower, and meditate. Inspired by Rinpoche, sessions on the cushion often extended longer and felt more tranquil — although some days, besieged by thoughts of London, I felt more agitated than ever. Three mornings a week I'd set out with Thor and Tiki to my new temporary job at the Ruwa Buddhist Society. We'd take a shortcut through the bush — only a few posts marked the boundary between Aunt Carrie's property and the Society's. The dogs and I loved those morning walks through silver grass cool as the night, with gold light just beginning to filter through the butterfly-shaped mopane leaves.

From the moment we set out, the energy of a new day would beckon irresistibly: grey loeries sweeping through the branches with their alarm cries — 'G'way! G'way!' Ground-level skirmishes as the dogs set off in futile pursuit of 'African Chickens' — the local term for guinea-fowl, lizards, and skinks, or even, more rarely, root-grubbing warthogs. This was nothing like my usual London Underground commute to Bank Station.

Instead of all the faces of grim resignation or self-absorbed detachment, here the dawning of a new day was greeted with unfettered joy.

Similarly, my office with its vaulted thatch roof offered nothing like the glistening steel-and-glass skyscape I was familiar with. Here my window overlooked the lawn where Mampara might be grazing. Perhaps the warthogs too — or our inquisitive and truly omnivorous family member, the black goat Mbudzi, who wandered in and out of the homestead at will, incurring Gogo's wrath if venturing too close to the kitchen. Something was always going on.

And then there was my new employer. As I soon discovered, there were ways in which he was much more like my financial district colleagues than I would have imagined. For all his untroubled lightness, the boundless depth of tranquillity you felt in his presence, far from resting in a place of serene inaction, his activities were unceasing.

I came to learn that he went to bed only in the early hours of the morning and got up no later than five am. Throughout the day he moved between the guest cottage and his office, a converted sitting room on the other side of the hall from mine. He was constantly dealing with queries and sending messages to Dharma centres and students around the world. As different time zones came online, I'd catch discussions about fund-raising for the reconstruction of a monastery in Tibet, the delivery of supplies to an orphanage in Mongolia, a teaching tour of Europe and UK, and meditation retreats being planned in upstate New York, Colorado, and Costa Rica. He walked to his cottage for periods of the day during which I guessed he was meditating. I could always tell where he was by the presence of Bodhi, who was either sprawled on the lawn outside his office or on the deck of his cottage.

When he was working in the house, I couldn't help overhearing his conversations. I had the sense that he kept his door deliberately open, that observing him at close range was part of why he wanted me here. I'd never given any thought to what a yogi might do all day when not meditating. So I was surprised not just by the sheer volume of activities he was involved with but also by his global range. Through an attendant in India, who seemed to serve the role of virtual assistant, he segued effortlessly from one project and country to another, all the while conveying the ease of someone who had just come off a long and deeply relaxing vacation. There was something serenely untouched about his presence.

~

On my very first morning, as I crossed the hall in welcome, he had only one message for me. Feeling the need to acknowledge that I had overheard some of his phone calls, I made a remark about him being busy. 'Serving others,' he said. 'This is *the most* important thing to do.' There was a significance about his expression as he said it. A sense of urgency.

I instantly recalled a comment he'd made that night on top of Ruwa Rock when he'd first suggested we build a temple. Saying that he would support whatever decision we came to, he had used the words 'I am here to serve you.'

'Some people say that they yearn for a lama to help them meditate,' he continued that first day. 'But a teacher is one who inspires them to serve others. This is the *main* issue.' He made sure I got the point. 'The only way to true happiness.'

With that, he turned about, heading back to his office.

~

The service he'd asked from me couldn't have been easier, at least to begin with. After I went through all the computer files of the Ruwa Buddhist Society, along with paper records in an old wooden filing cabinet, it didn't take me long to create a member database. And using other Buddhist organisation websites as a guide, it wasn't difficult to draft a proposed website brief, and to short-list companies who could put it together.

Working on my personal laptop, I found emails from London about the new business. Legal documents to be scrutinised, amended, and signed off on. The acquisition of IT programs to be to negotiated. Recruitment and design matters requiring my attention. In the past, I would have responded immediately. But here under the thatch, I was curiously unwilling to give them my attention. The requests and queries came from a different world, one I was reluctant to engage with for now. I'd have to turn my mind to them, I knew. But for the moment, I kicked the can down the road, telling people in London that I'd need time to get back to them.

~

Towards the end of that first week, I noticed Harris with his GPS unit at the furthermost end of the property. I walked to the edge of the lawn and crossed the open bush to where he was working with Tinashe under the shade of a massive umbrella tree. The two of them had cleared and levelled a wide flat space. Into the sandy ground they'd hammered wooden pegs connected by twine.

Welcoming my arrival as time for a break, Harris lowered himself onto a large, smooth boulder, removing his worn panama hat with its guinea-fowl feather plume and fanning his large pink face. Tinashe remained in the distance, checking measurements with great concentration.

Harris gestured for me to join him and started to explain the importance of accuracy in setting out a building. How the measurements of its footprint arose from the ground. About how he and Tinashe had spent a lot of time with Rinpoche to ensure that the alignment of the temple was precise.

'So, this is 31 East?' I confirmed.

'Right here,' he nodded. 'The umbilical cord connecting human beings to the place of their birth.'

I mulled this over, studying the shape they'd marked out on the ground. 'The entrance faces up the lawn to the homestead?'

He nodded. 'And right behind it, the protector, Ruwa Rock.'

I glanced around me slowly. The whole clearing felt as though it had been ordained for exactly this purpose: a sacred meeting place of heaven and earth.

'You're keeping the tree?'

He nodded. 'It will provide cover.'

'Unique,' I said, taking in the vast sweep of acacia umbrella. 'Like Great Zimbabwe itself.'

He shot me a glance with those sagacious blue eyes. 'There are actually between five and six hundred stone palaces like Great Zimbabwe throughout Southern Africa.'

I raised my eyebrows.

'Much smaller, granted. For location and size, Great Zimbabwe *is* unique. The zenith of Zimbabwe culture.'

'I didn't know about the others,' I admitted.

'Most people don't,' he said. 'But Zimbabwe culture evolved for centuries before Great Zimbabwe. The first southern African state was actually at Mapungubwe, in what we now call South Africa. That was when the idea of sacred leadership first came into being.'

'Sacred leadership?'

'The idea of a leader, chief, living in a home *set apart* just for him, which is the meaning of "sacred". Unlike in earlier times, he no longer rubbed shoulders with ordinary people. There was a class structure and he was at the top. It was believed he had a strongly spiritual basis for what he did. He needed to keep his people in good standing with God, through their ancestors, because then there would be rain.'

'The ultimate rainmaker?' I asked.

'Most important job in the tribe.'

The rainy season, from November to March, was the basis of tribal wealth. It always had been, and it still was for many Zimbabweans. Abundant rain was needed for the maize fields tended by the women and for fresh pastures for cattle, an important store of wealth for any villager.

'In time, the king came to be supported by special rainmakers, his most powerful advisers.'

'Tough job when there's a dry season,' I murmured.

'Which is exactly why Mapungubwe came to an end,' said Harris. 'In around 1300 there was a terrible drought. It went on for years. Eventually, the people scattered in search of water, which was when the rival Great Zimbabwe state became dominant. There had been a rainmaking site there for over eight centuries. An auspicious place to build a city.'

'How do you think the builders worked out the 31 East location?' I asked.

Harris looked into the distance. 'We can only speculate. But we need to remember that by the fourteenth century, people here were already in touch with the world.'

From along the boulder, he regarded my questioning

expression with a droll smile. 'Archaeologists have found coins from pre-Christian times near ancient gold workings. Cowrie shells dating from about 900 AD. Copper coins from medieval Arab sultanates, glass beads from southeast Asia. Porcelain bowls from China. Great Zimbabwe was a nation state the size of France. The chiefs dealt with Arab and Indian traders in ivory and gold. Local settlements were linked internationally — and what they exchanged went further than only gold and beads.' His eyes became sharper. 'They also exchanged ideas.'

I recognised the truth in what he was saying. Just as I understood my mistake in assuming that Africa had comprised only vast tracts of empty space, the local inhabitants cut off from other civilisations.

'Who knows what information was shared around campfires between visitors and locals?' Harris continued. 'Or how far curious individuals may have travelled to discover more? It's not such a long journey up the east coast of Africa to Egypt and India. Traders were doing it all the time. You know,' he smiled. 'You can find yourself on the most remote kopje in the middle of Africa and notice a rock with rows of holes that were made there centuries ago. *Mancala*,' he said. 'The Arab game from ancient Egypt. It's played throughout Africa.' His eyes were penetrating as he told me, 'There's nothing more portable than an idea.'

Far from Zimbabwe culture arising in isolation, Harris was saying, other influences were also at play. To see Great Zimbabwe as purely parochial would be to misunderstand its place in the world. To diminish its significance.

'Visitors to Great Zimbabwe,' he continued, 'and to the other stone palaces usually focus on the stunning herringbone patterns on the walls and towers.

The absence of mortar. But for me ...' the faraway look that had come into his eyes the first time I met him had returned, 'the most breathtaking thing is what is encoded in the symbols. In particular, that most powerful symbol of all, the Zimbabwe bird.'

Eight statues of what came to be known as the Zimbabwe bird had been discovered at Great Zimbabwe by early explorers. Simple in design and sculpted in stone, there was a mystical quality about the bird that reached beyond time and space. A significance that was felt, even when it wasn't understood, by early European explorers and later by settlers from Britain.

The Zimbabwe bird, paramount among the symbols of Great Zimbabwe, continued to be supreme, at the head of every coat of arms through colonial and post-colonial times. It was on flags, coins, banknotes, a ubiquitous national emblem irrespective of who was running the country. You didn't have to spend much time in Zimbabwe to see it. And despite having grown up here, I had never given any thought at all to what it might symbolise. From Harris's look of significance, it was clear that I was missing something.

'I was once told it was a representation of the bateleur eagle,' I said. 'That's as far as I know.'

Having completed his measurements, Tinashe walked to join us.

'The bateleur,' confirmed Harris, 'was said to bring messages directly from God. It often flies in straight lines, you see?' he gestured. 'For the people of Great Zimbabwe, the eagle was at the top of the bird kingdom, in the same way that the lion was king of the beasts. If anything, the eagle was more transcendent, more revered, because it could go up high,' he pointed toward the sky. 'Omniscient.'

Tinashe nodded.

'Like a Buddha?' I mused hesitantly, knowing that a quality of the Buddhas is to be all-seeing.

Harris and Tinashe exchanged a glance as Harris gestured for him to reply.

'The Buddhas,' he said, 'are always shown sitting on lotus thrones, which are symbols. Our own Zimbabwe bird is the same.'

Zimbabwe birds were displayed perched on a plinth. And whether they were perfectly sculpted or roughly sketched, the plinth was always decorated in an identical way. With two emblems, I realised to my chagrin, about which I was completely ignorant.

Tinashe reached down and picked up a stick. Turning to face the same way as us, he used it to draw an outline of a Zimbabwe bird in the sand. The eagle itself, facing left. Below it, a plinth he decorated first with two circles, and then below them, with a pair of chevron-pattern lines. As he traced the lines, I had the powerful sense of being tugged out of time. Was it Tinashe's presence, or a sense of arcane transmission as he met my eyes with his own?

'These symbols may be interpreted in different ways, depending on context. And the wisdom of the one who reads them. But for me,' he pointed to the circles he had drawn, 'these seem obvious.' He gestured to his eyes. 'Perception,' he said. 'The eagle is lord of the sky. There is nothing he cannot see, nothing hidden from him. This represents the knowing nature of the enlightened mind.'

He gave me a moment to process before continuing.

'These,' he repeated the angular up and down pattern of the twin lines, 'mean energy. What Indian sages call "prana".' He made a gliding movement with his right hand, like an eagle soaring on thermal currents, while he fixed me with a gaze of piercing lucidity. 'The enlightened mind arises from consciousness and energy of the most subtle kinds.'

It was a moment of epiphany. As I sat on a boulder and stared at Tinashe's sketch in the sand, I pondered how the very last thing I had imagined when I'd made my way down the lawn this morning was to be shown how the Zimbabwe bird, an emblem I knew so well, might be a symbol of enlightenment.

'All this time.' I met his gaze, which melted into one of jovial good humour. 'I had no idea!'

Along the boulder from me, Harris chuckled. 'Like all the very best symbols!' he said. 'Hidden in plain sight.'

Later that same morning, Mr Nzou arrived for a meeting with Rinpoche. Most of the time I saw him, Mr Nzou was in the distance, dressed in green overalls, rearranging flowerbed sprinklers or raking up leaves. Today, he was in the same suit and tie he had worn to attend Yogi Tarchin's first meditation session. Evidently this was an official visit. Gripping the shiny rim of an ancient-looking trilby hat, he knocked timidly on Rinpoche's office door.

What emerged was quite intriguing: Mr Nzou had come to ask Yogi Tarchin to make the rains fall. For all Rinpoche's refutations that he could do such a thing, Mr Nzou persisted, before finally admitting that he wasn't only the local chief's occasional representative: he was also the local rainmaker.

The conversation I'd had with Harris a short while earlier suddenly took on a particular relevance as I imagined how responsible Mr Nzou must feel. And how desperate — to be held personally liable by the chief and all the villagers for the weather. Despite his own best efforts, he had failed to coax rain-laden clouds across the horizon while other parts of Zimbabwe were receiving torrential downpours.

There was much more talk about the late start of the rainy season, although I didn't tune in. The subject of jealousy came up. A short while later, Mr Nzou was leaving the house, brisk with purpose. In his hand he clutched a box of Treasure Trees Apothecary's premium Baobab products.

~

My favourite times were when, around mid-morning, if Rinpoche had time, he would come out of his office and beckon me with the words 'Coffee break!' The two of us would find a sunny spot on the veranda and a short while later Gogo would arrive bearing a tray with two mugs of coffee. No coffee break was allowed to go by without one of Gogo's home-made treats — cookies perhaps, *melk terte*, or banana bread.

Gogo presided over the homestead as a constant, bountiful presence. Food was her love language. It wasn't by accident that Football, the tabby cat, was spherical. A deeply religious woman who hummed and sang hymns as a constant accompaniment to whatever she was doing, if she had any qualms about having a Buddhist lama under her roof, she never showed them. On the contrary, she seemed as enchanted by Rinpoche as he was by her.

One particular morning, in the first week of my voluntary job, Gogo came through the house to the chorus of "What a Friend We Have in Jesus", before setting a tray of coffee and fresh scones before us.

'Hey-heyyy!' She clapped her hands together as we thanked her warmly. 'It's good to have someone to bake for, sure!'

~

On the surface, there might be nothing unusual about two men on a veranda drinking coffee, but I knew I was in the presence of an extraordinary being, and that sitting with him was a rare privilege. As the two of us sat together without saying a word, I found myself drawn, just as I had before, into a different state of perception, one in which the garden appeared as a place of wonder and every being in it as quite magical. I knew that the source of this rarefied view was sitting right beside me. That it came about not from the garden or the beings themselves, but from the mind apprehending them. A mind into which I was somehow absorbed.

Also, without the need for anything as coarse as speech, I came to understand a remarkable truth: that this same perception was available to me too. That there wasn't some hidden doorway to which I could never possibly gain access, that needed to be opened. That I wasn't in thrall to an esoteric magician without whom I couldn't find my own way to this state of gentle exaltation.

But how, exactly, to see a world filled with so much beauty without relying on the lama? How to awaken to such an enchanted vision? Rinpoche took a sip of coffee — or was it ambrosial nectar? — and looked at me with that heart-melting smile. Revelling in being here and not wanting the moment to end, I wondered how many such sessions we might have on the veranda together before I returned to London. Maybe only a handful?

Which was why I decided to seize the moment and ask about the subject that had been puzzling me since my first morning.

'Rinpoche, you said that our main task is serving others,' I said.

He nodded, as if he'd made the comment only moments earlier.

'Is that because we need to take the focus off thinking about ourselves the whole time? To cultivate compassion?'

He seemed glad that I had asked. Approved that I had pondered the message he'd so emphatically delivered.

'You remember why I said that serving others is the main issue?' he probed.

'The only way to true happiness,' I quoted.

'Yes,' he confirmed. 'Tell me, Rob, is there an object in existence which is a guaranteed source of happiness? An object that, whoever owns it, or wherever they live, or how many other of the same objects they possess, will always produce happiness?'

It didn't take me long to shake my head.

'What about a person? An individual who is an unfailing source of happiness whenever you are around him — or her?'

We both chuckled at the implausibility of what he was asking.

'What about a lifestyle?' he pressed. 'Houses, cars, private jets? A cabin in the forest? A mansion by the sea? Are these true sources of happiness for everyone? Guaranteed to create joy or wellbeing in anyone who owns them?'

'There's no such thing out there because we all have our own likes and dislikes,' I replied. 'And over time, even our own tastes change.'

'These likes and dislikes,' he said. 'Where do they arise?'

'Our minds, I guess.'

'And why?'

'Conditioning,' I suggested. 'Upbringing. And we're

constantly influenced by new information and situations and other people.'

'This coffee,' he held up his mug, 'you are enjoying?'

I nodded.

'Is the enjoyment coming from the coffee or from your mind?'

I thought of my former colleagues at Landers. The early morning run one of the executive assistants would make to a nearby coffee shop whose barista was the office's favourite. How demanding certain people were about their orders and how easily displeased when another barista was on duty.

'Some of my colleagues are coffee snobs,' I said. 'They wouldn't thank you for instant coffee. Perhaps we have different taste buds?'

'Perhaps,' he shrugged.

'Or we become conditioned to like certain things.'

He nodded.

'So, the enjoyment is less from the coffee than from us.'

'Correct. This,' he nodded to his mug, 'is *merely* a contributing factor. The main cause is the mind itself. The coffee exists conventionally. It has certain qualities we can agree make it appropriate to be called "coffee". But *the way* it exists for each one of us, *how* it exists, as good, bad, or indifferent — all this depends on our minds.'

Glancing over, he fixed me with a penetrating expression. 'It's the same with *everything*. External objects, people, situations. None of them can be true causes of happiness, because they are incapable of producing it. The happiness isn't coming from them. It never did. It never could. Whatever happiness they create, or not, depends on the mind of the perceiver.'

The logic was obvious. And yet completely at odds with the way we usually thought, our social beliefs, viewing things out there as having qualities that made them inherently desirable or undesirable.

'So, happiness comes from mind, yes?'

I nodded.

'And what causes it to arise is virtue.'

'Virtue?'

'The definition of virtue is "a cause of happiness". It is karma: the cause of a future result. Causes and results are similar. So, to create the causes to enjoy good food and drink in the future,' once again he held up his mug, 'we help other beings enjoy good food and drink. To have the experience of abundance, we offer abundance. To experience love and wisdom, we offer love and wisdom.'

His explanation of karma was a more refined one than what I'd heard before. It wasn't only the things themselves that arose from karma, but our experience of them also. I knew plenty of wealthy people who derived little contentment from their wealth, whose hard-working, stressful lives were joyless. According to Rinpoche's diagnosis, the reason was simple.

'So, you see why serving others is the only path to happiness,' he said.

I smiled ruefully.

'If we constantly create the causes to give delight to others we have no choice — karma will force us to experience reality as delightful. And if we share the transcendent wisdom of the Dharma with others, then we perceive reality as sublime — no matter what that reality may be.'

'*Merely* a contributing factor,' I repeated.

'Correct,' he agreed. 'Main cause,' he brought a hand

to his heart, 'mind itself.'

Reaching over, he clasped my arm briefly for emphasis as he looked into my eyes. 'One further thing. If, when you enjoy something, like drinking coffee while gazing at a beautiful garden, you recollect that the true cause of your happiness is *not* the coffee or the garden, but a virtue you created in the past, then your joy will become even greater! When we rejoice in virtue, we strengthen the habit and our affinity to it until, more and more, we embody the reality it produces.'

He returned his own focus to the garden, and I realised that he had just shown me the pathway to his personal reality. His mandala. Shared the cause of his uplifting presence. Why it was that something as simple as sitting and drinking instant coffee with him was so enrapturing: he constantly served others. The phone calls. The messages. The emails night and day. His tireless efforts to give others not only mundane delight but the benefit of his insights in teachings, retreats, and Dharma activities — these virtues were the cause of his own incredible lightness of being. Or at least, they were part of it. I had no doubt there was much more as well.

Gogo appeared on the veranda. 'Your phone, sir.' It was ringing and she passed it to him.

Yogi Tarchin glanced at the screen before putting down his coffee mug and standing.

'I must take this call,' he said, looking at me, fingertip poised on the screen. 'But we will have many more coffees together.'

I recalled my musing earlier about how many times we might sit here.

'More than a handful,' he chuckled, before swiping to receive the call.

~

One afternoon I invited Tinashe to visit me at home. It was shortly after three when we walked to the shed where he undertook a full inspection of what Uncle Adrian had left behind under a variety of dustsheets. By the time he came to find me an hour later, his face was alight.

'D'you know what you've got in there?' he asked breathlessly.

It was a revelation to see the usually still and silent Tinashe so animated.

Without waiting for my answer, he continued, 'Your uncle was rebuilding an XK150 Roadster.'

'Okay,' I replied. There had been a Triumph once in the past. I remembered my uncle's proud unveiling of it. And a Bristol before that. This time, it seemed, a very British sports car.

'I haven't done a full inventory. But it seems like he has all the parts.'

'He was methodical about that sort of thing,' I remembered. 'Meticulous.'

'You're not getting it, Rob.' Tinashe wanted to share his elation. 'Have you any idea how much a Jag like this is worth these days?!'

'Assembled,' I grinned, 'a lot, I'm sure. But not when it's spread across a shed floor in the middle of Africa.'

'I can put it together,' he offered. 'Perhaps you can sell it?'

I could see where he was heading with this. 'Or perhaps you can,' I told him. 'And take the tools. You'll be doing me a favour. I need to clear the place.'

Tinashe regarded me, speechless.

'Just one proviso. I'm returning to London in a month.'

'I can get the car moving by then,' Tinashe said, his expression animated.

'Then we have a deal.' I extended my hand, hoping that a handshake would convince him of my good faith. To my surprise, he ignored the hand and came in to hug me. 'You have no idea, Rob,' he said, stepping back after a moment, meeting my eyes with his own earnest gaze, 'how much this means to me. It can change everything.'

'I hope so,' I told him. 'Uncle Adrian would have been happy to see an enthusiast take over from where he left off.'

In the same instant I said the words, I recalled what Yogi Tarchin had said when suggesting that I thoroughly inspect the shed: 'Perhaps there is something helpful for you and others.'

~

Tinashe became a frequent visitor. I gave him the shed key so he could let himself in. This occurred almost always in the late afternoon. As I came to discover, he had a very busy life. He was up at three am every day to meditate for an hour, as required by Rinpoche, before setting out for his garbage pick-ups. After a four-hour shift, he'd return, wash and change into more formal attire to teach at a local school. Finishing mid-afternoon, he'd return home for more Dharma study and meditation. Rinpoche had, in the first days he was here, set him a rigorous program. Between four and five he might come to Aunt Carrie's to work on the car.

I got into the habit of visiting some afternoons as he lay in the inspection pit under the car. He'd usually have a small portable speaker playing Oliver Mtukudzi or another Shona musician. Beside the music, he'd leave what he termed his *katundu* on a table. This included his phone, watch, and a small white circular plate, the size of a wide teaspoon, with a spiral motif.

'A *ndoro*?' I recognised it immediately.

He nodded. 'A gift from my late grandfather.'

'Very special talisman,' I observed. Traditionally, *ndoros*, made from conch shells, had more than only symbolic importance. They represented status, wealth, and power of both the worldly and other-worldly varieties.

'He gave it to me the only time I saw him ...' Tinashe hesitated before correcting himself. 'The only time I *remember* seeing him. I was about eight.'

'On your father's side, right?'

He nodded.

Tinashe told me how he'd been brought up by his mother, a domestic worker in Chisipite. How he'd gone to Oriel Boys School, and because his mother was so strict and he was so determined, he had passed both his O levels and his A levels. He'd been one of an ambitious group of youngsters who'd earned enough money to buy airfares to Europe and work as stewards on Mediterranean cruise liners. In this capacity, over several years he'd earned enough to pay for his mother to retire from domestic work to a small home on the family land in Guruve.

'You don't talk about your father,' I observed.

'He died,' he shrugged. 'He wasn't much use to Mum. He was hardly ever on the scene when I grew up. She says he was a playboy. He died of AIDS.'

'I'm sorry.' Like elsewhere in southern Africa, AIDS had stripped a whole generation of communities. In some villages, it was only the elderly who had been left behind to bring up their grandchildren.

'My grandfather, Dad's dad,' Tinashe wriggled out from under the car, 'was very different. A *n'anga*, highly respected for divination.'

A n'anga! These were traditional healers who combined an understanding of herbs and natural medicines with spiritual capabilities to deliver healing, guidance — and occasionally more terrifying occult powers upon villagers. It intrigued me that Tinashe's own grandfather had been such a person. The lineage of n'angas often followed family lines, or so I'd heard.

As if aware of my thoughts, and wanting to divert them, he turned to face me directly. 'That *ndoro*,' he pointed, 'is over eight hundred years old.'

For the first time, as I held his eyes, I glimpsed an extraordinary strength beneath Tinashe's stillness.

I leaned to study the ndoro more closely. 'For land-locked tribespeople in the 1400s,' I observed, 'this would have been very exotic. Especially one so beautifully patterned.'

The swirl, which began at the centre of the disc, formed a perfect spiral to the circumference.

'My ancestors paid a lot of money for such things,' Tinashe confirmed. 'Between 1500 and the mid 1600s they traded about $250 million US dollars in gold and ivory alone.'

'I'm surprised the traders could find enough shells to satisfy demand.'

'They didn't,' he replied. 'What you're looking at isn't a shell. It is ceramic, made in Goa. The traders built factories to make these which they exchanged for gold.'

'Manufactured in India, circa 1400!' I exclaimed. 'Finding its way to the middle of Africa.'

Tinashe met my eyes thoughtfully. 'Other things from India also found their way here.' I instantly remembered what he'd revealed to Harris and me days earlier about the startling symbolic significance of the Zimbabwe bird. How Rinpoche had entwined his index and middle finger on Ruwa Rock. 'Africa and India are much closer than most people would believe.'

~

During one of my visits to the shed, Tinashe announced a project milestone: The engine, largely rebuilt by Uncle Adrian, was now supported by the other main mechanical components. He'd assembled the suspension, brakes, and steering system. The electrics were fully functioning thanks to a new battery. While the inside of the car was still an empty shell, Tinashe said that interior restoration was straightforward by comparison. With some ceremony he even turned the engine so that, for the first time in who knew when, it burst to life with a throaty growl that sent the bantam hens outside squawking in indignation.

~

That afternoon, for the first time, Tinashe allowed himself to celebrate when I handed him a bottle of Zambezi lager.

'Next milestone, I'm taking you to a jazz club,' I told him. 'That is, if there's such a thing in Harare.'

We had already established a mutual love of jazz.

'Oh, there is,' he replied. 'Enterprise Road. Next to the Italian Club. They have sessions every Friday night.'

'Done!' We clinked together the green glass necks of our bottles.

At the shed bench, a beer later, I returned to the question that had intrigued me since he'd mentioned his grandfather.

'Your n'anga granddad,' I asked him. 'The divination expert. You can tell me that this is none of my business, of course, but did he ever forecast anything about your future?'

Tinashe stared down at the floor for a while before meeting my eyes with an expression of mixed emotions.

He nodded slowly a few times before saying, 'He said it was my destiny to be a healer. A "great" healer, actually.'

I raised my eyebrows.

'But I don't have the STEM subject grades,' he shrugged. 'Therefore, I'll never be a medical doctor. That's not happening for me.'

He looked so downcast that I felt bad for having asked him.

'What about healing in a different way?'

He shrugged again. 'I must keep teaching to persuade Pema's parents to let her marry me. They value education. They'd never let their daughter marry a garbage collector.'

'*That's* why you're a teacher!' I had wondered why he devoted so much time and energy to a job that barely paid for a week's groceries in a month. I was struck by his dilemma.

'Meantime, Rinpoche has me studying and meditating every day.'

I knew that Rinpoche seemed to hold Tinashe to a higher standard than the rest of us. He was a much harder taskmaster when it came to Tinashe. There had been an intensely personal relevance to the insight Pema had shared, in her beautiful words about the guru: 'It is challenging when our master pushes us beyond the limits we would accept if we were trying to find the way on our own.'

'I have no regrets,' continued Tinashe. 'I just feel ...' he trailed off.

'Torn?' I suggested after a while.

He acknowledged this, leaning back in his chair, staring at the Roadster for a long time before meeting my eyes. 'Like you.'

I was ever so gently ambushed.

'You have a life and house and a big job in London. But this is your home.'

'That obvious?' I smiled ruefully.

'Yes,' he returned a wide smile.

In an instant I thought about how my future in London was assured: the job I'd spent my whole career preparing for. The opportunities I knew it would unlock. The wealth it would deliver.

But Tinashe was right: I did feel at home here, in so many long-forgotten ways. If Tinashe's destiny was to be a great healer, I thought, he had revealed an uncanny knack for diagnosis. He placed his finger, ever so lightly, on a subject I had done my best to avoid.

I smiled before taking a sip of my beer. After I swallowed I told him, 'I guess I do feel a little conflicted.'

He nodded. 'This is your *kumusha.*'

'Kumusha,' I repeated the word with relish. There was an earthiness to it. A grounded-ness. The Shona meaning of 'home' meant a lot more than where you lived. Kumusha was the place of your ancestors, the land of your birth. It was the very soil of which your body was made — who you were.

I met his eyes, nodding. An acknowledgement not only that I knew and understood the meaning of kumusha but that in an important way we were the same. Beneath the surface ran a powerful undertow calling into question the directions of our lives.

~

The following morning I received the fateful call. The imperative voice of Mr Kachingwe, an official at National Parks, boomed with importance.

'We need your help looking after a female elephant calf,' he said without preamble.

'Elephant?'

'You are the manager of the Ruwa Buddhist Society?'

I was startled that we were even on his radar.

'You already have a cheetah? Giraffe? Wildebeest?'

From the window I could see Mampara chasing the warthog family off the lawn.

'They live on the property,' I said. Not much 'looking after' was required.

'You are close to the airstrip?'

'Uh-huh.'

'The elephant is being transferred from Mana Pools. The aircraft will be there in two hours.' Kachingwe was assuming my consent. 'I'll get Tembo to call you.'

'Wait!' I replied. 'Why isn't the calf with her mother?'

'She was found alone. We are investigating.'

'At Mana Pools?'

'Yes.'

'Why don't you keep her up there until you find her herd?'

'We don't have the facilities.'

'So, when you *do* locate them ...?'

'We'll keep you posted.'

As the little calf's arrival became more imminent, I also tried finding Mr Nzou. Despite my lamentably poor knowledge of Shona, I knew that "nzou" meant "elephant", and so he might have some special interest in our new arrival. After searching for him high and low, I eventually learned from Gogo that Mr Nzou was on a bus from Mutare and not expected home before nightfall. This was the first day that Rinpoche hadn't been around. The only time that Mr Nzou had also been absent. What were the chances?

A couple of hours later I was in the passenger seat of a *bakkie* near Ruwa airstrip. Seeing the Cessna

Caravan come into view, I stepped out of the cab, shielded my eyes, and watched it circling low above the treetops.

The people I would have leaned on, Yogi Tarchin and Mr Nzou, were both off site. Through Luke, Riley's boyfriend, I'd tracked down the country's top expert on elephant adoption, Tessa Brenthurst, in the middle of transporting her own herd of orphans to a rewilding site. She had been very supportive. But what she'd said about the time ahead filled me with concern.

Chapter Five

AS SOON AS the small aircraft came to a halt on the landing strip, the door swung open. From inside, two men turned with urgent expressions as I hurried towards them.

'She's stable,' said Dr Tembo, 'but the sooner we get her out of here the better.'

In the semi-darkness of the cabin, I could see only blankets and drip tubes behind them.

I gestured to Simba to reverse the *bakkie* as close as possible to the plane. Simba had called by at the Ruwa Buddhist Society on an errand just as I was putting together a support team for elephant transfer from the airstrip. Even though we'd never met, when the large jolly fellow said he could drive, I'd recruited him on the spot.

~

He backed the vehicle carefully across the open ground. Marvellous was using hand signals from the open back of the *bakkie* to guide him. Dr Tembo stepped out of the plane. The two of us had already spoken. He'd called me soon after I'd received the call from Mr Kachingwe. With calm deliberation, he delivered a list of instructions above the drone of the aircraft engine. As his experience in running such missions was evident, I became acutely aware of my own complete lack of it. Now he was gesturing that I should get in the plane to help his colleague with the other end of the stretcher.

As I stepped up into the cabin, eyes adjusting to the light, nothing prepared me for what I saw. She was an elephant calf, a few feet tall and, according to Dr Tembo, about four weeks old — a perfectly formed miniature more exquisite than I could possibly have imagined. But seeing her sedated on a green canvas stretcher, hundreds of miles from her herd, was a palpable shock. Alone and vulnerable, she was in a place that no baby elephant should be.

~

Dr Tembo's assistant signalled for me to take one corner of the stretcher. At the other end, Dr Tembo was leading the operation. Next to him, Marvellous, who'd climbed from the *bakkie*, gripped the fourth corner.

Simba opened the tailgate as we headed towards him. The bed of the vehicle had been lined with mattresses and thick blankets as instructed by Dr Tembo. Soon, the four of us were carrying the stretcher the short distance from the plane to the truck. After carefully loading the sedated calf on the back, we climbed in around her. Dr Tembo at her head leaned over to check where lines were going into her ear.

At the steering wheel once again, Simba drove carefully from the landing strip along a dirt road that wound through the msasa trees. Pressed against the side panel with Marvellous, I faced Dr Tembo and his assistant on the other side.

'You got the formula and bottles?' checked the veterinarian. He was a large Ndebele man with a round face and a serious expression.

'From Tessa Brenthurst,' I confirmed.

Both Tessa and he had explained that you couldn't give regular milk to baby elephants. Much higher levels of glucosamine and other elements were needed, missing from cow's milk.

'We've also fixed up a place for her with straw and an infrared light,' I pre-empted another of his earlier directions. 'Used to be a stable.'

He nodded.

'Do you know how she was found?' I nodded towards the calf. 'The circumstances?'

From the moment Mr Kachingwe had ended his call to me, I had the strong sensation of having been set up. Played for a gullible foreigner. This brief time with Dr Tembo might be my only chance to get to the truth of things.

'They said she was being driven away.'

'By her own kind?'

'Bachelor herd.'

'I don't get it,' I shook my head. 'I thought elephants were very protective.'

'Breeding herds are female. Matriarchal. This one was seen being chased by young males.'

'Where was her mother?'

Dr Tembo shrugged.

'Mr Kachingwe told me they are investigating,' I said, tasting the falsehood of the words in my mouth as I repeated them. 'If they find her mother, her herd, will you take her back?'

He looked down, shrugging. 'That's up to Parks.'

This wasn't a conversation he wanted any part of. But I felt he knew more. What had happened that a baby elephant had found herself abandoned by her mother and herd? And why would neither National Parks nor Dr Tembo say what that something was?

~

Simba sped up as we headed along the smooth straight track behind the homestead. As we travelled towards the stables, I noticed late-blooming lucky bean trees growing in the middle of the parched bush. Coral-red blossoms spangled the sepia sky. We pulled up outside a solid whitewashed outhouse comprising four box stalls on one side of a cobbled courtyard, and storerooms, a toilet, and a washroom on the other. The outhouse was surrounded by a low white wall. Within moments we were manoeuvring the stretcher off the vehicle.

~

Preparing for the arrival of the baby elephant had been a collective effort. Ubuntu. Diva had arranged to fetch the special milk formula and feeding bottles from Tessa Brenthurst's centre across town. Luke had sorted out the loan of the infrared light and electric cable. Gogo had cleaned out the stable and spread a protective layer of straw across the full length of it.

As soon as the calf was on the floor, Dr Tembo opened his medical case to draw a dose of reverse-sedation into a syringe. Simba, Marvellous, and I watched in silence as he inserted it into a small cannula going into the little elephant's ear, steadily pushing down the plunger.

'It will take ten to fifteen minutes,' he said, disposing of the syringe and logging the dosage. 'Try to keep her upright when she's awake. That shouldn't be a problem. She will be hungry.'

I hadn't realised how quickly we were to be left on our own. I'd imagined that Dr Tembo would stay longer.

'What about the infrared?' I asked. 'Should we have it on?'

'Won't be cold tonight,' he shook his head. 'Best keep things natural.'

'Are you available for questions?' I tapped the phone in my pocket. 'If something happens?'

'I'm a translocation specialist.' He was non-committal. 'I move animals from A to B. Raising elephants,' he was shaking his head, 'that's not my thing. Best you call Tessa.'

~

One of the calf's legs was beginning to twitch. Then her other limbs. We were focusing intently when it occurred to me to ask, 'Where was she found, Dr Tembo?'

'Not far from the Zambezi River,' he replied. 'Near Vundu camp.'

The elephant's legs began flailing, her eyes flickered open, and suddenly she was trying to get up. Five pairs of hands were there to help. Even though she was only a month old, she weighed one hundred kilograms, or so Dr Tembo had said on our first call.

Gogo arrived from the house, her large bosom rising and falling to the hum of 'Amazing Grace' as she brought a tray of food bottles she'd helped prepare. She held one to the calf's mouth. Eyes still half shut and unsteady on her legs, the little elephant started sucking from it immediately. As Gogo held the bottle upright and steady, the strength of the calf's movements took her by surprise.

'She likes it,' she said, getting to her knees to be on the same level as the calf. At that moment the elephant pulled away from the teat, regurgitating formula onto Gogo's uniform.

'Let me.' I relieved her of the bottle so that she could wipe herself down. I felt the strength of the calf myself. She was desperate with hunger, and disoriented.

She had no idea where she was, craving food and contact. I remembered my conversation with Tessa Brenthurst. 'Food is only fifty percent of what an elephant calf needs,' she told me. 'She will also need love. Elephants touch each other continually. They're very tactile, especially with the young. A baby elephant needs constant physical reassurance, even when asleep. If an orphaned elephant doesn't feel loved,' she explained firmly, 'she will die of a broken heart.'

~

I reached out, caressing the little elephant's head and neck as I held the bottle to her. She tugged at the teat, famished. It seemed hardly any time and she had gone through the whole bottle. Gogo handed me a second. Absorbed in what was happening, it was only when I heard the stable latch being opened that I looked up to see Dr Tembo and his assistant at the door. He met my eyes and inclined his head in farewell. There was a finality about his expression. He'd made the delivery on behalf of National Parks. Now it was over to me.

'I'll take the guys to the plane,' volunteered Simba. 'They need to get to Charles Prince Airport before dark.'

I'd been too caught up in things here to give any thought to Dr Tembo and his assistant, or to Simba. I nodded as they left.

I fed the calf a second bottle of milk, and then a third. After a while, as with Gogo, she broke away, regurgitating some of it over me, stumbling till she came to the wall, trunk extended, bewildered and searching for what wasn't to be found. This was all completely foreign to her. The place. The milk. All of us. Who knew what horrors she had been through just before she was sedated? What trauma she had so recently endured? All I knew was that she woke up here, in my care. Suddenly I was responsible.

She bumped unseeing against the stable walls, floundering this way and that. Her eyes were open, but she was still coming out of sedation. I had no doubt that she was searching for her mother, her aunties, the herd members who were all she'd ever known. I exchanged glances with Gogo and Marvellous. Like me, they were doing their best to guide her away from the walls, stroking her head, her body, her trunk, trying to reassure her that she was safe and protected.

~

It would take time for the drugs to wear off, and for her to become fully conscious of where she was. I felt quite desperate not knowing how best to help or what I should be doing. Taking care of a baby elephant was completely outside my range of experience — but I so wanted her to feel cared for, to know that we were here to look after her.

It seemed like an age before her directionless struggle began fading and she at last stood still for long enough for me to put my arms around her chest and neck. Speaking in a low voice, I tried to soothe her, to tell her that things were going to be okay. As we stood there in the stillness, it occurred to me that being inside and in this semi-darkness wasn't a natural place for an elephant. Under the sky, among trees and plants, would be more natural. But I was also apprehensive about what might happen. What if she decided to run away?

'Shall we take her outside?' I suggested, getting up. Placing my hand on her shoulders, I guided her towards where Marvellous was opening the stable door. He and Gogo stood on either side, stroking her as she passed.

'Eish!' Gogo shook her head as she touched her, motheringly. 'She is *kadiki*.'

'Very small,' nodded Marvellous, translating for me.

The four of us were outside, walking tentatively across the paved courtyard and through posts on either side of an opening in the low white wall. I watched the little creature walking among us, lifting her feet in that uniquely relaxed, almost casual gait of elephants. Looking about her, she seemed to brighten. Outside, a lawn gave onto a flowerbed where a large marula tree was surrounded by lush ferns. The rear of the homestead and the kitchen door were twenty yards away.

~

We gradually made our way to the lawn, the calf pausing to sniff the grass with her trunk. Gogo and Marvellous went to sit a short distance away as I remained with her. She raised her trunk to sniff me, briefly running its tip up my sleeve to my neck and around my ears, taking in my scent. It was the first time she'd really paid me attention. It was a novel sensation and felt like a rare but decided privilege. She was *noticing* me.

Shaking her shoulders from side to side, it seemed that she was coming back to life. So focused on how she was responding to being outside, I was taken by surprise when, from through the ferns bounded the black goat, Mbudzi, who scampered directly towards us, halting only just in front of the elephant. The two sized each other up curiously for a few moments before the goat prodded her in the side with the curve of his horns before skipping away. The calf took up the invitation, instantly chasing him. Stopping when the goat froze. Starting off in a different direction.

And so a game began. A friendship was made. The intensity of the afternoon began to lift. As goat and calf dashed about the lawn, I noticed how the little elephant kept glancing my way. When I took a few steps to the side, she would change the direction of her skirmishes to keep me in view. As we headed around the side of the house to the front lawn, I knew that my fears of her running away were completely unfounded. She had already anchored herself to me.

And her spontaneous play date with the black goat led to a wider circle of friendship. Seeing how well the two were getting on, I decided to let out Thor and Tiki, who were secured in the house. When they came outside, it was the large and usually boisterous wolfhound Thor who was initially the more diffident, holding back from Kadiki — as we began calling the calf — even when Tiki, the Jack Russell, skirmished playfully about her legs. But as the two dogs were already playmates with the goat, it wasn't long before they had cheerfully accepted the elephant calf as their comrade.

From time to time, I checked my phone. Still no response from Rinpoche, who remained out of range. In the initial minutes after Mr Kachingwe's call, I had made determined efforts to call him back. I felt blindsided by Mr Kachingwe and railroaded into a much bigger commitment than I was prepared for, a decision involving the Ruwa Buddhist Society that wasn't mine alone to make.

~

As the sun's rays lengthened, Kadiki started to tire visibly. I asked Gogo to help feed the dogs and goat, then led our motley crew to the back of the house and into the stable. I offered a new bottle of milk to Kadiki and she accepted it immediately.

Unlike the first feeding earlier, this session was less frenzied. For my part, I knew more about what to expect as I sat on the straw, back to the wall for support. Her mouth open and tiny trunk raised out of the way, Kadiki kept her eyes on me as she suckled. She gazed closely, for the first time really taking me in. Once again, I felt that curious sense of being honoured by her attention. More than honoured. How few people ever had this experience? How few got anywhere this close to an elephant calf?

I stroked the soft smooth skin on her forehead and her perfectly formed ears that contrasted so completely with the ridges of her trunk. I noticed the way her cheeks and body were already deeply etched with criss-crossed lines. Even though she had been alive for only four weeks, the wrinkles gave her the appearance of being already ancient and knowing. I reached behind her ears, where her skin was soft as velvet. The place behind an elephant's ears is enormously sensitive, capillaries coursing close to the skin surface to release heat. I remembered learning at school that this was an important way that elephants keep cool in the hot summers. Even better is a trunk full of water directed over the head and streaming across this plush smoothness.

As she finished her first bottle and started on a second, I stroked her brow, taking in those bushy black lashes. Her earnest watchful eyes. As fascinated as I was by her, she seemed equally enthralled by me. Sucking on the bottle, she was staring into my eyes with complete trust, studying me with an open and unaffected reflection of my own feelings for her right now. Our connection didn't require me to be an elephant expert to understand, or to have any training as an animal communicator: She was adoring me.

It was a long time since I had felt so wanted or needed. In the deepening shadows of the stable, I was completely pulled into her world, absorbed by the simplicity of an emotion that made everything else irrelevant. It was just Kadiki and me, connected at this moment, beautiful and complete. Nothing else mattered.

After she had taken a third bottle, she settled on the straw and blankets beside me, head resting on my lap. Thor and Tiki came to join us, Thor pressing his back against her belly while Tiki lolled around her neck. Mbudzi knelt a short distance away, munching ruminatively.

The bottom half of the stable door was closed, and through the open panel the last light of the day was fading into darkness. Thinking about the night ahead, I realised I didn't have enough milk. I had underestimated how much she'd drink. Tessa had told me that I would probably need to feed her every two to three hours. If she carried on at the current rate, we'd get through the remaining six bottles by midnight. There was milk formula in large urns at the house, but how to get one of them here without unsettling Kadiki or leaving her alone?

~

I worked through the different options, checking the signal on my phone. Then came the sound of footsteps on the pavers outside. A woman's voice, 'Rob, are you there?'

It was Lakshmi, Riley's yoga student and friend whom I'd met briefly at Treasure Trees Apothecary.

'When I came to deliver food for Rinpoche I heard about the new arrival,' she said as she appeared at the stable door.

'He's back?'

'Not yet.' She spoke softly in the presence of the sleeping elephant. 'He's still in town. Mum insisted that I bring a delivery of food for him.'

On my lap Kadiki was opening her eyes and moving. I needed to shift, my left leg having gone completely numb.

'Come in,' I murmured. 'She's been resting.'

I had seen Lakshmi only once. Now, as then, even in the few steps she took from the door, there was something of the maharani about her, not that she seemed afraid of getting her clothes dirty. In jeans and a light jacket, she crouched on the floor as I shifted under the calf's weight.

'Oh, she's beautiful!' she said, reaching out to stroke the elephant.

The only light came from a single lantern glowing in the courtyard, but it was enough. Kadiki blinked her eyes a few times, and Lakshmi's face was filled with awe as she touched Kadiki's forehead. 'It's all right, little one,' she murmured softly. 'Just sleep.'

After she'd spent some time doting on the calf, I told her, 'You've come at just the right moment.' Soon after, Lakshmi set out to the house to collect milk. I remembered how Riley had first mentioned her to me. It had been Lakshmi who'd recognised me on the lawn the day that Yogi Tarchin arrived. Asking my niece if she knew me, Riley had told her who I was. Between them, they'd worked out that our paths must have crossed at Landers, where she had a temporary job a few years ago.

Subsequently we met at Diva's shop where I was also struck by a familiarity I couldn't place.

She returned with an urn, and I got up to decant formula into bottles. Kadiki was lying on the straw, curled up with Thor and Tiki, half awake. Lakshmi joined them, stroking the calf as we spoke.

'We must have met at some company 'do,' I told Lakshmi, as I held one of the bottles to the urn. 'I can't remember exactly.'

'That's the weird thing,' she replied. 'Me neither.'

'Which team at Landers were you in?'

'Fixed interest. Three years ago. July to September.'

'Miles Hodgson?' I named the team head.

'Yes.'

'Nice guy, Miles. But Fixed Interest? I wish we could have found you something more exciting.'

'The pay was good.' She was pragmatic. Then she added, 'Maybe it was the Fixed Interest Committee meetings — where we met, I mean?'

'Wednesday afternoons. Four pm.'

We both chuckled as she said ironically, 'Highlight of the week!'

~

Usually at least half a dozen people attended the meetings, with Miles and me at one end, and various people from the team ranged around the large oval conference table. If Lakshmi was one of his staffers, that would explain it.

'What took you to London?'

'Career.'

'In finance?'

'That was the day job,' she admitted. 'My passion is singing.'

'Really?'

'Since I was a little girl. Mum said I sang before I could talk.'

'I guess there are more opportunities in London.'

'I thought that too. I don't regret the eighteen months I was there. You know it's funny — it was only when I came this side that things started taking off for me.'

Many Zimbabweans spoke about "this side" and "that side" the binary distinction between home and elsewhere that was part of local jargon.

'It was like I had to spend time there to find out that I was meant to be here.' She paused for a reflective moment. 'Plus, I had to come home to find my man,' she smiled.

'A musician?'

'Sculptor.'

'That's unusual.'

'You met him earlier.'

'Did I?'

'Simba.'

'Ah, he arrived just when we needed an extra pair of hands.' I recalled the tall, obliging young man. 'He was a big help. Very well spoken.'

'Went to St George's.' The private, Jesuit-founded school was one of the best in the country.

'It shows,' I nodded.

'As a boy he studied with some of the greats, like Henry Munyaradzi.'

~

Hearing the name was like running the eye along a shelf of books and rediscovering a forgotten but much-loved volume like an echo through time. "Henry Munyaradzi". We had one of Henry's pieces. It had pride of place on a pedestal next to the front door. Dad had been a keen supporter of the Workshop School at the National Gallery of Zimbabwe headed by Frank McEwan, which brought global attention to the Shona sculpture movement.

'Munyaradzi's from around here, isn't he?'

'Ruwa,' confirmed Lakshmi. 'Our home too. Well, Marondera.'

I glanced to where she knelt over Kadiki. With the references to singing and sculpture, I was about to suggest that maybe we knew each other from here in Zimbabwe rather than London. I checked myself. Our family would have migrated before Lakshmi was even born.

~

Lakshmi explained how she visited her parents each week. I had already met her father, memorably. She told me that her mother, a spiritual woman and active senior, had heard about a yogi from India visiting Ruwa Buddhist Society. She had prepared half a dozen generous meals for him, each in its own self-contained dish. At the house, fetching the urn of milk, Lakshmi had also put two meals in the oven — one for Rinpoche and one for me. When I filled up the milk bottles, she insisted on fetching my food.

'You have to eat,' she reasoned. 'I can sit with Kadiki in the meantime.'

It was a delicious korma with a side of saffron rice, and I was hungrier than I'd realised. In the monochrome light of the stable, I sat on a chopped tree stump that served as a seat, grateful for Lakshmi's thoughtfulness, and for her mother's cooking. Close by, Kadiki raised her head to check on me. As she rested it back on a blanket, Lakshmi caressed her face. 'When I fall in love,' she sang the words of the Nat King Cole song in a sultry voice, 'it will be forever.'

~

As Lakshmi continued serenading Kadiki softly, I became aware of something quite different. Surprisingly strong, the emotion caught me completely unawares: I felt suddenly protective. I knew that Lakshmi meant well and was doing her best to help. But I wanted Kadiki back.

~

It was the most curious thing — getting jealous over a calf who had only just arrived. Until that moment, I wouldn't have thought myself capable of such a reaction. But once the emotion reared, there was no stopping it. As soon as I'd finished the meal, I told Lakshmi she should return to Harare before it got dark, the road conditions being terrible. Brushing aside her offer to continue babysitting, I thanked her and asked her to latch the lower part of the door on her way out.

A short while later it was just us: Kadiki and me, the dogs, and Mbudzi. And so began our first night together. Knowing nothing of the calf's sleeping patterns, I was unprepared for what might happen — when would she wake? How would I know if she was hungry or just shifting in her sleep? And how best to try getting some sleep myself while lying with her on the floor?

I tried a number of positions, using blankets and straw as props. Resting behind her on my side, an arm draped over her shoulders and around the front to her chest, I felt the rhythmic swell and ebb of her breathing. In the darkness of the stable, lying on straw and blankets, I was torn by contradictory instincts. Aversion for the discomfort and the disruption into which I had been thrown. And yet there was something strangely important and quite miraculous about lying here with my arm around a baby elephant, listening to the moist, almost wheezy sound of air passing through her trunk, smelling her sweet, earthy smell.

~

I came to learn that when she was hungry, she'd use her trunk to lift my hand into her mouth and suck my fingers. Time for me to get up and fetch her bottle. I tried sleeping between feeds but found it hard to get comfortable. Every time I was nodding off, she stirred, wanting to be fed again. With an aching shoulder I tried shifting position, lying to face her with my arms about her front legs. She rested her trunk on my neck. The unfamiliar rugged wrinkles were heavy on my skin. I followed the sound of her breathing in and out through the tip of her trunk. Thor was snoring heavily. Tiki remained silent, but occasionally would spasm, her

111

legs twitching in her sleep.

As I lay, fatigued and foggy, the events that had brought me here returned to mind in that vivid, foreboding way of the early hours. How Mr Kachingwe from National Parks had deliberately caught me unawares. Dr Tembo's reluctance to comment on that conversation. How, in my brief call to Tessa Brenthurst, she'd mentioned how Parks received precious little government funding. In a situation like Kadiki's, if requests for help were refused, the consequences didn't bear thinking of.

Now, here she was, having undergone some unspeakable horror on the banks of the Zambezi River during which she had lost her mother and herd. Investing her faith, her love, in me. I could see it in the way she gazed at me as she suckled. How she closed her trunk around my neck and pulled me to her in the night. She needed me in a way I had never before known.

~

In my mental jumble, I recalled the emails continuing to come in from London. A variety of people wanted me to comment, advise, direct, or decide. The tone was increasingly urgent. Initially, I'd asked for a few days' consideration. More recently I simply ignored them. In some cases, they went unread. I was being asked to do as I always did: take charge. To reach out and put my hand on the tiller. I needed to get back in the game and take action. I couldn't expect the team in London to keep waiting for me.

Amid the swirl of thoughts, I recognised that time was running out and I still hadn't visited my godmother Kay in the Nyanga mountains, one of the priorities of my visit to Zim. We had spoken a few times on the phone and every time I'd promise her that it wouldn't be long. She was, after all, only a three-hour drive away.

In the early hours, something Lakshmi had said surfaced: 'Three years ago. July to September.' It was when she'd worked at Landers on Miles Hodgson's team. The time it seemed our paths must have crossed. With sudden clarity I recollected how, three years ago, I had spent summer out of town. Justine and I had just parted ways, after twenty years as a couple. She had moved to Germany to be with her daughter, who was about to give birth to her first granddaughter. I had opted for a circuit breaker, spending July in the Landers Paris office and September in New York. I'd taken off August to be with friends in the Caribbean. Lakshmi might very well have attended Fixed Interest Committee meetings every Wednesday at four pm. But not me.

~

Throughout the night, whenever I looked out at the panel of sky, revealed through the open stable door, it seemed to be the same: pitch-black canvas with a spray of distant stars. Getting up time and again for a bottle to feed Kadiki, I was groggy yet unable to sleep. But I must have slipped off, because I was in my office at Landers — everything hyper-real in the vivid way of dreams. I walked to look out the window, but instead of the familiar skyline of City towers, including the Shard and the Cheesegrater, I was gazing down on Ruwa Buddhist Society lawn. It was verdant green, and I could see Mampara grazing on it, along with a small herd of kudu. Sonny and Cher were perched on the roof.

The lawn was beginning to fill with people. For the first time I noticed that the area was scattered with glittering jewels. Riley and Luke were there, accompanied by the dogs. Tinashe and Harris were diligently bending to collect rubies and emeralds, diamonds and sapphires, some the size of oranges, and placing them in sturdy sacks. I saw Diva and Bruno and Mr Nzou, Gogo and Marvellous, Lakshmi and Simba, plus others whose names I didn't know but whom I'd met through the Ruwa Buddhist Society. All were picking up the priceless gems, stuffing them in backpacks, in their pockets, using any available bag or container.

'You are unspeakably special, Rob,' Rinpoche had said that day as we sat on the veranda drinking coffee. 'You are so close! After lifetimes on the path you are almost there. The human life you have at the present, it is as though you are living on an island of jewels. Compared to the lives of most other beings, it is so easy for you to collect treasures of extraordinary value.'

What he was saying was true of me. It was also true of the others. All those on the lawn had come to understand that if we wish to experience the immaculate reality of the lama, the most direct way to do so is to create its causes. Jewels are gathered by serving others. And who better to serve, first and foremost, than the guru himself? 'Whatever you do,' he exhorted me, 'don't leave the island empty-handed!'

~

I wanted to get down onto the lawn. In my dream I was trying to open my office window, but I couldn't. On the thirty-fifth floor, it wasn't designed to be opened. And when I walked out to the elevator, it was out of action. I had to use the stairs. Everyone else was having to use the stairs too. It was like rush hour at an Underground station as people hurried down.

I worried that it was getting too late. That by the time I descended to the lawn there would be no jewels left. Perhaps the whole place would have gone by then?

Disappeared. Was this a vanishing opportunity?

Somehow, I managed to find my way to the lawn, which was like the morning in a garden after a party the night before. There was a scattered detritus of celebrations and in my exhaustion it was hard to see if there were any jewels left. But as I scrabbled about, hands and knees damp from the wet grass, eventually I found something: a single, large, overlooked ruby. I placed it carefully in my right pocket.

~

Next thing I knew, Kadiki was stirring and, muzzily, I sat up. I was about to collect a fresh bottle for her, when I saw that Rinpoche was there, a milk bottle in his hand, approaching and greeting us softly. The dogs were wagging their tails. Kadiki stood to feed and, even though she had never met Rinpoche before, she quickly accepted the bottle from him, eyes half closed.

'Diva told me about this one,' Rinpoche nodded towards Kadiki. 'Go home, Rob. Get some sleep.'

I glanced outside. It was pitch black.

'What's the time?'

'Just after three.' Rinpoche's usual wake-up time. The time that, since he was a boy in the monasteries, he was in the habit of rising for early-morning meditation.

I was about to tell him that I would see the night through when I felt his hand on my shoulder, his gaze penetrating mine. 'Come back when you're rested,' he told me, his tone appreciative but firm. 'We will make a roster to care for this one.'

~

Kadiki seemed drowsy and comfortable as she fed from him. Half asleep, I led the way outside, Thor and Tiki following me through the night, nonplussed. Mbudzi was still asleep. It was well before dawn. The bush was dark and silent. Even so, as the three of us took our familiar route home I had the sense that we weren't alone. That we were being protected in some way I was too tired to understand. Back at the house I went straight to my room, took off my shoes, and collapsed on the bed.

Not that I slumbered for long. I woke at what had become my usual time, around six am, sun already filling the bedroom with a golden glow, brightening moment by moment. I'd hoped to rest for longer, but I couldn't. Instead, I got up and showered, trying to awaken fully.

As I was putting yesterday's clothes in the wash basket, I felt a bump in the trousers. I turned out the pockets. At the very bottom of the right one, etched with a smooth, black eye, was a large and shiny seed from a lucky bean tree. Ruby red.

Chapter Six

IN THE KITCHEN I made a plunger of coffee, poured out a bowl of muesli, and switched on Aunt Carrie's vintage Roberts radio. The room immediately filled with upbeat morning music. The news came on, mercifully brief, before a sing-song weatherman promised us another warm day in Mashonaland, with sunny skies to continue for the next week. Not great news for Mr Nzou's rainmaking. Munching on my breakfast, I stared at the lucky bean I'd placed in the saucer of a small brass candle holder in front of me. What *that* was about I'd need to figure out when I was more alert. Meantime, I felt a strong pull towards Kadiki. A care roster was a good idea, but for the moment she was my responsibility.

~

The dogs were delighted to accompany me back through the bush, bright-eyed with the prospect of fresh adventures. When we reached the stable, we found the elephant calf lying on the floor with her head on Rinpoche's lap, her eyes closed, as he sat meditating. It was a scene of sublime serenity and I didn't want to disturb it. But the door latch rattled.

Kadiki looked up. And the moment she saw me, she scrambled to her feet and rushed to me, trunk reaching up to seize me around the waist and draw me to her. I knelt, stroking her softly.

'Yes, my baby,' I reassured her. 'I'm back.'

The fierceness of her welcome was so moving that I felt myself welling up. Rinpoche looked directly at me. He folded his fingertips together. I nodded. It was true. We were entwined, and in a way I would never have imagined.

~

We walked into the garden, Kadiki less tentative than her first time, yesterday. In the company of her new friends, she took in the scents of the morning, moving her trunk nimbly among the shrubs as she walked through the flower bed under the great marula tree.

'I wasn't given much choice.' I wanted to explain to Rinpoche about Mr Kachingwe's call.

'She's here now,' he interjected. 'We must look after our fellow sem chen.'

His words were simple, but consequential.

'It will take a while to work out how,' I said.

'We have seen,' he gestured to Kadiki. 'You know.' He looked at me directly. 'All sem chens are the same. We all want to feel loved,' he brought a hand to his heart. 'That is the *most* important.'

I didn't doubt what he was saying, but it seemed to me that there was more, so much more to taking care of a creature as socially intelligent as an elephant.

'Some animals show qualities like compassion. Altruism. Fairness. They grieve for lost love,' he responded directly to my thoughts. 'They are complex. They communicate — not using words. This is why it's important to learn to be like them.'

'In what way?' I asked.

'Non-verbal,' he said. 'Humans have words. Words give rise to thoughts. And we are so conditioned to thoughts that we can't imagine a different way of being. Generally, humans constantly crave mental stimulation.

~

'Animals are not like this. They have no words. Fewer concepts. They are as advanced in non-verbal behaviour as we are in our world of ideas. They detect shifts in mind and mood so subtle we may not even be aware of them. They may not understand why we are anxious or depressed or caught up on our devices, but when we are so absorbed that we are unavailable, we upset them. So, with a sem chen like this one,' he nodded towards Kadiki, 'it helps to let go of thinking. To allow the mind to rest.'

I smiled at what he said — as well as at the difficulty of the challenge he set out with such inexorable logic.

'Remember Tilopa's six words of advice to Marpa,' he continued, naming two great masters. 'Well, in the Tibetan language they are just six words:

Don't recollect: let go of thoughts of the past.

Don't imagine: let go of thoughts of the future.

Don't think: let go of thoughts of the present.

Don't examine: let go of the need to analyse things.

Don't control: let go of the need to manage things.

Just *rest*.'

'Rest,' I nodded.

'To begin, you may find it hard.' Was I imagining it or was he referring to the way I'd spent last night on the stable floor?

'When we are addicted to distraction, a peaceful mind is hard to find. We may wish for it, even with all our heart, but our mind keeps doing what it has always

119

done. Thinking, thinking, thinking! There is no easy solution. No magic I can offer, except simply to be aware. Whatever you keep doing, you become better at. With acquaintance, everything becomes easy.'

'And then?' I was curious. 'When you *are* able to experience it, how do things change?'

I felt an expansive benevolence as he looked at me. 'Our subdued mind becomes so tranquil that it is a beautiful place to abide. We like to stay there. To soak in this state of wellbeing. We become better at identifying a movement of mind before a thought fully emerges so that we can avoid it arising. And we *do* wish to avoid it, because we discover for ourselves that a peaceful mind, free of conception, has a radiance that is delightful. A boundlessness that has no limits. We see for ourselves that our mind is truly not the size of our heads!'

We chuckled.

'Most of all,' he held my gaze, 'in this space of clarity that has no beginning or no end, we come to experience the wellspring of serenity directly for ourselves. A treasure that has been there all along, only we never knew it. A way of being so sublime that the more we taste it, the longer we wish to stay.'

~

The state he was describing sounded close to ineffable. Literally, beyond words. I tried to imagine being in this state all the time — was this how reality appeared to him when we sat on the veranda looking out at the garden? On top of Ruwa Rock? Even during moments of humdrum daily activity? It would explain the lightness I felt in his presence. The feeling that even though he shared the same physical world that I did, there was always something untouched about him.

~

'I guess that's when you create space ...' I was working through the implications of what he was saying.

'You make more room for the others,' he continued for me. 'You are more sensitive to them. How they feel. What they may be trying to communicate — perhaps even able to hear them without sound.'

'You mean, like telepathy? Clairvoyance?'

Yogi Tarchin's eyes twinkled. 'These words. They are "woo-woo", yes?'

He seemed uncomfortable with terms implying something otherworldly to a process that was straightforward. Being able to read the moods, even the minds of others, was unexceptional if your own mind was clear.

At that moment, Kadiki looked up at us from the flowerbed and shook her shoulders playfully before coming over.

'For this one ...' he said.

'Kadiki,' I named her. 'Shona for "very small".'

'Kadiki.' He leaned over, brushing her with his hand. 'You can use the meditation I have already shown you.'

I didn't understand at first. 'What meditation?'

'The day I arrived. The golden lotus blossoming at the heart.'

'Oh, *that* meditation.'

'She will feel love. She will like it.'

~

Looking down, I became aware of how badly I had failed her. So caught up in my own agitation yesterday, not for one moment had I even considered how my mental state might affect her. She arrived, desperate for her mother and all that she knew, struggling to understand this strange reality. And what had I been doing? So utterly consumed in thoughts about myself, I'd cleared no mental space for her. How had *she* felt, tuned into all my turmoil?

At the same time, I was recognising another thing. 'She will feel love.' That very first afternoon when Yogi Tarchin had arrived, and we all sat on the lawn as he guided us through the golden lotus meditation, it had seemed magical, bordering on the impossible, when we opened our eyes to find Bodhi stretching out casually in front of us. John Elliott's cheetah, who had disappeared into the bush the day he'd died. Three years later, having been neither seen nor heard of, there she was again.

But what if her re-appearance had a simple explanation? What if she abandoned her home when the love left, and returned when she felt it again? Could a visualisation be that powerful? Could we change things in the material world just by imagining?

Later we were on the front lawn with Kadiki and the other animals when from around the side of the house came Mr Nzou, accompanied by a tall, spare-framed young man in his twenties. Mr Nzou wore his usual gardening uniform, the younger man similarly dressed. On seeing Rinpoche, both adopted the most reverential postures, clapping their hands together in a traditional show of respect.

As they came closer, Mr Nzou formally introduced us to his nephew, Ezekiel. He was here, the groundsman explained, to help look after the elephant. We all turned to watch Kadiki, who was tugging at one of the low-hanging branches of the flamboyant tree with her trunk. Evidently word was getting around about Kadiki. There were others to support her and perhaps soon there would be even more. As Ezekiel went to play with Kadiki, Rinpoche walking to watch over them, Mr Nzou stood beside me.

'Perhaps you have brought us rain?' I observed, as we looked up to where deep blue folds of rain-bearing clouds were gathering on the horizon, contrary to that morning's weather forecast. There would be much excitement in the lands and villages all around us.

'This is not me,' he pointed upwards, ruling out all personal involvement.

'But you are the rainmaker.'

'*Aiwha*,' he shook his head. 'Not this rain.' Mr Nzou glanced secretively towards me before jutting his chin in Rinpoche's direction. 'This one gave me strange advice.'

Mr Nzou told me that Rinpoche had discovered his jealousy of his contemporary in Manicaland. Success Domba was as well known for his reflective sunglasses, sharp suits, and slimline briefcase as he was for inducing vast quantities of rain. Such resentment must be overcome, the lama said, directing Mr Nzou to visit his rival to congratulate him in person.

Mr Nzou had made the long bus trip to Success Domba's village near Mutare, where he'd encountered a man quite different from the arrogant know-all he had imagined, encountering instead one who was touched by the visit of a fellow rainmaker and delighted by his gift of baobab tree products. Success Domba had humbly asked advice from him, as his elder, about rainmaking, fearing what would happen if his own run of good fortune was to change.

Mr Nzou wagged his finger towards Rinpoche. 'He knew my jealousy.' A rueful smile appeared on his face. 'Now, it is gone.'

'And because it is gone,' I prompted him, 'there is no problem for you making rain?'

'Ah, no!' he shook his head, once again. 'If there is rain, it is his. *I* know this.' Wizened face frowning with concentration, he continued enigmatically, 'The great ones and the ancestors, *they* know this. They feel him in the land. He calls animals out of the bush,' he gestured first to where Bodhi was yawning widely, then to Kadiki, who was chasing Tiki across the lawn at high speed. 'He can call rain from the sky.' There was finality in his voice as he declared, 'That is why we call him Africa Buddha.'

'Africa Buddha,' I murmured. It was the first time I had heard the title. It wouldn't be the last. And as I repeated it, I wondered by what strange magic it was that our rainmaker, Mr Nzou, his ancestors, and those he termed 'the great ones' recognised Yogi Tarchin as a Buddha. Simultaneously, I recalled Kay saying how those who saw the teacher as a Buddha received the blessings of a Buddha.

'He is the one!' Mr Nzou agreed emphatically.

~

A short while later, when Ezekiel led Kadiki towards me, Mr Nzou went to speak to Rinpoche.

'Are you also a Nzou?' I asked Ezekiel, kneeling next to the elephant.

'Like this one,' he nodded, chuckling.

'There are quite a few surnames, aren't there, the same as animals?'

'Mbizi — zebra,' he confirmed. 'Mvuu — hippo. Nyati — buffalo. Shiri — fish eagle. Yes, these are the totem names.'

I had forgotten about totems. We had learned about them at school, but sketchily. In a society without a written language, totems had a particular importance: On no account were you to marry someone from the same totem, because you were blood relatives.

'Totems were to avoid interbreeding, weren't they?'

Ezekiel glanced over. He had a cheerful demeanour and ready smile. 'Ja. That was part of it. But even now when there are other ways to do such things, totems are still important. Even more important.'

'Really?'

He nodded vehemently. 'It is our job to look after our totem animals and the land where they live. To keep them safe. To make sure they have enough food and water.'

'Different people look after different animals according to their clan totem?' I was seeing a broader picture.

'It's our job,' he confirmed, and I recognised the young man's sense of purpose. 'Our personal job. Some young ones today, eish, they don't understand,' he shook his head, expression turning sombre. 'In olden days, the times of our forefathers, the clan gathered around the fire at night. African TV!' he joked. 'We'd sing praises to our animal totem. Because of the strong connection, these praises were about ourselves also,' he touched his heart. 'We could feel them.'

'People knew who they were?' I recognised the identity, the sense of belonging that would come with such practices.

'Ehe,' he agreed.

~

I guessed Ezekiel understood more than most about animal totems, given his uncle's high standing with the chief, and that his passion for the subject came from a deep knowledge.

'When you say, "strong connection",' I asked, 'how is it that you feel connected?' Was it from a sense of knowing, I wondered, of telepathic contact along the lines Rinpoche had been talking about?

Ezekiel surprised me. His answer was more direct.

'Because they are ancestors,' he said simply.

I raised my eyebrows. 'Our grandfathers and grandmothers. Our aunts and uncles. All the mothers and fathers of them,' he indicated a family tree stretching infinitely upwards.

'Shona people believe in rebirth?'

'The animals of our totem are their spirits. This is why we would never kill a totem animal.'

'You could be killing your own grandmother?' I confirmed.

He nodded.

'If you do so, and eat the meat,' he looked at me ominously, 'you may lose your teeth. Even your life. For sure,' he shook his head, 'as long as you walk on this earth you will be cursed!'

I had no inkling of these ideas. What Ezekiel was explaining didn't sound so far removed from eastern notions of rebirth. It was a curious spiritual alignment. And the more deeply I considered it, the more the system of animal totems seemed a radically good idea. What if every person in the world was brought up to feel an affinity for a particular animal and a duty of care for it? What if, between the families in a place, we had all the species covered? Collectively — through ubuntu — the whole ecosystem would be protected.

~

On a personal basis, how much better would people feel if, instead of taking on labels of victimhood or mental dysfunction, they first and foremost identified with the inspiring qualities of their totem? If they had a conviction of their place in the world? Of possessing archetypal abilities to navigate their way through life? How much better would it be if we all had a heartfelt bond to the place we were from and the beings who lived there?

'This one, she is my clan,' said Ezekiel, as Kadiki searched him with her trunk, before she turned to me with evident curiosity.

Remembering what Tinashe had said about home, kumusha, being about much more than only a physical place, but also one of belonging to one's land and ancestors, I realised that your totem animal was vital to that connection. When you were with your totem animals you were with your kin. Their presence defined you as being at home.

Ezekiel watched how Kadiki, so close that her leg was touching me, slipped her trunk down the front of my shirt and was sniffing my chest. I was becoming more used to this form of intimacy with her. She had searched my limbs and torso with the tip of that trunk — fascinated, in particular, by a small, black mole just beneath my right knee. I remember feeling the same intrigue as a child studying my father's mole in exactly the same place. The mole ran in the family.

'Ah! I think you are also with us,' he said. 'The *nzou* family.'

I felt a tug at the heart. It was such an unaffected remark. But with everything that was going on, and after the night I'd been through with Kadiki, being adopted into the *nzou* family felt like the greatest of privileges. Not trusting myself to speak, I nodded.

~

Later that morning, I led Kadiki to the stable so that I could sit with some back support as I fed her. This was all still so new, but in another way we were already becoming familiar with each other. Not only familiar — we shared something that defied being put into words. I recalled Yogi Tarchin's suggestion that I use the golden lotus visualisation to connect more deeply with the little calf.

~

After she'd finished feeding, she lay on the floor beside me. I placed one hand on her chest, the other on her forehead, as I tried my best to imagine the petals of Rinpoche's radiant golden lotus bud peeling open at my heart — waves of loving kindness bursting forth from it, passing through not just my own body, but Kadiki's too, like blissful shivers, subtle but tangible. I tried imagining the transformative powers of those rays, removing all pain and suffering, enveloping us in an infinite abundance of love, compassion, and hope. It felt real to me. And I had the sense that in some way she could feel it too. For the longest time she remained, unmoving, her small but perfectly formed elephant head resting on my lap.

I dozed off. Kadiki too. Fatigue was catching up with us. But when I woke, I felt the strangest sensation — it was dark outside. Surely we hadn't slept into the night? Then I realised that it wasn't nightfall causing the skies to darken. Through the open stable door I watched cumulonimbus clouds gathering, deep blue grey, swollen with rain. There came the low moan of wind, the sound of branches and debris scattering across the courtyard pavers. Reaching over, I felt Thor's furry body pressed against Kadiki's and stroked him gently before reaching across to Tiki. Mbudzi watched the three of us, utterly unconcerned.

~

I was still only half-awake. I guessed that the dogs were probably okay with thunderstorms. I knew that Aunt Carrie used to sit on her veranda, drinking Tanganda and relishing the immersive sensation. As for Kadiki, she was more cosseted here than she would be in the wild. Nestling in blankets and straw, she was safe and protected.

From outside came the raised voices of Gogo and Ezekiel shouting to one another, footfalls as Ezekiel pounded to Mr Nzou's nearby cottage. Wind howled through the trees and the groaning outspread limbs of the marula. Second by second the sky was deepening even more apocalyptically. Then we heard the first, electric crackle, and a few seconds later, the rumble.

As a boy I'd learned how to tell how quickly a storm was approaching by the delay between lightning and thunder. This was my first African tempest in decades, and even though I was drowsy, I relished the power of it. The next lightning strike, a dramatic fork through the darkness, was followed, much more closely, by thunder so loud that the stables shuddered. I was relieved that Kadiki, the dogs, and the goat seemed at ease where they were, content to witness this tumultuous spectacle from our place of warm comfort.

Outside, a first spray of rain exploded onto the cobbles and roof, drops sounding as if they were the size of small grapes, so forcefully were they flung from the sky. There were further sporadic strikes, rain tattooing the corrugated iron roof. The phosphorescence was becoming ever more blinding, the roar that followed swifter and more furious as the storm drew near.

Then the scattered assaults of rain joined to form a sustained downpour, turning the roof into a drum. The tumult was directly above us, deafening in its elemental power. Having gasped through the seemingly endless dry days of early summer, Mother Earth was offered not simply relief, but glorious satiation.

~

It was a magnificent outpouring. For minute after glorious

minute, the generosity of the heavens was utterly mesmerising. And along with the rain came the smell that instantly connected me to my earliest moments. Unique in its sublime potency, that sudden, clean, freshness as a torrent of water purged the trees, the rocks, the sky itself of dust. The unique scent of petrichor swept into the stable, earthy and sweet.

In an instant I was back in my childhood room in the warm glow of the bedside lamp as Dad read from *The Wind in the Willows*. Outside was a cataclysm of rain and wrath. But with that pungent smell of renewal coming from the garden, and my father's arm around my shoulders, I had never felt more cosily protected. Just as I hoped that, in this first storm of her life, with my arm about her, Kadiki felt the same deep reassurance.

When the rains begin in Zimbabwe, they mark more than just another season. They transform. Water is life. After the seemingly endless dry comes the time of deep quenching. Within a day the bush blushes pale green. Puddles glitter in previously dry riverbeds. After further downpours the whole landscape turns verdant, iron-rich soil and summer heat giving birth to prolific fast-growing grass, weeds, shrubs, and all manner of fecundity. Pools turn into trickles, trickles into streams. Empty water tanks, ponds, and lakes fill day by day. The world becomes a different place with abundant lush grass for the wildlife to feed on. A place where fields can be ploughed and corn seeds planted. Where there is a future again.

~

Within our little group at Ruwa Buddhist Society, change was visceral. Following that first prodigious torrent, Gogo, Mr Nzou, and Ezekiel spent every spare moment between the deluges planting seasonal crops in the plots behind their staff cottages. At night, snatches of song gusted with the breeze from the local village where the men ended another day of promise drinking beer and the women ululated. Hope and purpose burbled through the community, free as laughter. On Sunday, the white-clad Apostolics under their winter thorn acacia, having forgiven the Lord for His prior intractability, raised their arms aloft to chorus and praise Him with zeal.

Gogo was all 'What a Friend We Have in Jesus' as she busied herself about the homestead with renewed gusto. When she took time out from her labours, I would find her bent over her phone at the kitchen table. At first, I thought she must be messaging friends, until I discovered she was doing a puzzle of some kind.

'*New York Times* Wordle,' she told me. 'It helps my vocabulary. But today,' she sighed, 'I have only three letters and I have run out of lines!'

Tinashe travelled to spend the weekend helping his mother sow mealies in her land at Guruve. Harris Gould climbed the ladder of the water tank, raised on stilts behind the homestead, to check on its readiness. Luke came out to help choose a site for a purpose-built shelter for Kadiki. Elephants weren't used to four walls, he noted, and Kadiki would soon outgrow the stable.

~

Rinpoche created a roster for Kadiki, with shifts taken not only by Mr Nzou and Ezekiel, but also by Gogo and Lakshmi. It was a new routine for us all, and Rinpoche insisted on playing his part. I volunteered for most of the night shifts, and we settled into a pattern where Kadiki would usually wake twice to feed, first around midnight and then when Rinpoche arrived at three in the morning. After the feeding, he'd conduct his morning meditation with her head on his lap, sending me away so that I might get a few hours of sleep in my bed. The early hours tramp through the bush with the dogs became a regular ritual.

~

As with the first night walk, I had the same feeling of presence, of guardianship, when the dogs and I made our next three o'clock return. And the sense again, the night after that. It was only after several early morning walks that I caught an amber glint out of the corner of my eye.

'Bodhi?' I called out.

The path turned, and there she was. Back to us, she was leading the way as if she had been heading our procession home all along. I realised that she'd been playing a game of hide and seek these past few nights. It was probably only when she allowed herself to be revealed that I'd spotted her.

When we got home, she crossed the garden to the veranda as if to say, 'I know where you live.'

I opened the door and the dogs went in. Before stepping inside I turned to where she'd hopped on the low veranda wall.

'Thanks.'

I recalled Rinpoche's instruction to imagine gold light reaching from the lotus in my chest, stretching through the darkness to where she stood. And it may have been only my imagination, but what I felt return was like a fire trail of energy racing back, a burst of primal power clutching my heart as she stared into the darkness, poised and watchful.

There was a novelty, a thrill, about having our own cheetah escort. It happened every night. The only difference was when she chose to reveal a glimpse of herself. Then I'd call her name, and she would appear. It was always the same procession: Bodhi followed by Tiki the fearless, me, and then Thor. My very own nocturnal Praetorian guard.

~

Bodhi remained distant from Kadiki in the early days. If she was lying on the lawn outside Rinpoche's office when I brought the calf to the front of the house, she didn't move. Nor did she ever approach her. I knew her detachment to be more apparent than real.

One day I was making my way alone from stable to office, walking quickly around the side of the house, lost in thought, when my foot struck an obstacle that sent me sprawling.

Even in the instant it took me to go from vertical to buckling onto the lawn, I recognised the obstacle. I had evidently been too tempting a target for Bodhi, reclining by the window. With that swift yet casual insouciance of cats, she slipped out her paw and watched me tumble. Picking myself up, I looked over. Her head facing Ruwa rock, she studiously ignored me. Who said that cheetahs don't have a sense of humour?

The emails from London grew increasingly urgent. Text messages began arriving. Depending on the time of the day, or night, I would read and respond to some. Since Kadiki's arrival I hadn't had a full night's sleep. I was fatigued, disoriented, and powerfully conflicted.

When I had first arrived in Ruwa, everything in Zimbabwe was a novelty. There were nostalgic moments, of course, and flashbacks to my childhood. But none of it felt real. Not in the sense of my normal working life with all the meetings and decisions and commutes through the city.

Now that I had been here, experiencing things for which I was completely unprepared, London itself began to feel somehow unreal. And difficult. Having jumped off the treadmill, for the first time I found myself reluctant to return.

~

Nevertheless, I was taken by surprise when Nick Berkeley phoned me at seven one morning after another night of not much sleep. Sitting at the kitchen table, he must have seen I was online, because next thing, my phone was ringing.

'Busy time in Zim?' he asked.

We had spoken only briefly after Aunt Carrie's death. I told him about Kadiki's arrival, recognising how distant the idea of sleeping with an elephant calf must sound. I also mentioned Rinpoche. Nick was an acute observer, but he was also a traditionalist, and he found my interest in anything Eastern somewhat baffling.

He soon got to the nub of the matter. 'Are you coming back?' he queried in a tone free of judgement. I hadn't expected to be asked so bluntly. Nick had no interest in delving into the details of missed messages or emails I hadn't replied to.

It was a while before I said, 'You know, Nick, it's turning out to be a tough call.'

I explained myself as best I was able. He was his usual probing, challenging self. Without any accusations, he worked through what was going on, as well as what might be done about it.

~

He already had a replacement CEO in mind. Paul Churchill had been my protégé at Landers before moving to Frankfurt. Apparently, Paul was missing Britain and wanted back. Arrangements for the new business were too advanced not to move forward —

with or without me. Nick was emphatic in reminding me about how the company would be the biggest job of my career, and the most lucrative. How everything that I'd worked for paved the way to this particular role. How he'd prefer me in the job over anyone else.

When I asked him, 'Taking your chairman's hat off, how would you advise me personally?' there was a pause from the other end before he said, 'I've got ten years on you, Robbie.'

Our birthdays, both in February, were exactly a decade apart.

'What becomes very apparent, if it isn't already, is that we're in the last quarter of the game, you and I,' he continued. 'If there's anything you really want to do in this life, whatever that something is, you'd best crack on and do it. Another chance may not come along.'

For a while after our call ended, I sat staring at the round red lucky bean in the brass candle holder.

~

My reveries were interrupted by the sound of a car in the driveway and the dogs yapping excitedly. It was Diva. She announced that she'd come to make me breakfast. Brushing aside objections that I could look after myself, she swept through the house in a magnificent red dress, with matching coral-coloured eyeshadow, wafting a bouquet of Treasure Trees aromas, and unpacking a tote bag of groceries.

'You must be exhausted from all the nights looking after Kadiki?' her face was a portrait of sympathy.

'Well ...'

'Who cares for the carer?' she demanded.

She wasn't asking my permission. She had already decided. Tying an apron around her waist, she busied herself about the kitchen, talking about the arrival of the rains in Mashonaland, how she and her husband, Herbert, had been besieged by flying ants.

I noted the coincidence that the rains started only days after Mr Nzou had consulted with Rinpoche.

'My dear,' she waved a spatula in my direction. 'They started *only* because of our Rinpoche, as Mr Nzou will be the first to tell you.'

Moments later, through the window I saw Tinashe crossing the backyard. I looked at my watch. 'Shouldn't he be on his way to school?'

'On a Saturday?' she queried.

I put my face into my hands and shook my head. 'Didn't realise.'

I had lost track of the days.

Diva soon called Tinashe to join us.

~

Breakfast was a scrumptious meal of richly yellow-yolked eggs, laid by our own bantams, accompanied by fried mushrooms, onions, tomatoes, and hash browns, served with thick slices of toast and coffee. Compared to my usual bowl of Kefalos muesli, it was a feast.

~

Over the meal, Diva told us about her most recent conversation with Rinpoche when she had asked if he'd be willing to lead a refuge ceremony. He had accepted.

'What's a refuge ceremony?' I asked.

'When you take refuge in the Buddha, Dharma, and Sangha,' she said.

Across the table, Tinashe put his cutlery down. 'We do this every day,' he said, dabbing his lips with a napkin, 'as Buddhists. But a refuge ceremony with the lama formalises our practice.'

'You become a card-carrying Buddhist?' I confirmed.

Tinashe smiled as he nodded. 'Usually, we take

pratimoksha vows at the same time.' Seeing my bewilderment, he explained, 'There are five of them. To abandon killing, stealing, lying, sexual misconduct, and taking intoxicants.'

'You don't have to take all five,' said Diva. 'Just the first one.'

'So, I can still enjoy a glass of wine in the evening?'

'Every vow is entirely up to you. Most of us take the first four.'

I pondered this for a moment. I hadn't ever considered what might constitute becoming a Buddhist. 'When did Rinpoche say he'd offer the refuge ceremony?' I asked.

'As soon as the temple is finished. Early January.' Alert to my interest, Diva met my eyes across the table. 'Might we persuade you to extend your stay?'

I held her expectant expression.

'I really don't know.'

~

I hadn't seen much of Tinashe since Kadiki arrived, and he was preoccupied that morning. He told us how he was busier than ever since the rains began. He was still working on the car, he assured me, and progress was good. I tried drawing him out with a few questions but, polite as usual, his smooth sculpted face remained enigmatic as a Buddha's.

~

Far less deferential, after munching on her toast Diva turned to him, earrings jingling colourfully.

'You're very quiet, Tina. Are you okay?'

So all-engulfing in manner, and so manifestly kind, Diva was impossible to resist. It took her a few minutes, but then Tinashe began telling us about the encounter that had created a great predicament.

Earlier that week, Yogi Tarchin asked him to collect

137

chili seedlings from a nursery at Ruwa. Such a request from one's guru was to be willingly accepted, whatever the inconvenience. On his way to the nursery, Tinashe found himself in his truck, stuck in a one-way street in which a car driven by an elderly man travelling in the wrong direction, had broken down. It was raining heavily.

Tinashe had no alternative but to climb from his cab amid the downpour and diagnose the cause of the stalled Renault: a dead battery. He always carried jump leads, so the problem wasn't hard to fix. While attaching cables from his own battery to the other car, its elderly driver, fussing and fretting beside him, picked up on the way he pronounced "Renault". Where had he learned to speak like that, he demanded? Tinashe told him that he'd worked on a cruise ship in the Mediterranean. Which prompted the other man to bemoan the country's brain drain.

Rain continuing, and Tinashe returning to his cab, needing a couple of attempts to get the alligator clips positioned correctly, the old man began speaking about a friend in his home village. How his grandson had gone to work on ships in the Mediterranean, never to return. How much the old man missed him. The great wisdom he wished to pass on. How his dearest wish was to see his grandson.

More concerned about getting the other car out of the way, Tinashe had only been half-listening. Until, in the midst of the monologue he heard the old man say, 'He is a n'anga, you know. Famous for his divinations with *hakata*.'

Hakata were the divining tablets used by n'angas — a technique in which Tinashe's own grandfather had been an acknowledged expert. Tinashe had interrupted the old man to ask who this n'anga was.

The wizened senior had spoken the name of his grandfather. Wondering if he had got this right, Tinashe asked several more questions about the n'anga. The answers confirmed his grandfather's identity.

~

Until that moment, Tinashe had believed his grandfather to be dead. Long ago his mother told him so. Stunned by the revelations, he was further shaken to discover that the old man lived near Centenary — only a few hours' drive away.

'He is yearning to see me,' he told us over the kitchen table. 'And I want to visit. But what to do about Mum? She lied to me about him. For all these years she let me think he had passed away, when he has been alive all the time!'

~

When we got up from the breakfast table half an hour later, much had been discussed but not a lot resolved. Most of it, for the moment, couldn't be. Diva was soon on her way to Treasure Trees Apothecary in Chisipite, and Tinashe to the shed. I went out to the veranda with the dogs, my laptop, and a fresh mug of coffee. The morning was warm, the sky dazzling blue, and Aunt Carrie's garden was brilliant with impatiens blossoms. In the distance, Ruwa Rock loomed cleansed and propitious in its setting of succulent euphorbias.

Focused on my computer screen, it wasn't until I heard Thor's tail thumping heavily on the floor that I looked up to see Bodhi strolling casually along the veranda. Moments later, Yogi Tarchin appeared in the garden. I took off my glasses and pushed the screen away. About to stand, he motioned me to stay where I was. As he approached, it was clear from his expression that he'd come to deliver a message.

'You need to rest, Rob,' he told me. 'Have a few

nights' proper sleep. I have made arrangements.'

It was an instruction, not a suggestion. My first thoughts went to Kadiki, and how she'd feel. Was I being presumptuous to think that she couldn't live contentedly with the support of others in her *nzou* family?

Next I wondered about Kay, a three-hour drive away in Nyanga.

'I could visit my godmother?' I suggested.

'You are here to connect with your family and,' he brought a hand to his heart, 'your true purpose.'

Turning, he crossed the lawn back into the bush. Glancing over the veranda, Bodhi was nowhere to be seen.

Chapter Seven

THE DRIVE TO NYANGA gave me time to think, to reflect on the decision I had to make. One so consequential that part of me was incredulous I was even considering it. But with the driver's window rolled down, the dogs in the back with a head at each window eagerly taking in the landscape flying past, in another way nothing felt more natural than being here now. Nor more warmly anticipatory than visiting Kay at her home in the highlands.

I called my godmother soon after Rinpoche's instruction. She was delighted by the prospect of a visit. When I told her I had to plan for the dogs, she suggested that I bring them too. Her faithful golden retriever, Cara, had died two years earlier, and as Kay was eighty-one years old, she didn't think it wise to take on another dog. A brief interlude with Thor and Tiki would be a pleasure, she said.

I tried not to mull over Kadiki. I was her primary carer, but even in the short time she'd been with us I knew it was a relationship that went way deeper. I was unable to describe it, having never felt like this about another living being. But it would be an absence of only three nights. I knew that Mr Nzou, Ezekiel, Lakshmi, and Rinpoche would take excellent care of her while Kay and I explored old haunts.

The rains that afternoon mostly took the form of two heavy downpours. The first, just after we started, came before we'd even reached Marondera, and the second as we drove through Headlands about half an hour later. But from the time we turned left at Rusape and began driving through more undulating landscapes, the sky began to clear.

~

There were few scenes lovelier than these. Sweeping curves in the road led us past towering granite castles, majestic in their green-season mantles. Msasa-clad vistas, rising as far as the eye could see, taking us ever-eastwards towards the distant blue mountains. It was the first time I'd made this journey in nearly forty years and the feeling was both dazzling and deeply nostalgic.

I had last made this trip with Dad and sister Kate just before leaving the country. Mum had stayed at home overseeing the packing. Dad, I calculated, would have been around the same age that I was now. He would have known that this was the last time he'd be travelling to Nyanga to visit his friend. I could only try to imagine how he must have felt.

The word that kept coming to mind as I drove through those changing landscapes was kumusha. Home. How much I truly remembered from earlier times, or merely believed that I remembered, was hard to tell. In the end, I supposed, all that mattered was that the feeling was undeniable. In Dad's case, I knew that he had left at least part of his heart in Africa. Even years later, settled into life in Scotland, he'd harboured the deepest longing for these sacred vistas.

Over the years I'd met plenty of expats in Britain

just like Dad. Whether they defined themselves as Rhodies or Zimbos, and no matter the colour of their skin, they never got over leaving. There had been civil war in this country during the 1970s, and after it ended, most of the country's white population migrated to South Africa, Britain, or Australia. The country's European population that peaked around 300,000 in the mid-1970s had reduced by ninety percent within thirty years.

This white diaspora was as nothing compared to the black one to come. After economic collapse in the early years of the century, most Zimbabweans found it impossible to get a job. Five million of them, a third of the population, followed in their white compatriots' footsteps, with precisely the same motivation that had impelled whites to escape post-war Britain: to earn money. To support their families. To risk the many evident threats of an alien land because they'd lost hope in a future at home. So many now live in London that it is jokingly called "Harare North". But how they all yearn for the warm, beating heart of the Motherland!

Kay lived at the closest part of Nyanga, in Juliasdale. I had put her address into a map app, but as we drew closer, I found that I didn't need it. Even though it was forty years since I was last here, the memory of the turn-off from the main road was etched in my mind. And the instructions she'd given me over the phone were easy to follow once I was on the dirt track. For moments, the car was engulfed in clouds of *guti*, misty showers common in the mountains, and visibility was poor. Thor and Tiki were intrigued by the novelty of the fine, vapoury gusts, shoving their faces even further outside than usual.

Sun broke through the clouds at just the right moment. As I remembered, Kay's surname 'Hartman' was neatly painted, dark blue on a white background, on a round ploughshare at the roadside. As I turned into the short driveway, I found her cottage wreathed in rainbows.

It was a modest bungalow, a single rectangular strip with living areas at one end and bedrooms at the other. I recalled a paved veranda stretching the full distance on the far side, lending the house its only extravagance — the view of a spectacular valley with a river running through it and, in the distance, soaring mountains.

I stopped the engine and let the dogs out. They yapped excitedly, dashing into lush green undergrowth. Alerted by their barking, Kay emerged from the open front door. To me, she had always seemed the same: tall and slender with curly hair, now tending more towards pearly than flaxen. That radiant, fey intelligence to her blue eyes. She'd been a great beauty and in her younger days had travelled the world modelling for a cosmetics company. But along with her assured poise there was always something indefinably different about her, an inner energy that made her sparkle.

We hugged for a long while, before I collected a few things from the car and she showed me to the guest bedroom. I had last seen her just under a year ago when she passed through London. She had spent about a week with me as had become her habit. And we spoke at least once a month on the phone.

Whenever we met it was the same, as if we had just stepped away from one another for a few minutes, rather than months. And although it was so very long since I'd been to her home here in Nyanga, everything felt very natural, easy. There was a constancy yet a lightness as I glanced about, taking in things about the place that I had forgotten. She watched me with a bright-eyed gentleness.

'Just as I remembered,' I told her.

Her sitting room was filled with shelves and shelves

of books on three walls, and in the fourth wall were French doors leading onto the veranda. As we passed through, I noticed, in one of the gaps between books, a gleaming white shell the size of a large bread roll, one end forming a spiral that circled to the right. I paused to trace it with my fingertip. 'Is this ...?'

'A conch,' she said. She gestured to a framed picture on the wall nearby. 'One of the eight auspicious symbols.'

I looked from the shell to its representation.

'You find them on temple doors throughout the Himalayas,' she explained.

'Auspicious symbols,' I mused. 'What does the conch represent?'

'The sound of Dharma. Buddha's teachings. The highest, purest sound,' she held my gaze. 'But all eight symbols as a collection go back long before the time of Buddha.'

I raised my eyebrows.

Kay had spent her lifetime meditating and studying spiritual wisdom. She would come out with intriguing revelations in the most matter-of-fact way.

'They're called the Ashtamangala, collectively,' she told me. 'The special attributes of enlightened beings. In Hinduism, Lord Vishnu is often shown holding a conch. When deities hold things, it means that they possess that particular quality. In Vishnu's case, divine sound — the power of creation.'

What she said resonated with school chapel. '"In the beginning was the Word",' I quoted.

'That's a version of it,' she nodded. 'The same idea percolates through the great spiritual traditions. Vibration as the most subtle manifestation in the physical realm. The thought becoming the word. The word becoming the deed.'

'Om?' I asked.

'*Aum*.' She repeated the three syllables, elongating them: A – U – M. 'Buddha, Dharma, Sangha. Father, Son, and Holy Spirit. Whichever trinity represents your idea of totality. Aum is the primordial sound from which all else flows.'

I paused, staring at the spiral shell. 'I recently met a Shona guy, Tinashe, who showed me this ndoro he'd been given by his late grandfather. Hundreds of years old, he said. Made in India.'

'Rare, I'd imagine,' Kay's eyes shone.

I nodded. 'Back in the day, apparently ndoro represented real wealth here. And some kind of spiritual power.'

'Connection to the ancestors,' confirmed Kay.

'They look like they have the same spiral as conch shells?'

'They do,' she agreed. 'To begin with, ndoros were made from sea snails, *Conus Turbo*, treasured because of their rarity in the interior. Arab and Portuguese traders found that they could get a lot of gold for them. There was so much demand that they started having ceramic versions manufactured in Goa and even Holland.'

The idea of international trade in medieval times still felt somehow astonishing.

'Symbolically,' said Kay, 'the conch and the ndoro have parallel meanings, interpreted according to local cultures. The ndoro represents contact with the divine realm of the ancestors.' She met my look of surprise with a twinkle. 'The conch and the ndoro both signify sacred sound and spiritual insight.'

'Sound making manifest the divine in the material world?' I confirmed.

'The material, outside world,' Kay nodded, eyes gleaming. 'The inner world too. This spiral shape,' she reached out, tracing the shell with her own fingertip, 'it is a shape traditionally used to gather and intensify *prana* in Eastern visualisations. Think propellers. Turbines. Vortices. How do we draw divine energy within? Through this. N'angas,' she referred to traditional healers, 'who know the old ways use the same process to manifest the divine in themselves, usually in the form of ancestral spirits. They become oracles.'

I contemplated this for a moment. 'There are oracles in Buddhism also, aren't there?'

'Some very famous ones.' Her eyes narrowed as she followed my thinking. 'The Nechung Oracle, consulted by the Dalai Lama even in recent times. The Karmapa's Oracle. And of course, others with *siddhi* powers.'

We walked onto the veranda, the view stilling conversation. This was a different Africa from the veldt around Ruwa. Higher and more temperate, the landscape had a softness fed by lakes and mountain streams. Ferns, proteas, and native orchids thrived in the milder temperatures. Rhododendrons, roses, and camellias, incomers from the Northern hemisphere, had taken this craggy terrain to heart. Conifers clad distant valleys as far as the eye could see, and from these rolling green oceans came the bracing scent of pine. We gazed to where the mountains were indigo thumbprints on the horizon, including the highest and most fabled peak in the country, Mount Nyangani. From where we stood, there was no sign of human habitation to be seen.

The air itself seemed somehow brighter up here. Like champagne, people said. Early visitors had instantly found in this place a resonance of the old country, particularly the Highlands and Islands of Britain. Settlers' place names still evoked the Celtic spirit: Troutbeck Hotel after the village in Cumbria, and many a Scottish lodge. Melsetter from the distant Orkneys. The Connemara lakes named for the rugged vistas and rolling hills of Ireland.

'I'd forgotten how beautiful it is,' I murmured.

Kay looked over at my expression of wonderment. 'Never forget where the beauty is really coming from, young man,' she said.

In an instant I was recollecting Rinpoche as we sat on the veranda drinking coffee. 'This,' he had gestured to his mug, 'is merely a contributing factor. The main cause is the mind itself. The way it exists for each one of us, *how* it exists, this depends on our minds.'

'Mind itself?' I confirmed.

She nodded. 'Not everyone loves Nyanga.'

'But you and I have the karma to.'

'We do,' she nodded.

'Rinpoche says that if we're able to remember at peak moments — when we're revelling in the beauty of anything — if we can recollect that the true source of happiness is our mind, not the thing outside us, then we amplify our joy. We are even more appreciative.'

It was true! I could feel the upwelling right now — the intensity of the moment being heightened, the sublime panorama before us charged with a vibrancy that elevated my mood almost to a state of rapture.

~

Afternoon slid effortlessly into evening as we sat gazing over Caledonian Africa. We'd had a few long conversations since I'd come back, and she knew all about Rinpoche and the Ruwa Buddhist Society, but not Kadiki. I told her what had happened, and the intense time it had been since the calf's arrival. How Yogi Tarchin had prescribed a few days' rest. My conversation with Nick Berkeley. The life choice I faced.

Kay didn't voice an opinion. Her usual method was to open up pathways of conversation that might help me find my own answer. That afternoon, however, we didn't venture far. I think she realised how much the accumulation of sleeplessness over the past week affected me. Instead, I fetched Dad's sketchbook that I'd wanted to show her as soon as I'd discovered it. I told her about finding it in the old map cabinet of Uncle Adrian's shed. And I watched as she leafed through the pages until reaching the sketch of the woman, that image of sultry allure and deep longing, with the miniature Zodiac bowl in her hand. Drawn back through the decades, she paused.

Kay and her husband Roger had known my parents when we all lived in Marondera. Roger had died not long after our family left for Scotland, which was when Kay had begun her migratory lifestyle, following the sun to Italy each year. During her transits through London, there wasn't anything about our families we hadn't discussed, including Dad's female friends, of whom he'd had many. There were those who found refreshing the company of a man who had that gift of only the most exceptional teachers, the ability to enthral you with his subject. Those who, like Kay, found in him a kindred spirit, someone as willing to spend the morning throwing pottery as exploring tai chi.

And there had been a few with whom he'd become more intimate: he'd confessed as much on that final visit to Nyanga. Alcohol-fuelled encounters that should never have happened. A couple of short-lived affairs. He'd tried shielding Mum, he told Kay. He didn't think she'd found out about them. Until the last one.

Kay looked up from the sketch book.

'This was the one, I think, who troubled your mother.'

'You mean, who forced the family move?'

Kay nodded. 'Euan said she was the most fascinating woman he'd ever met. He had this impetuous urge to know her.'

I held her gaze.

'He told me once how he'd asked her to sit for a portrait.'

'Looks like a working sketch,' I nodded towards the pad.

'Definitely.'

'How can you be so sure?'

'Because of this.' She pointed to what was in the woman's hand.

'The Zodiac bowl?'

It was a shallow roundel featuring a wisdom crocodile. Around its rim were the arcane symbols of what seemed like a forgotten astrology.

'It wasn't just in the drawing.' Glancing up, she met my eyes. 'He made it as a gift for her. It was a pendant.'

'An actual ...?' I placed my fingers to my chest.

'Yes. The most remarkable piece of craftsmanship,' she nodded.

'You saw it?'

'He showed it to me once when I was coming through Marondera. He didn't tell me about the intended recipient, of course. I didn't know about her then. But afterwards,' she drew back from the sketch, 'the piece of the jigsaw was pressed into place.'

'The signs around the rim of the bowl are of the heavens, right?'

'Just not our Western symbols,' she agreed.

'So, symbolically?' I was remembering Lord Vishnu holding the conch, the symbol of divine creation. As my father was an artist, his inclusion of the pendant would have been deliberate.

'The zodiac in one's hand?' Kay held my eyes. 'It represents entirety.'

'He gave her the world?'

'The universe.' She handed me the sketchbook to look again for myself. 'When he showed me the miniature he made, he explained it to me as "Aum made visible".'

The turn of phrase sounded exactly like Dad in full, extravagant flow.

'I didn't know he was so interested in esoteric subjects,' I observed.

Kay's eyes narrowed. 'Perhaps his friend was.'

I thought back to a time that seemed both long distant yet, in this moment, vitally present. 'I just hope Mum wasn't crushed.'

'Your dear mamma was very accepting,' said Kay. 'She knew your father better than anyone. Him and his ... his free spirit.'

'D'you think?' I met her eyes. We'd never spoken about this directly.

'"Least said, soonest mended",' she replied. 'Wasn't that what your mum believed?'

I nodded. Neat, petite Mum who devoted so much effort trying to tame the wilderness, or at least to creating her own family island in it. Who struggled so hard to recreate her Scottish properness in a land that defied order. What didn't conform was overlooked, minimised, never mentioned. Instead, she took refuge in the company of her compatriots. She would insist we join her at Highlands Presbyterian Church where

Padre and Jean Nesbit provided an encouraging link to the old country. She would find solace in thriving, Scottish-run concerns like Sanders department store, or Meikle's hotel, or Chisipite's Howff restaurant. An 'island hopper' before the term had been invented, she'd discovered that there was only so much hopping you could do before facing the irrefutable truth that most of the time you were at sea.

'I expect she was worried Euan was falling for this one.' Kay pointed to the sketch. 'That's why she was determined to go.'

'I think he already had fallen for her,' I nodded, remembering the strip of light under the closed studio door that night I'd gone to speak with him. His muted sobbing coming from within. It turned out that he was facing the same wrench, the same heartache I was in having to leave my first love, Mandy. Only his was a forbidden passion, a betrayal he must hide.

How extraordinary to be making such a discovery about Dad, years following his death. Absorbing Kay's revelations after all this time. When we'd last sat on this same veranda, it had been the three of us together at the end of an era. one about which I had known so much less than I had realised at the time.

~

In the gloaming, Kay and I ate eggplant parmigiana and sipped Kumusha Pinotage. Ahead of us, the mountains drew their gauzy bedsheets from the valleys below, and the stars paradoxically felt more distant and muted from this high vantage. Thor and Tiki, well fed and exhausted after their mountain scrambles, lay relaxed at our feet.

As we ate, I told Kay about the last thing Rinpoche had said. How I was here to connect with my family and my true purpose.

'Perhaps he wasn't being literal about "family",' I said.

'You've been visiting Kate?' queried Kay.

'Lunch every few weeks.' After a pause I shrugged my shoulders. 'Just like it's always been.'

Kay well knew how my sister and I lived in different realities. That we saw the world through different lenses.

'I would love to have that feeling of family, that connection other people have.'

'Uncle Fraser?' prompted Kay.

I chuckled. Mum's much younger brother, Fraser, had migrated from Scotland to Zimbabwe the very same month that our family had moved the other way. His choice of destination was in no way connected with us and he was such a terrible communicator that over the years we had inevitably lost touch with him. We weren't even sure he was still alive.

~

Two glasses of wine, the mountain air, and Kay's nourishing food had me feeling drowsy. I struggled to stifle my yawns. Knowing that I was already sleep deprived, Kay insisted I go to bed.

'Wake as late as you like,' she told me, waving me down the short corridor. 'I'll see you whenever you surface.'

~

It was the strangest sensation closing Kay's guest bedroom door. The last time I had been here, my whole adult life still lay ahead of me. Now, in Nick Berkeley's words, I was in the last quarter of the game. During the intervening forty years, Kay's cottage had assumed a place in my mind that was almost mythical. Whether because of its extraordinary setting in the misty orchid-strewn wilderness of the African highlands, or the refuge it had once offered from tortured emotions, or the soothing benevolence of my godmother herself, her home had always seemed like a haven. One I would return to in my mind, especially in times of calamity. A state, as much as a place, where I found refuge, sensing a compassion as constant as the rainbows that shrouded the cottage in spectral light.

I knew this place by heart, and the physical reality had turned out to be much as I remembered, only smaller and more achingly vulnerable, as places from the distant long ago often turn out to be. But there were things I had forgotten. As I reached out to the bedside lamp, I noticed a copper plaque on the wall, the kind that had been so popular in the 1970s. I knew it had occupied the same space for the past forty years because the moment I saw the words printed on it, I remembered them. The aphorism attributed to Franz Kafka had seemed mysterious when I'd first encountered it. Closing my eyes, it felt more powerfully resonant now:

'From a certain point onwards, there is no longer any turning back,' it read. *'That is the point that must be reached.'*

What was that certain point, I wondered? And how would you know when you had reached it? Though, as I sank through the gathering *guti* of sleep in that mountain darkness, I had the sense that I was drifting ever closer towards that nameless and pivotal landmark.

Chapter Eight

I WOKE, as usual, around six o'clock, and my first thoughts were of Kadiki. How was she doing in the stable? I figured that Rinpoche would be handing over to Mr Nzou or Ezekiel about now. I slipped into tracksuit pants and a sweatshirt, emerging from my room to find Kay up and dressed, playing with the dogs.

'We've already been for a walk,' she told me as Thor and Tiki bounded over in high spirits.

I took in their tail-wagging as I bent to pat them.

'Coffee?'

'I'd love some.'

There was a freshness to the morning as the sun rose over the mountains. The vast sweep of sky from horizon to horizon was a clear, ethereal blue. The fragrance of honeysuckle was sweet in the morning coolness. Bees hovered about the fresh pink petals of a hibiscus bush. As Kay brought out not only coffee but also a plate of rusks, I was reminded of Diva Derembwe treating me to her breakfast. I told Kay about the conversation we'd had around the kitchen table on the subject of taking refuge — the recognised term for formally becoming a Buddhist. She listened keenly.

155

'If Yogi Tarchin does offer refuge — or clear direction, as I like to think of it,' she said, blue eyes shining, 'I would love to come.'

'I thought you took refuge decades ago?'

'From the marvellous Lama Yeshe,' she nodded. 'And from other lamas since. But taking refuge is like receiving initiations. It's good to refresh them. Refuge is one of the most powerful forms of purification.'

'Really?'

'There's a quote,' she continued, 'from the *Perfection of Wisdom Sutra*. It says:

"If the merit from taking refuge had form, the three realms would be too small to accommodate it. The great ocean, the source of all water, cannot be measured with a cup".'

'Wow!' I was astonished. 'Why so enormous?'

'Because when we take refuge, we are making a commitment to our future selves to strike out in a new direction. We're saying: "I've had enough of the ups and downs of life. Instead, I'm going to use *dukkha*, dissatisfaction, to motivate my journey to transcendence — just like the lotus uses the mud of the swamps to rise to the surface".'

'Which is why the lotus is big in Buddhism?' I prompted.

'Most images of Buddhas show them on lotus seats,' she confirmed. 'Because it's the symbol of renunciation or turning away from the causes of suffering. When we take refuge, that's what we're doing.' She held my gaze with a clarity of intent.

I recalled my times with Yogi Tarchin, and my developing awareness that although we might be sharing the same physical space, we occupied entirely different realities. Sitting on a different veranda with

Kay made me understand what all the years of study and meditation in peaceful seclusion had done for her too. The lightness I sensed in her presence, the feeling of warm acceptance that illuminated her whole being — none of this was without cause.

'What people take refuge in,' I wanted to be clear, 'is the historical Buddha and his teachings, right?'

'That's the traditional way they talk about it.'

It was typical of Kay to leave conversational breadcrumbs. 'There's another way?'

'You've described *cause* refuge, when we place our confidence in the Dharma as the cause for our own future enlightenment. But there is also *result* refuge, where we take refuge in the fact that we already have Buddha nature. We don't need to manufacture something or go in search of it or pay someone else to help us find it. The true nature of your mind,' her eyes held mine, 'and my own mind's true nature is boundless. Radiant. Pristine. When we take refuge, we're also reminding ourselves that even though we are currently human beings, our true nature is very different. As different as a vast oak tree is from the single acorn from which it grew.'

For a while we sat in silence, sipping our coffee, as I absorbed what she'd said. Eventually I told her, 'I really do hope you have a chance to meet Rinpoche. He's an extraordinary person.' Recalling a conversation we'd had years before, when she'd told me how Buddhists trained to think of their teachers, I said, 'A real-life Buddha!'

She smiled in recognition. 'If you think of your teacher as an ordinary person, you receive the blessings of an ordinary person. If you think of your teacher as a Buddha,' she nodded, 'you receive the blessings of a Buddha.'

'I think you'd like all of them down at the Ruwa Buddhist Society,' I said. 'Tinashe — there's something unusually tuned-in about him. Diva is a force of nature, passionate about trees! Harris Gould is a source of the most remarkable esoteric knowledge. And, of course, Kadiki and the Nzous.'

Kay nodded slowly. 'Your metaphorical family?' she reminded me of our conversation the previous day.

I smiled.

~

We hadn't discussed our plans for the day. I imagined we'd drive through the mountains and visit somewhere I could treat Kay to lunch. The sacred Nyanga mountains were a place of unique enchantment. Occupied since antiquity, their ancient history, along with their extraordinary beauty, made them redolent of a promised land — one yearning for rediscovery.

But after coffee when I went inside, I found a text message from Mr Nzou. 'Kadiki not eating. Very sorry. Will keep you informed.'

I phoned him immediately. It turned out that Kadiki had stopped accepting milk late in the afternoon the previous day. She hadn't eaten anything in the evening or overnight. Usually she left the stable at sunrise, but today she was lying unmoving in the straw. Mr Nzou wasn't asking me to return, but he was clearly anxious.

I said I would head back right away.

~

Kay understood, as I knew she would. This was an emergency. I couldn't do anything for Kadiki from here. As much as I wanted to roam the mountains with her, and reconnect to their intriguing energy, I was needed in Ruwa. For her part, Kay needed to stay in Nyanga to support a convalescing friend in the coming days.

I packed quickly. Kay and I talked about a rescheduled visit. Calling the dogs, I returned to the vehicle, and we were soon reversing out the short driveway to the track beyond. Turning, we headed towards the main road.

~

I needed to stop for fuel at Juliasdale service station, where I was so absorbed in my thoughts that I didn't even notice the man standing in the forecourt, much less recognise him, until he gestured to me.

'Roberto, yes?' he approached.

I knew that rugged face. I was trying to place him.

'Bruno. From the Buddhist Society.' Of course! The organic tea farmer from Nyanga! I glanced at his truck, which had a Bobcat machine loaded on the back.

'I've been grading the temple site.'

I nodded. Diva had mentioned it.

'I hear you have an elephant?'

Part of me was startled to be thought of in this way. Was it even possible to 'have' an elephant?

'You'll be staying in Zim?'

'For a while.'

'You don't want to go back there,' he jabbed his thumb in a northerly direction.

Bruno's family owned a *fortezza* in Tuscany and he was wealthy enough to live anywhere in the world that he pleased. Or so I had been told. His forceful rebuff of Europe made me curious.

'Why don't I want to go back?' I asked.

He threw his arms open. 'In Africa there is space for everybody. You can breathe!' He demonstrated, taking a deep inhalation, before exhaling with a contented expression. 'You are free.'

I smiled at his enthusiasm, at the same time

remembering the expressions of some of my sceptical friends. 'Not everyone back home would agree,' I countered.

Bruno's forehead creased. 'Europeans used to call this place "the Dark Continent",' he said. 'Some still do. Like the first explorers, they think Africa is backward. Barbaric. But what kind of men, finding people ignorant of worldly ways, try only to exploit or enslave them? And when they see amazing animals, want only to kill them to mount their heads on the wall? Is this not the definition of darkness?'

I raised my eyebrows.

'Many who came here, and who still come, *they* are the ones with hearts of darkness. *This*,' he was emphatic, 'is a continent of light!'

Once again he spread his arms, relishing the brilliant clarity of the morning. 'I'm telling you, Roberto,' he said after a moment. 'Think carefully: do you want to be a battery cage hen?' He thrust his jaw out defiantly. 'Or live free range?'

~

His incisive summary preoccupied me as I drove back to Ruwa. As did my concern for Kadiki. Several times I tried calling Tessa Brenthurst, the elephant expert, but her phone was out of range. I had more success getting hold of Luke, currently with guests in Gonarezhou, who gave me the details of a vet in Harare with elephant experience. Luke recommended I spend some time with Kadiki before getting vets involved in case she was simply pining, a possibility I had considered but didn't want to contemplate too much.

It being a Sunday morning, there wasn't much traffic and I made quick progress. Turning off the main road, I drove directly to Ruwa Buddhist Society and took the dirt track towards the stables. As soon as I parked the car and opened the doors for them, the dogs followed on my heels. Reaching the stable, I could see Rinpoche, Mr Nzou, and Ezekiel sitting in a semi-circle around the elephant calf, a sombre quietness about the place. As I undid the latch, they looked up. As did Kadiki.

Suddenly, she was barrelling towards me. I got onto my knees, reaching out. She hit my chest so hard that I fell backwards. I hugged her to me, reassuring her that everything was okay. Reaching around my neck, she pulled at me desperately. As she held me in her tight trunk grasp for the longest time, I felt the urgent beat of her elephant heart gradually slowing after a while. I breathed in that rich, loamy, elephant aroma and felt her breathing beginning to slow. I remembered the golden lotus visualisation, imagining love and bliss reaching from my heart to hers.

When I offered her a bottle, she accepted it immediately, draining it in record time. I gave her another. Wordlessly, Rinpoche nodded, squeezing my shoulder as he left the stable. I told Mr Nzou and Ezekiel that I would take over.

When she'd had her fill of milk, I led her from the stable, Thor and Tiki accompanying us. The garden was lush and burgeoning in the warm morning. Under the marula tree, the rains had brought forth all manner of weeds and shrubs among the ferns. Behind them, a row of canna lilies, previously so desiccated I hadn't noticed them, were now resplendent in rubbery, carmine foliage, pluming with succulent orange buds.

It wasn't long before Mbudzi found us. Trotting over, beard twitching and a mischievous glint in those strange, rectangular pupils, he urged Kadiki to play, prancing and bleating and horn-butting her flanks. Kadiki had her trunk around my right leg and wasn't letting go. She kept looking up at me with her great brown bushy-lashed eyes. It was only when we had gone all the way round to the front of the homestead and I sank to the lawn that she allowed herself to be distracted. Even then, she kept close watch on me.

Sometime later Mr Nzou appeared from around the side of the house, his shrunken figure and grizzled features belied by a surprisingly youthful stride.

'Tonight, I can look after this one,' he gestured towards Kadiki as he approached.

'I'm worried about leaving her again.'

He shook his head fiercely.

'You don't think it will be a problem?'

'She knows you are close,' he gestured, motioning the direction of Aunt Carrie's place with his arm.

'Really?' I was interested. 'How?'

He held up his palm towards me, representing the bottom of her foot. 'Here,' he said, pointing towards it. 'And here,' he touched his heart.

I looked at Kadiki tugging at a stalk of agapanthus. I knew that elephants communicated via seismic vibrations below the threshold of human hearing. The thick pads of their feet, those same pads that enabled a whole herd to walk by in near silence, were filled with sensitive nerve endings enabling them to exchange messages with their own kind even miles away. The arrival of new elephants to an area. The presence of predators. Signals of a river in flood or other natural disaster. They sensed all this through their feet.

What I hadn't considered was that Kadiki was using her feet to track me. That she knew the difference between my walking to Aunt Carrie's and getting in a car and driving out of range. That she knew, without having to be told, when I was lying asleep next door or in the mountains.

And then there was the heart. Mr Nzou probably didn't have the words in English, and I certainly lacked the Shona vocabulary to discuss intuition. Perhaps no discussion was needed. The knowingness he indicated went beyond words. It was even more subtle than infrasound. Kadiki *knew*, was all that mattered. So long as I didn't go far, he was saying, she would be okay.

'You are the mother of Kadiki,' he confirmed, sitting on the grass nearby. We both watched her pulling and pulling before eventually plucking out the entire agapanthus stalk, complete with teal flower. She turned, bringing the flower to me, then flicking it away whimsically. And then, with familiar intimacy, turning my right leg to inspect the mole just under my knee with the tip of her trunk. If I hadn't known it before this morning, I understood it now. And of all the job titles I'd had in my life, it was the most daunting.

~

That afternoon, I sought out Rinpoche. There was no sign of Bodhi at his cottage or at the front of the house. Hearing an unfamiliar engine cranking up, I looked down the garden. The site of the new temple was abuzz with activity. A concrete mixer, the source of the new sound, was churning, and around it a dozen workmen wielded shovels. As I walked down the lawn I could see where Bruno had graded out a path from the parking area up to the temple. The temple area itself was also meticulously levelled, deep trenches dug in places around the perimeter, metal caging inserted in them.

Evidently, I was arriving at a moment of significance. On the far side of the site the builder spoke loudly over the engine to Diva and Harris, gesturing as he did. Gogo Margaret and Ezekiel watched on from the sidelines. And Yogi Tarchin was there. Standing alone, some distance from the commotion with his back to me. As I got closer, he sensed my approach and turned.

His eyes met mine — and in that instant I understood that he already knew what I had come to tell him. Standing on the lawn not far from a noisy concrete mixer hardly seemed like the ideal place to be doing this. But as I was here now, I wanted to tell him — and to make my request.

'Rinpoche, I've decided to stay. In Zimbabwe.'

He nodded, matter-of-factly. Not exactly the response I had expected. A momentous decision for me seemed almost like one that he had assumed. In an instant he punctured the psychodrama playing out in my mind. The analysis, hypothesising, and heart versus head. All the on-the-one-hands versus on-the-others. They all went pop ... and it was just Rinpoche and me standing together.

After a pause I continued, 'I'd also like to take refuge with you.'

'Good, good,' he said, reaching to take my arm in one hand, while gesturing with the other to where workmen tipped out a barrowful of concrete, spreading it along the trenches.

'Like this,' he said.

Not for the first time with Rinpoche, I realised that I was exactly where I was supposed to be. What more appropriate metaphor could there be, how more memorably emblematic to be asking for refuge, than when the foundations of a new temple were being poured? He glanced over with a hint of mischief. Get out of your head, he seemed to say, and into the moment.

Only when you do can you fully appreciate what's really happening!

We watched the pouring continue. Barrow after barrow loaded and wheeled and tipped into the deepest holes in the trenches where the temple posts were to be set. There wasn't anything inherently mesmerising about the process, so much as understanding what was happening in its most sublime form. The foundations of a Buddhist temple at 31 degrees East were being set in place before our eyes. That, in itself, was a marvel. The creation of a unique symbol of virtue, a spiritual powerhouse to complement the most spectacular natural stupa in the district towering behind it.

And on a different level, as Rinpoche had noted, holding my arm to make quite sure I didn't miss the meaning, by taking refuge we would be entrenching the foundations, creating the bedrock of a new way of being.

'"If the merit from taking refuge had form",' Kay had quoted the Buddha, '"The three realms would be too small to accommodate it. The great ocean, the source of all water, cannot be measured with a cup".'

~

Something shifted and I knew it was time to make my particular request.

'Rinpoche, please will you be my guru?'

'Really?' he turned, his eyes alighting on mine with that fine clarity.

'Of course.'

'You are sure that you want me to be a mirror?'

I nodded.

'We can't become masters on our own,' he told me, a forcefulness in his eyes, 'because our minds are not visible to us. We need someone who can show us.

Including correcting faults that perhaps we can't see ourselves.'

'I know.'

'If I am a teacher, I may reflect things my students don't want to see when I show them.'

I swallowed.

'For that we must be humble,' he was regarding me closely. I knew he wanted to make sure I was making my request only after due consideration. 'It may be painful.'

'Yes.'

For a while he looked towards Ruwa Rock before saying, 'Are you sure you want to learn what I teach?'

I knew this was a test. That he wanted to check what I had already absorbed. I could give him a conventional answer about respecting his wisdom, but as he asked the question, I remembered the message he'd delivered with such vigour that very first day. Drinking instant coffee that morning when I'd asked him to explain it further.

'I want to learn how best to serve others,' I said.

'Why?' he probed with a severe expression.

'Because it is the only path to happiness.'

'Why is that?' he persisted.

'Because the reality we experience, moment by moment, comes from the karma we create. Only if we give happiness can we experience it.'

'Very good,' he delivered a gleeful smile. 'Then I accept. You are opening the door to new possibilities, Robbie.'

~

My encounter with Lakshmi that evening was brief. Preparing Kadiki's special milk in the kitchen, I was about to pick up pails of stacked bottles in each hand when there came the sound of footsteps approaching swiftly down the corridor. We greeted each other simultaneously. Resplendent in traditional dress, with kohl eyes and gleaming gold jewellery, Lakshmi was carrying a wicker basket.

'Haven't seen you in a sari before,' I smiled. 'Magnificent!'

'Oh, thanks! I'm off to the Indian Ladies' Club dinner with Mum.' Placing the basket on the benchtop and opening the fridge door, she quickly stacked meal boxes on a shelf. She and her mother had continued to ensure that Rinpoche had a steady supply of homemade food even if, like tonight, it meant the inconvenience of a detour.

Closing the fridge door, she grabbed the basket and turned to leave. As she did, I had to stop her. Something caught my attention.

'Your pendant!' It was a perfect miniature of the Zodiac bowl.

She leaned over briefly, holding it up for me to study more closely.

'Exquisite!'

'Twenty-first birthday present.'

'I've never seen one like it.'

'Given to Mum by an old friend.' She strode to the door. 'Always been my favourite.'

Chapter Nine

FOR THE REST of that night, while Kadiki, the dogs, and Mbudzi snored contentedly on the straw, I sat propped against the stable wall, soaking in the reality of my decision to stay, imagining how people back in London were going to react. And threaded through all the musings, remembering my encounter with Lakshmi.

Her Zodiac bowl pendant looked just like Dad's — but that didn't make it the very same one. Just as Zimbabwe's master sculptor Patrick Mavros created gleaming silver jewellery in homage to other national icons like the ndoro, perhaps another local craftsman manufactured Zodiac bowl pendants?

When I saw Lakshmi again, I'd be sure to ask her about the 'old friend' of her mother's. But it did seem an extraordinary coincidence, one reaching directly to the chapter of my family's past that I knew least about.

~

Tessa Brenthurst came to visit. I had been asking her to come since Kadiki's arrival. Zimbabwe's leading elephant expert, who successfully rewilded herds of once-orphaned elephants, she had been a constant source of advice and reassurance on the phone. Now, suddenly she was here, climbing out of a Land Rover and striding across the lawn to where Luke and I were discussing the location of a new elephant shed. Although we had never met, I felt as if I already knew her. She was tall and slender, wearing chinos and an olive-green blouse, and there was an openness about her face and almond-shaped brown eyes. A sense of vital presence, and at the same time, a capacity to perceive more than was immediately evident.

Some distance before reaching Luke and me she paused, watching Kadiki chasing Thor across the lawn and into the flower bed.

'Good to see!' she chuckled, as Kadiki paused for just a moment to take her in, before throwing her head to one side and continuing her pursuit.

'Thanks for coming.' I approached her, introducing her to Luke, who was climbing through a board fence to survey the bush beyond the garden. At the bottom of the lawn, a group of workers were gathering to inspect the concrete slab on the site of the new temple. Skellum, the three-limbed vervet monkey, was sitting on a fence post, stretching his legs in the sun.

'They need lots of play.' Tessa watched Kadiki and her friends.

'I worry that she'll lose her 'elephant-ness' if she spends too much time with these ones.'

Tessa shook her head. 'It will make her more tolerant of other species.'

Kadiki returned, bumping her forehead into me before lifting her trunk curiously to inhale Tessa.

Tessa leaned in, caressing the calf's neck. Kadiki scrutinised her with her huge elephant eyes, the two of them connecting with a wordless understanding. 'Nice chubby cheeks,' she murmured, touching them.

Then responding to my blank expression, 'The best way to check on a calf's condition.'

'Is it?'

'Most reliable indicator,' she said. 'How much milk is she drinking? About twenty litres a day?'

'Exactly.'

'D'you know how much weight she's put on since she arrived?'

I shook my head.

'Is she gnawing a lot?'

'Funny you ask. She was chewing sticks before going to sleep last night. And this morning again.'

'Diarrhoea?'

'It was quite runny yesterday.'

'Teething,' confirmed Tessa.

'So young?' I was startled.

'D'you know if any teeth have erupted yet? You have to put your hand in her mouth, right at the back.'

'Can't say I've tried.'

'Be careful. If she nips by mistake, the bruising lasts for weeks. But teething can be a dangerous time for little ones. Life-threatening, even. You need to keep an eye on their temperature. Watch for signs of pain, like irritability. Get some baby paracetamol. If she needs it, give her the amount for a six-year-old child, not an elephant-weight dose.'

Tessa asked me how Kadiki slept: restfully or did she seem to have nightmares? While elephant calves were usually happy little souls, those orphaned, especially in distressing circumstances, might suffer post-traumatic stress disorder. It was not always easy to detect, but one way it became apparent was, just as in humans, dreams haunted by the horrors of the past.

Plenty of cuddles, love, and a soft voice at bedtime, Tessa said, could help avert night terrors.

Then she asked about swimming and mud baths. For elephants, water wasn't simply for drinking. It was for washing and frolicking — and it was never too soon to start! There was a dam with a pool at the bottom of the property, but I hadn't taken Kadiki. I began to understand how important it was that I do, just as I also needed to spend time teaching Kadiki how to pull leaves and fruit off tree branches. What Tessa explained seemed obvious when she pointed it out. Increasingly, I was coming to understand that there was a lot more to nurturing an elephant than providing food and love.

The two of us settled in the shade. A dozen blue waxbills fluttered their glossy sapphire feathers at the birdbath as they took turns hopping out of the surrounding tickberry bushes to drink and bathe.

'I know you're still getting to grips with all of this,' said Tessa. 'And I don't want to overwhelm you. But have you any more thoughts about Kadiki in the longer term?'

We had discussed this the very first time we spoke. How Tessa, her elephant orphanage bursting at the seams, had been unable to take on Kadiki — which is why Mr Kachingwe had ambushed me. There had been talk of Tessa taking on Kadiki at a future time when she had some capacity. But that was before I got to know Kadiki, and the two of us had bonded.

'I wanted to ask you about that,' I said. 'I don't know what's best.'

We both watched where the calf and the dogs continued playing chase. 'Part of the reason we feel so drawn to elephants,' Tessa mused, 'is because they're just like us. Especially how they form such intimate bonds with each other. Social connection is all important.'

'She needs a family?' I sensed where Tessa was going.

She nodded. 'Right now, she's all about you, and the dogs and her other carers. But keeping her alone ...'

'Isn't natural?'

'We can try our best to teach them. Some things they know instinctively. But there's a lot that can only be learned by imitating other elephants. Exactly how to pluck food off a branch. Plants to avoid. How to get in and out of watering holes. How to act around others in the herd.'

'Elephant social skills?'

'Normally their mum and aunties soon bring them into line if they're not behaving.'

The scope of my inadequacy as a single, ignorant, human parent was increasingly revealed.

'How do we get from where we are now to Kadiki being part of a herd?' I asked.

'One step at a time.' She paused, holding my gaze. 'Beginning, as soon as possible, with an aunty.'

I raised my eyebrows.

'A young female, say seven to ten, who has also been hand-raised. An elie who will be very happy to take on Kadiki as her companion.'

Another elephant! This was unexpected. But given what Tessa had just explained, also self-evident. 'How easy would it be to find such an elie?'

'You'd be surprised,' shrugged Tessa. 'Lots of things happen on farms and in concessions that most people never hear about. I can make inquiries. People talk to me.'

I understood why.

'A new female would need to come with her carers so that she doesn't have to go through the trauma of losing them.'

'I'm thinking about costs,' I replied.

'A lot to consider,' she agreed. 'Also making sure staff are properly trained. *I* can help with that. Send someone over regularly to support your team until the time is right to bring Kadiki and her aunty into our herd.'

Yogi Tarchin's request for me to manage the Ruwa Buddhist Society was starting to feel a lot less innocuous than it had at the time.

'But you're doing well, Rob, so far. Everything can't happen at once. Kadiki is healthy and happy. We've time to work out next steps.'

'I'm glad you said "we"!'

'I'm here to support you,' she smiled. 'What you're doing, what we're both doing, is important. Much bigger than about only us.'

~

Diva emerged from the homestead wearing a cotton-linen dress with a striking floral pattern. We exchanged waves. On her way to the car park she crossed towards us as Luke appeared behind the flowerbed at the white wooden fence.

'I've found just the place for an elephant boma,' he called excitedly, pointing towards a winter thorn tree. 'Right here!'

Tessa and I were joined by Diva. This being Zimbabwe, it turned out that Tessa and Diva had already met, Tessa being a keen consumer of Treasure Trees Apothecary *muti* — the generic Zimbabwe word for any health-related substance. Joining Luke, we climbed through the fence, walking a short distance along a narrow path towards the outstretched branches of the winter thorn.

Luke halted underneath. 'Ja — I'm thinking right here!' Under the rim of his worn buff cap, his green eyes glinted with enthusiasm. 'There's *maningi* cover already and it's close enough to bring water and power across from the house.'

Tessa and Diva were nodding in agreement.

'We'll follow the same design as your place,' he told Tessa. 'The enclosure running down here. Storage and wet rooms at the end.'

I was relieved he was so assured. Practical tasks were never my forte, but Luke seemed more than equal to the task of building a new home for Kadiki. And Kadiki's aunt-to-be. As Luke and Tessa talked about building requirements, Diva's attention was caught by a coppice of trees on the other side of the winter thorn, thirty-three feet high, with gnarled silver bark and branches studded with vivid green leaves. I recognised the dangling cylindrical pods.

'Drumstick trees,' I remembered from my childhood.

'Moringa.' She used the correct name appreciatively. 'With many exceptional qualities.'

'Anti-inflammatory, right?' I remembered.

Diva fixed me with her wide-eyed, avid expression. 'They are the most super of super foods!' she said enthusiastically. 'Even a single leaf of moringa has seven times the vitamin C of a whole orange, four times the calcium of a bottle of milk, twice the protein of a bowl of yoghurt, and three times the potassium of a banana.' She delivered her pitch with brio.

'Just in a leaf?!'

She nodded, laughing. 'The whole tree is amazing. Our ancestors didn't have the science, of course, but they knew that these ones keep you strong and fit.'

'I love your passion for indigenous trees!'

'I *am* very passionate. But these,' she gestured, 'are not indigenous.'

'No?' There was nothing more innate to the bush, I had always believed, than a moringa tree.

'They came maybe thousands of years ago from India.'

'Really?'

The more deeply you looked, it seemed, the more you discovered roots that stretched back through time to other places.

'The foothills of the Himalayas,' Diva said, 'is where moringas are said to have originated.'

'Just like the Buddha?'

She held my eyes, her whole being glowing. 'Even more fitting that we call it "the miracle tree",' she said.

Then responding to my look of wonder, 'The trees of Zimbabwe have many secrets to tell. Like Dichwe forest, near Mangula, where rough lemons have been growing for many centuries. And Tingwa Raphia Palms at Guruve where you feel like you're in Jurassic Park. Palms and rough lemons are not from Africa. They were brought by other people long ago.'

Her eyes revealed a fervent connection not only to living trees and their unusual qualities but also, it seemed, to their deeper significance. Beneath all the verve and ebullience, I sensed a Diva connected to immemorial times, to an ancient lineage of apothecarial secrets.

~

We returned to Tessa and Luke.

'Diva was just pointing out the moringas.'

'We'll fence them off,' nodded Luke, 'or the elies will chow them.'

'Treat rations,' proposed Tessa.

'You approve of the location?' I prompted.

'It's gorgeous!' she effused, with a glance at Luke. 'A short walk to the dam that way,' she pointed in one direction. 'The homestead right there,' she gestured in the opposite direction. 'Plenty of bush. Ruwa Rock,' she nodded. 'If I were an animal, I'd be happy here.'

As if on cue, Debbie and Kim appeared in the distance beside an umbrella tree, pausing to stare at us.

'Our own Sisters Sledge,' I told Tessa. John Elliott's humour — and age — was evident in his naming various animals after 70s pop stars.

'Kim's expecting.' Luke raised binoculars from the case on his belt, while musing. 'Ja, they *are* lucky. No predators to *shupa* them. Food. Water.' Lowering the glasses, he grinned. 'Good karma, hey?'

'When this place is built,' suggested Diva, 'perhaps we should name it that.'

We turned to her.

'The Good Karma Refuge,' she said, 'for elephants.'

We chuckled as I added '... and other sentient beings.'

'Oh yes,' she agreed, making a generous gathering-up motion with her arms. 'We must not forget the other sem chens too.'

~

I glanced towards where the temple was being built and Kadiki was playing. I contemplated how there would soon be an elephant refuge and that I had taken it on myself to manage an incipient organisation which was evolving in all manner of unforeseen ways.

'It's amazing,' I found myself saying aloud, 'how Rinpoche has changed so much around here. And so quickly.'

'For the Ruwa Buddhist Society,' said Diva with feeling, 'and in our hearts.'

'He's certainly changed me,' I agreed emphatically.

Diva regarded me with a gleam in her eye, 'You are describing the mind of faith.'

'Really?'

'"The state of mind",' she quoted, '"that arises when you reflect on the realisations the lama has given you".'

'I like that,' I replied.

'Ja,' said Luke. 'Based on fact. Not wishful thinking.'

Tessa nodded.

'Faith,' said Diva, encouraged, 'is when we reflect on the realisations the lama has given us. And reverence, when we reflect on the kindness he has shown us.'

The pause while we contemplated this was broken only by the soft cooing of a Cape Turtle dove in the warm morning.

'And what kindness it has been!' she murmured.

We walked to the fence and across the lawn. Luke headed towards the temple site to discuss the elephant shed with the builders. Diva bade her goodbyes and went to her car. Tessa said she had something to give Kadiki before she left. The little calf, never far away, was in a flower bed, being regarded with some alarm from the lower branches of a jacaranda tree by the crowned cranes. Tessa took a paper bag out of her pocket.

'Blueberries?' I observed as she showed me what was inside.

'Elies love them.'

It was true. As soon as Kadiki smelled them in Tessa's hand she was nuzzling her, opening her mouth, a bright gleam appearing in her big brown eyes. We both chuckled as Tessa fed her a few, watching her mash the berries lustily in her mouth before swallowing.

'You've made a friend,' I murmured.

'That's the idea.'

~

After lunch together I saw Tessa to her Land Rover. It was a vivid blue December afternoon and as I watched her drive along the dark brown track through the grass into the distance, I thought what a very different sight this was from only weeks earlier. The veldt had been so parched, before Biblical downpours brought the irrepressible explosion of the green season. It was a sequence I remembered from childhood. Back then, the break of rain would herald an even greater excitement to come: Christmas!

With everything else going on in my life, I hadn't given much thought to the festive season. By now the London party round would be in full swing, with all the planning and invitations and making sure you went to the right events and entertained the right clients and intermediaries.

Glancing to where Bodhi appeared from the homestead to survey her domain, accompanied by Football, and where Mampara the wildebeest grazed nonchalantly, I was relieved to be here. For all the decisions to be made and the uncertainties about the future, I was where I was meant to be.

Kadiki hadn't left my side. More specifically, her trunk hadn't left the wrist of my right hand, in which I held the packet of remaining blueberries.

'I know, I know,' I said. 'There'll be no rest until you've eaten the lot.'

She responded to my teasing by tilting her head to give me her most heart-melting flutter of eyelashes. She might just be a baby, all her teeth yet to break through, but she already knew exactly how to do make me do her bidding. Responding to my laughter, she did a kind of jig, dancing in a circle around me, tugging my hand more insistently.

~

We hadn't walked far from the trees of the car park, and as I opened the brown paper packet, I had no idea that Kadiki wasn't the only one interested in its contents. I popped a few berries into her mouth, absorbed by her beatific expression as she merrily munched. Tessa had brought a generous supply and several handfuls were left. I wondered if I should keep some back for later in the day. As if aware of what I was thinking, Kadiki grabbed the packet with the precise and powerful tip of her trunk. She was trying to tug it from my grip. I resisted. In an instant, the bag ripped open, flinging an arc of blueberries onto the lawn.

Fixated, Kadiki immediately scooped several that had fallen right next to her, collecting them in the tip of her trunk. Out the corner of my eye, I was aware of sudden movement. I glanced to see a large male baboon. Face close to the lawn, he was seizing handfuls of berries, shoving them in his mouth. Kadiki turned, shaking her head and throwing her trunk towards him. He leapt forward, barking and aggressively baring his teeth.

It was suddenly dangerous. The baboon also wanted the berries and seemed willing to attack. I must get Kadiki away. The last thing I wanted was for her to get bitten. But how to remove her with blueberries glistening on the grass? The baboon was scraping them into his mouth even more vigorously than she had. I tried tugging Kadiki by the neck. She wasn't budging. Instead, she trumpeted. The baboon snarled, revealing massive incisors.

I strained to pull her.

'Kadiki, *please!*' I begged.

Suddenly, the baboon about turned and scampered. A moment later came a sinuous gold flash, Bodhi racing in pursuit. Thinking this was a new game, Kadiki joined in, forgetting the blueberries for the present.

Bounding towards the trees, glancing behind him, the baboon veered right. Bodhi stayed on the most direct route, running directly across the recently poured concrete floor of the temple. Despite my calling, Kadiki followed seconds later.

The concrete wasn't soft, nor was it fully cured. As I ran around the site in pursuit of Kadiki, several of the builder's team were pointing, expressions aghast.

~

In the protective canopy of the trees, the baboon unleashed a torrent of outraged hooting. I had no idea where Bodhi was — maybe pursuing him upwards, but unlike leopards, cheetahs aren't good climbers. After her initial excitement, and losing sight of Bodhi, Kadiki seemed to have forgotten what the whole thing was about. As I approached, she turned, bewildered.

'Close shave, little one,' I told her, getting her to turn back with me. It could have gone very badly wrong.

We paused by the temple site. There was no escaping the two distinct lines of tracks running the full length of the temple floor. Labourers from the concrete firm were gesturing towards them with loud 'eishes!' and 'maiwes!' But even in that moment I didn't think it was entirely a bad thing that Bodhi's rescue was memorialised. Until now I had wondered what Bodhi's attitude towards Kadiki might be. I had been concerned, even. She pretended to ignore the baby elephant, just as she appeared to ignore most of us except Rinpoche. But what did she *really* think? In the wild, elephants and cheetahs occupied such different places in the ecosystem that they didn't have much to do with each other. But all big cats were a danger to vulnerable others. I was relieved that Bodhi literally came running to the calf's rescue. Even if it had been sport for her, and territory-marking, she protected Kadiki when I was unable to.

Having returned to the scene of the drama, Kadiki paused, searching for any remaining blueberries. I got on my hands and knees to gather up those I could find. As I did, Kadiki's trunk curling about my left arm in the search for fallen berries, there was a sudden press of warmth on my right, a slide of muscular power clothed in fur, from hip to shoulder, as Bodhi stalked past, a flick from the tip of her tail across my face.

A few paces on she paused, looking back.

'Thanks, Bodhi,' I said.

After I said it I realised I was doing something I had never done until then: looking straight at her. 'Don't meet her eyes directly,' Rinpoche had instructed that first time I'd sat with her. 'Not until she is ready.'

'How will I know she is ready?' I had asked.

'It will happen naturally,' he said.

For what felt like the longest while, she faced me with that rare, enigmatic scrutiny of cats. Then she turned, strolling with silken nonchalance to the homestead.

It had been a single meeting of the eyes lasting only a few seconds. But the impact of the exchange stayed with me. Bodhi had bestowed the rarest of gifts, the meaning of which wasn't to be fathomed in words but felt. As Rinpoche had reminded me, the language of animals wasn't one of thoughts and ideas. Bodhi's message was primal: 'I protect you. I keep you and your dependants safe.' It was an acknowledgement. An acceptance. Without uttering a sound, she had conferred on me what felt like the most extraordinary blessing.

~

That evening, as I walked home through the bush with my personal Praetorian guard, the enchantment continued. I had stayed late with Kadiki, making sure she had teething sticks and showed no sign of pain, before leaving her to spend the night with Ezekiel. It was dark by the time the dogs and I set out, but no matter what time of the night we started, it wasn't long before Bodhi appeared in front. Cloud veiled the moon and much of the sky in a blue-grey wash, but we were familiar enough with the way home for it not to matter. Instead, the diminished light had the effect of heightening other senses: the earthy aroma of petrichor as the ground soaked up that afternoon's deluge; the rippling, rising trill of fiery-neck nightjars as we brushed away leafy tendrils that had sprung across the path.

As we arrived at the bottom of Aunt Carrie's place, it was to a display that seemed to have manifested especially for my enjoyment. By some strange alchemy of rain and heat, conditions had ripened for the lawn and shrubs to be garlanded in sprays of shimmering luminescence. Glow worms! I knew them from my childhood, and, like so much else from that time that I'd forgotten I even knew, I suddenly remembered how intrigued I'd been by them. 'The larvae of the firefly,' Dad had explained them to me, leading me onto the veranda at bedtime to see them for myself. I must have been all of five or six years old. 'But it's more magical, isn't it,' he had continued, 'to think that they've come to visit us from a far-away world?'

It *was* more magical! Just as, right now, it was as if Dad himself was visiting from a distant plane to witness the unlikely Milky Way settled on the garden. Ahead of me, Bodhi paid no attention to the dots festooned erratically about the place. Instead, she followed her usual practice after seeing us safely home: sauntering along the veranda, hopping over the low wall, and vanishing into the darkness. The dogs' only interest, meanwhile, was in me opening the door, going to the kitchen, and serving them dinner.

But I returned straight after to the veranda and sat taking in the other-worldly yellow-green haze. Glow worms weren't really worms at all, but soft-bodied beetles, emitting lucent pinpricks to attract mates. If I focused on any individual glow, I could watch it gleam and fade from moment to moment, poignant and ephemeral, looking for love.

And perhaps because of that first memorable encounter of glow worms with Dad, and the revelations about him in recent days, I was reminded of the pendant he'd made to place around the neck of his lover, and his own yearning for intimacy. I recalled Lakshmi in the splendour of her sari, and the feelings of connection I'd sensed in the past weeks to our small community of humans and other beings.

As Thor and Tiki, my now-familiar companions, came to rest beside me, the night felt quite fantastical. From the distant homestead roof, Sonny and Cher wailed plaintively in the darkness. Closer to home, nocturnal galagos — 'bushbabies' — chirped and grunted in the tree canopy. The glow worm display would last only a night. There might still be some tomorrow, but it would be a much-reduced spectacle. This was an evanescent moment, the performance of a single night. Without any bidding on my part, Rinpoche's wisdom surfaced in my mind: *The reality we experience comes from the karma we have created. Only if we give happiness can we experience it.*

It was a wisdom that made the moment feel even more transcendent. Nothing that I was perceiving was fully coming from "out there". The glow worms and the bushbabies, the comfort of dogs, and the rippling nightjars, even the memory of Bodhi's benediction — all these were merely contributing factors. The true cause for my wonder came from an earlier time, a kindness offered deep in the past by my unknown benefactor of a previous life. I felt that such causes were ripening with an abundance I had never before known.

Faith, I recollected Diva saying, was the state of mind that arises when we reflect on the realisations the lama has given us. Reverence, when we reflect on his kindness. I now had the words to give to what I experienced, but what mattered more than those was the state of heart itself. The wonder, that larvae-lit night, as I realised how the lama's sublime presence was becoming available to me. And the welling-up of gratitude within: *How lucky am I?*

Chapter Ten

'LET'S TAKE A WALK,' suggested Rinpoche, stepping into my office.

It wasn't yet nine in the morning. I was at my laptop under the thatch dealing with a flurry of overnight emails.

Things at Ruwa Buddhist Society were never busier. It wasn't only Kadiki, although she continued as my main preoccupation. The 'Taking Refuge' ceremony, planned for early January, was gaining momentum in a way I had never imagined. Instead of attracting only a few Harare locals, Rinpoche's presence was igniting interest among groups as far afield as Colesberg in the South African Karoo, and Ixopo in Natal, from Vilanculos in Mozambique and Lubumbashi in the Congo. I was managing inquiries for an event to be held in a temple still under construction, while also trying to get a grip on future funding for a proposed elephant aunty and carers. Milk alone, for an elephant calf, added thousands of dollars to the monthly budget. I was willing and able to pay for these expenses personally for the time being. During my time in London, I'd earned enough to live here for the rest of my life

185

without having to worry about money. But Rinpoche said that Ruwa Buddhist Society must be self-supporting.

He looked at my furrowed brow with a puckish expression. 'There's something I want you to see.'

~

We stepped into the clear morning, Rinpoche leading the way towards the car park, while Bodhi, stretched in the early sunlight with Football, rose sinuously to accompany us. Ezekiel was with Kadiki around the back of the homestead. The two dogs scampered to join in.

Down the lawn, the temple was quickly taking form. The foundation was fully cured, the imprints of Bodhi and Kadiki indelibly preserved. Sturdy support poles had been bolted into their cages and rafters attached. The site was a hive of activity as workmen strapped panels of thatch into place. A steep, gold-coloured A-frame of roof was taking form against its backdrop of ancient granite.

'What are you working on?' Rinpoche asked, tilting his head in the direction of my office.

'Emails,' I replied.

'Problems?' he responded to my flat tone.

'Stuff in London,' I said. It wasn't Ruwa Buddhist Society stuff that was causing me distress so much as extricating myself from life in London. What I hadn't expected was the amount of venom I was getting about moving to Zimbabwe. 'Some people are being very prickly,' I told him. 'They're saying that by moving here I'm showing support for the Zimbabwe government.'

'Politics,' he nodded.

'Yes.'

Some of the moral indignation I had received might have had more to do with hurt feelings and personal upset. But the distress in one of the emails this morning from a friend felt genuine. 'They're saying things like a government so corrupt and repressive as this one should be shunned. That simply being here normalises a regime that no decent person should tolerate.'

As I spoke, I realised that politics wasn't something I had discussed with Yogi Tarchin. For as long as I could remember, the state of government in this country was the subject of intensely felt, polarised convictions. A roller-coaster of oppression, hope, and brutal violence led to a state of affairs where the near-complete collapse of government services was presided over by ministers who seemed to own spectacular personal fortunes.

Rinpoche had never so much as mentioned the subject.

'Buddhism is apolitical,' he shrugged. 'This politician. That party. Does everyone have exactly the same view? Does everyone agree they are corrupt? Or trustworthy?' he asked hypothetically, before shaking his head. 'There are always many views. And where do these views come from?'

'From the minds of the perceivers,' I replied.

'They are the ones who are suffer,' he confirmed, 'the ones who see injustice and hatred. They are the ones we can help.'

'You're not saying some politicians *aren't* crooks and gangsters?'

'No,' he said as we walked under the trees, disturbing a pair of Cape doves, warming themselves in the sand. They took off with a mellifluous flutter of wings.

'Surely,' I persisted, 'we should rally around leaders doing the right thing — or at least trying to?'

'Of course,' he nodded. 'But having good leaders is not always possible. The karma of those we live among, the group karma, may be too strong. Perhaps you get stuck with rulers you can do nothing about — just like us Tibetans with the Chinese since the 1950s. None of us want them. We only want to be left to ourselves. But they are in charge. There is nothing we can do. So, do we spend our lives allowing evil beings to harm us even more by allowing them to occupy our minds? *They* won't be harmed if we do, but we are damaged greatly. The more we obsess about them, the more we allow them into our thoughts, then the more habitual our anger and bitterness becomes. If we do this, we let them destroy our happiness — and not only in this life. We may create causes to be propelled into the worst possible rebirths.'

Rinpoche was leading the way on the track that led from the car park behind the homestead and former stables. 'What becomes of a consciousness in the habit of resentment when it is no longer anchored to a human body?' He shot me a foreboding expression. 'There are no limits to the realms of suffering such a mind can create.'

~

It was the first time I'd heard such consequences spelled out, the potentially devastating impact explained with such stark clarity. It would take me a while to fathom. In the meantime I had to ask, 'What about the idea that all it takes for evil to triumph is for good people to do nothing?'

'Good people shouldn't do nothing,' he returned.

'But from what you've been saying ...'

'We don't have to be doormats or allow ourselves to be trampled on. But as Buddhists, our interest is in the mind, in consciousness. Our first priority is to make

188

sure that when we can we create virtue and merit, not negative karma. Taking a stand can be most useful. Worthwhile. Even,' he shrugged, 'if the solution is only temporary.'

'Why only temporary?' I asked.

'External reality *is* temporary,' he shrugged. 'All products are impermanent. Governments, politicians especially, are impermanent. People who seemed so powerful and important even thirty years ago — now we sometimes can't even remember their names. *Much better*,' he turned to me, expression emphatic, 'to look after what endures: mind itself. Serve others. Create virtue and merit. Seek a more enlightened state of being. *Then* we can be of true benefit.'

~

We continued walking through the emerald veldt. Bodhi had long since become invisible, but the dogs darted into the bush on either side. From the branches of a stately palm tree, heavy with swaying nests, came a cacophony of masked weaver birds, their dazzling yellow plumage contrasting sharply with their jet black faces. I still had no idea where Rinpoche was taking us, or whether this was simply a leg-stretching exercise. In the distance, the track came to a T-junction. Turning right took you to the main Mutare road. A left turn headed to Aunt Carrie's and, farther on, to the village.

Was it my imagination, or could I see Lakshmi in the distance, driving in the direction of the main road? I'd caught glimpses of her several times in recent days. Impatient as I was to speak to her, our paths hadn't crossed directly. And I didn't want to make a big deal of what might only be a curious coincidence. We'd bump into each other again soon enough.

At the junction of the two dirt roads, a few rickety branches were bound together to create a stall. Humble pyramids of tomatoes were arranged on two straw shelves presided over by a village woman. Informal vendors like this were found in the most unlikely places — traders and subsistence farmers doing what they could to earn a few dollars. Another woman stopped to chat to the stallholder, a baby strapped to her back and a bright pink bucket balanced on her head in the traditional way.

Rinpoche turned. 'It is a sign of an evolved person to endure hardship without bitterness. To experience poverty and pain — and yet still to be able to feel joy.'

I was reminded of what he'd told us that first moonlit night on Ruwa Rock. How the local people might have no formal knowledge of Buddhism, or identify in any way with that label, but where it mattered, their behaviour bore many of the imprints of Dharma practices. As if on cue, the two women burst out laughing, clapping their hands. On the head of the woman with the baby, the bucket rocked from side to side.

'You see this about Zimbabwean people,' he said. 'They are resilient. Many suffer greatly and yet,' he gestured to where the women continued the hilarity, shouting to each other as the woman with the baby headed to the main road, 'they already understand much about equanimity. Patience. They have strong minds, much stronger than elsewhere.'

'You mean, like us snowflakes in the West?' I queried drolly.

Rinpoche wasn't smiling. 'Problems like anxiety, attention disorders, and so on — these aren't on the same scale as having no food or shelter. They are modern problems of material success. In some ways *more* difficult, for there is no external cure.'

~

Because this was a road I had only driven along, when I approached the T-junction in the car I was usually on the lookout for pedestrians and locals on bicycles. Accordingly, I had never looked beyond a glance at two disused buildings on the left-hand side of the road. Mostly concealed by trees and shrubs, one looked like it may once have been a small barn for drying tobacco. The other was a local store of the kind that used to exist throughout rural districts in the heyday of commercial farming. Its doors and windows had long since been boarded over.

Rinpoche approached the stallholder, who greeted him respectfully, clapping cupped hands together. She was a slim, middle-aged woman in a lime green dress that had seen better days, with a *doek* tied about her head.

'You want tomatoes?' she called out encouragingly, face breaking into a smile. 'They are sweet, sure! Only two dollars,' she indicated one of the piles.

Rinpoche tilted his head, looking deeper into the lower shelf. 'Watermelons — five dollars.'

Stepping beside Rinpoche, I murmured, 'She's expecting you to bargain.'

'And this?' He pointed to flimsy plastic packets containing small brown tube-shaped items.

The woman explained something in Shona.

I peered closer. 'Mopane worms,' I told him. Seeing his expression cloud, I explained, 'Collected from Mopane trees. Fried and salted, they're like bar snacks, quite popular. Rich in protein.'

Rinpoche reached inside his pocket and took out a five-dollar note.

'Two lots of tomatoes.' He stretched out his hand.

'*Aiwha.*' She looked at the note, concerned. 'No

change.' She picked up a packet of mopane worms and proffered it instead. In Zimbabwe it was common practice, even in grocery chains, for a cashier to offer a banana, candy bar, or other small item in place of non-existent coinage.

Rinpoche shook his head. 'Keep the change,' he told her. 'Christmas box.' It was the local term for a seasonal gift.

The woman's face broke into a broad smile. 'He-heh!' she sang out, delighted, taking the bill from him and tucking it into her bra before he could change his mind. 'May God bless you!'

Gleefully, she scooped two piles of tomatoes into a brown paper packet and handed them over with a thankful bob of the head. But as she did so, her happiness shifted into something quite different. Pointing behind us with her right arm, she raised her left to her mouth, her eyes widening in alarm. 'Maiwe!' she cried — *oh my goodness!*

We turned to see that Bodhi had emerged from the grass nearby and was standing in the road, the sun on her face.

Rinpoche gestured to her. 'She is a friend,' he told the woman. 'Her name is Bodhi.'

The woman looked shocked and confused in equal measure — as much by Rinpoche's composure as by the appearance of the cheetah.

'Bodhi,' she echoed after a while.

'Bodhi the cheetah.'

'Bodhi *dindingwe*,' I told her.

The two of us turned, Rinpoche leading the way, Bodhi dissolving into the bush, and the stallholder staring after in disbelief.

'We have them in India too,' observed Rinpoche,

conversationally. 'Cheetahs.'

'Really?' I always thought them unique to Africa.

'Also, elephants, lions, buffaloes, monkeys and others,' he continued. 'The land bridge connecting Africa and Asia used to be much wider. Humans and animals travelled. So did ideas.'

'My godmother says that India and Africa share many things,' I said.

'She is wise,' said Rinpoche.

~

He returned on the same path. But as we passed the derelict buildings, he turned, following a space between trees that once would have been the track leading to them. As we got closer, I saw that a great, sliding barn door in the larger of the buildings was open. And was I imagining things, or could I detect a familiar but out-of-context smell, something that took a few moments to place. The faint wisp of baking.

We emerged from behind a thicket of moringas shielding buildings from the road, and I saw a familiar car parked beside it — Diva's. She had been visiting Ruwa Buddhist Society almost daily. I'd overheard talk of a small annual fundraiser she organised for the society but faced with more consuming tasks I hadn't paid it much attention. Now things fell into place. Christmas Cake! That was the smell.

Rinpoche, bright-eyed, led the way up a couple of steps and into the large brick building. It was dimly lit inside, narrow panes high above us, supplemented by a few dangling industrial pendant lamps. The place had been built as a tobacco barn, I guessed forty or fifty years ago. But as my eyes adjusted to the subdued lighting, and my nose to the richly aromatic melange of cinnamon, spices, and sweet fruits, I saw how it now was repurposed. Three large industrial ovens stood against the wall. In front of them was a row of bench tables where African women wrapped cakes in cellophane.

'Welcome to the Christmas Cake Bake-off!' Diva waved to us.

'Smells great!' I called as we approached.

In apron, cap, and gloves, she looked the part of a baker. 'I had no idea.' I shook my head as I took it in.

She was soon offering us a plate of samples. It was my first cake of the season, deliciously rich and moist. As we munched appreciatively, Rinpoche prompted her to explain how the Christmas Cake fundraiser came to be.

When John Elliott was still alive, he'd heard that a businessman leaving the country needed to sell three large-scale ovens. This was back during the first wave of hyper-inflation and business confidence was plummeting. John bought the ovens for a bargain. He had the idea of turning the barn into a bakery, with a ready-built shop next door, convenient both to the main Mutare Road and the local village.

There were obstacles at every turn. Despite dire food shortages, bureaucrats withheld permissions for no good reason. Only after a long while did John realise that they were waiting for a payoff. One time a local political bigwig showed up in his shiny Mercedes Benz and spoke ominously about 'sharing' the investment: John's financial risk required the kind of protection only he could offer — in exchange for a cut of the profits.

So, John gave up on the idea. He wasn't going to spend his retirement subject to bribery and blackmail. He would find other things to do. But he was stuck with the ovens. Later, when Diva had proposed, with delightful irony, that baking Christmas Cakes was a great way for the Buddhist group to raise money, John surprised everyone by saying he had the perfect facilities. Ruwa Buddhist Society Christmas Cake had been an annual tradition ever since, with the cakes beautifully wrapped and ribboned and sold at Treasure Trees Apothecary in Chisipite.

After we'd enjoyed the cake samples, Rinpoche guided me on a walk around the boarded-up shop next door. It was an old worn building, once whitewashed, with a wide concrete veranda inevitably taken over by plants. I studied a great bougainvillea bush growing around a tree on one side of the shop, forming a vast purple curtain and completely enclosing one end of the porch. The floor was covered with a variety of debris, thick with weeds.

'You are a very good organiser, Robbie,' Rinpoche told me.

I valued any compliment from Rinpoche, although in the circumstances this one seemed random.

'So many people coming to the refuge ceremony,' he said.

'Oh, that,' I nodded. 'All we did was set up a website and reach out to a few centres online.' One of Riley's friends was a wizard on social media targeting, and helped drive traffic to the new website.

'You know how to manage things,' he persisted.

I shrugged.

'There are many Buddhist centres that don't have such skills. They are limited in what they can do. But with you managing, the Ruwa Buddhist Society can do wonderful things.'

I suddenly realised what he was doing. The same as when we'd watched the temple foundations being poured: showing rather than telling, allowing what was physically apparent to point directly to an intention.

'Are you saying I should resurrect John Elliott's bakery?' I confirmed.

'There will be many expenses with the elephants and other things.' He met my eyes.

It felt as much an observation on his part as a response to what I'd explained after Tessa Brenthurst's visit. When I'd shared my concerns about rising costs, I wasn't sure he had understood the scale of what I was saying. Now I realised that I had misread his unaltering lightness of being. For him, increasing outgoings weren't so much a problem as a dynamic to be countered with increasing incomes. But I wasn't convinced: a bakery to make money to support the animal refuge?

'If John Elliott couldn't make the bakery work,' I said, 'what chance do I have, being so new to the country?'

'You have Diva,' he countered. 'And Diva's husband, Herbert.' Herbert Derembwe was a high-profile lawyer and fixer in town with the reputation for being able to cut through obstructionist obstacles and make things happen.

'Anyway,' he shrugged his shoulders, 'times change. Things move on. Those people from twenty years ago are no longer with us.'

This was undeniable. And in a different way, challenging. Not only did he want me to manage a growing refuge for elephants and other beings, he also wanted me to establish a thriving bakery to subsidise their activities. No pressure then, Rinpoche!

He struck out briskly along the path home. 'You can do it easily!' he announced as I walked beside him. 'For you it will be something different.'

Bodhi appeared on the path in front. Beside us, Thor and Tiki responded to her in a way I hadn't seen before. Ears pricked up and eyes glinting as she glanced back towards them, the impulse was confirmed. She began running — and they raced after. She allowed them to catch up before speeding effortlessly ahead as they drew closer. Dogs chase cats — a timeless game that kicked in with effortless instinct. One they had perhaps played when they were much younger and Aunt Carrie was visiting John Elliott. One they launched into with avid enthusiasm — even if it was a pursuit the dogs could never possibly win.

Rinpoche and I burst out laughing as Bodhi disappeared around a bend in the distance, closely pursued by an Irish wolfhound and a Jack Russell.

Something different, to be sure.

During the day, we were getting Kadiki used to moving further and further away from the manicured world of the homestead and into the veldt. The plan was to guide her all the way to the dam — a goal that was almost within reach. Tessa's recent visit clarified for me that as close as I felt to Kadiki, it wasn't my place to turn her into a pet. She hadn't been born in the world of humans, but in the wild. Some unfathomable quirk of karma brought her into my life, and the connection I felt for her was profound. Miraculous. But if she was ever to return to the bush, for her sake our bond must also be temporary.

Kadiki would outlive me by decades, maybe even half a century. The thought of leaving her dependent on people, some kind of plaything or zoo exhibit, was monstrous. Much better that she fulfil her destiny in nature. Become part of a matriarchal herd. In time, all being well, perhaps she would become a mother with her own calves. Even though it was only a few weeks since she'd arrived, my feelings for her ran so deep I didn't want to contemplate the future too much.

Better, that sunny afternoon as I led her through the bush towards Aunt Carrie's, to abide in the present moment. With Bodhi leading the way, followed by Tiki, me, Kadiki, and Thor bringing up the rear, we walked through the Christmas veldt pulsating with promise. The rains hadn't simply transformed barren scrub into lush greenery — African daisies clad in riotous colours shimmied through the viridescence. Wild hibiscus vied for attention, swaying flirtatiously in pink and scarlet petals, enticing insects towards their waiting stigma.

There were pollinators of all kinds, from bees humming diligently from flower to flower to African monarch butterflies dancing distractingly. Within weeks of the rains, the bush had spawned phalanxes of beetles, including shiny brown peanut-size cicadas. "Christmas beetles", we used to call them, because they always appeared at this time of the year. With them and an abundance of other insects came the attendant predators, like the pair of African hoopoes diving from the branches, their russet crests striped with black and white tips, hoop-hoop-hooping as they swooped and vaulted.

And along with the call of the wild that afternoon came a very different sound as our procession arrived in Aunt Carrie's garden. A Jaguar engine burst to life with a roar. This was followed by the sound of warming up, a resonance we had become used to in recent weeks as Tinashe worked in the shed. Then came a different cadence, one which I listened to for quite a while before realising: the car was moving!

Bodhi had dissolved into the bush by this time, and the dogs went to see Marvellous, who was tending to his vegetable patch. My hand draped on Kadiki's neck, I led her towards Marvellous and the dogs, wanting her to have as little contact with vehicles as possible.

As I returned to the gravel driveway, from around the side of the house Tinashe appeared, at the wheel of the XK150 Jaguar Roadster. It was an open sporty two-seater with both doors missing, but for the rest, the vehicle looked in showroom condition, glistening and purring throatily. His expression intense behind the wheel, Tinashe didn't see me at first. But when he looked up, he grinned widely.

'To think this was just a collection of parts scattered in the shed a few weeks ago!' I congratulated him.

'Every part was there.' He was modest as always. 'Your Uncle Adrian was thorough.'

'You've done him proud.'

'I wanted to get her moving.' He looked apologetic about the car's unfinished state. 'The doors will go on easily.'

I watched him demonstrate shifting the car into reverse, sliding it back a short distance, before changing gears to return.

'The engine.' He formed his middle finger and thumb into a circle, beaming. 'Just listen to that sound.'

'Celebrations are definitely in order!' I told him.

'Zambezi lager on the veranda?' he queried.

'I think we can go one better.' I recollected a previous conversation. 'Didn't you say there was a jazz club on Enterprise Road?'

~

Which was how I came to be driving into town that evening, with Tinashe in the passenger seat beside me. In Levis and a long-sleeve white shirt, there was nothing remarkable about the way he dressed, but as always he was the carrier of a perceptible stillness.

I remembered our conversation at the breakfast table when Diva visited — how Tinashe had been unusually withdrawn until our effusive friend coaxed out of him his recent shocking discovery about his grandfather.

'Did you speak to Rinpoche about your granddad?' I asked as we sped along the Mutare Road into town.

'Yes.' He turned toward me, before saying after a pause, 'He said I should get a flowering pot plant and give it to Mum.'

'Oh?'

A brightness appeared on his face. 'He described in detail the flowers it should have. Turned out he was talking about flame lilies.'

'Ah — *gloriosa superba*,' I named our national flower. As its Latin name suggests, the flowers are outstandingly beautiful: six vibrant red petals with wavy yellow edges that form a bowl shape, bright yellow anthers protruding beneath.

'He was very particular about it being in a ceramic pot.'

'Did you get a plant?'

He nodded. 'I'll give it to Mum when I visit her tomorrow. Don't know what to expect.'

'Did he suggest what you should say?'

'That's the weird thing.' He shook his head. 'No message at all.'

In the Friday evening darkness, taillights glowing on the road ahead while a stream of weekend traffic poured out of town, our conversation flowed from one subject to another. Tinashe told me proudly about how well Pema had done in her university exams in Britain. How much he hoped she'd come to Zim next year. We spoke about the boma near the moringa trees being built under Luke's supervision. How rapidly The Good Karma Refuge for Elephants was coming into being.

As we got closer to town, I asked him about my conversation with Rinpoche about the resilience of Zimbabweans — how the hardship they endured had made them more patient and better able to practice equanimity. 'Do you agree?' I asked him curiously.

'He has a point.' He shrugged after thinking for a while. 'We've always been ruled by chiefs. For all of Bantu history we had chiefs. Then when Europeans arrived, they made themselves chiefs. After that, liberation movement leaders took over as chiefs. We have never *not* had a chief.'

'So, democracy?'

'Not an African idea,' he shook his head. 'Personally, I like it. Many do. But it's a foreign import. A recent one. Anyone can tick a ballot box every four years, but democracy needs more. If leaders still have loyalties to clan and tribe when they are elected, they will be corrupt. If ordinary people allow the party to stay in power so long that it becomes the same as the army, the same as the electoral commission, you have a one-party state — and a chief,' he said. 'Things may change, but it will take many years. Until then, we must practice patience or risk making ourselves bitter.'

Rinpoche had made the same point, but from a different starting place: finding ourselves in a group with opposing beliefs, our first priority was to guard the wellbeing of our own mind. It was our most precious treasure, the only thing that would endure.

I wondered, too, if the tradition of having chiefs who were 'sacred' — set apart from their people —

made it somehow seem right to get off the road when a presidential cavalcade appeared with its bullet-proofed Mercedes and motorbike outriders. Was there something in the magnificence of such a display that resonated with the same awe as when the elaborately gilded gold state coach was drawn by eight horses down the mall to Westminster Abbey?

~

We drove past Haka Game Park and I got ready to turn right into Harare Drive. Talk moved on to the temple. In recent days the floor had been polished to a lustre, with special care taken to preserve the footprints left by Bodhi and Kadiki. Thatching was all but complete. We would have a purpose-built — if empty — temple ready by the time of the refuge ceremony in early January. The progress was amazing since our small group had met on top of Ruwa Rock just weeks earlier.

'The location.' I had wanted to ask Tinashe about this for some time. '31 degrees East. How is that significant, to local people?'

'I have little knowledge.' He shook his head. 'That's the kind of thing my grandfather might understand.' After a pause he continued, 'I *do* know that folklore stories tell of an underground river travelling all the way down the continent, north to south.'

'You've discussed this with Harris?'

'Many times. He is very interested in Chinhoyi Caves. You know the pool at the bottom of the main caves goes very deep.'

I had visited the legendary caves two hours north of Harare as a child and seen the crystal-clear waters for myself. I also remembered feeling the other-worldly presence of the main cave.

'An underground river runs through it, some say as far as Lake Malawi in the North and Durban in the south. Ancients believed that the river flowed through a series of underground passages and caverns all the way to distant lands. Others said that the river connects us to the realms of our ancestors.'

I was reminded of how much about this country remained unexplored, how much remained shrouded in myth, from the highest peak of the much-fabled Mount Nyangani to the subterranean river that could be accessed only via the metaphysical portal of Chinhoyi Cave.

'Maybe it's a myth,' I suggested after a while. 'A kind of metaphor?'

In the dim glow of the dashboard, Tinashe was silent for a few moments before saying, 'Whatever it is, it has always attracted visitors.'

'Just not on the scale of Victoria Falls!' I joked. Zimbabwe's main tourist attraction had its own airport and a steady stream of international traffic. Chinhoyi Caves, by contrast, was hardly known outside the country. But from his pensive expression I began to realise that Tinashe was suggesting something different. 'How do you mean, visitors?' I probed.

He pointed up to the sky. 'Our people have always known about them,' he said. 'When white farmers settled the area, they noticed them too. At night. They used to speak about the Ruwa lights.'

'Are you talking about UFOs?' I was astonished that the buttoned-down Tinashe was being so matter of fact.

He pulled a face. 'Tribal people didn't have such concepts. Or worry about what they might or might not be. They just saw these ... these things appearing, sometimes very close. We have always known about them. They are controlled by a higher intelligence — you can see from the way they move.'

'I really didn't know!'

'In 1994, they visited Ariel School.'

I was flummoxed. The turn-off to Ariel School was only a few hundred yards from Aunt Carrie's!

'You didn't hear about it?' he confirmed, taking in my thunderstruck expression.

As I shook my head he told me with a smile, 'It was such a big event that a documentary was made about it. One of the closest recorded encounters. *The Ariel Phenomenon*. You should watch it.'

I didn't know what astounded me the most. An unexplored continental river running for thousands of miles underground, an invisible longitudinal meridian connecting Great Zimbabwe to the Egyptian pyramids, UFOs from distant planets paying regular visits to Ruwa, or the fact that none of this came as any surprise to the ever-tranquil Tinashe.

His dispassionate nature made what he went on to say even more extraordinary. 'There are many unusual things about this place that have been lost in time. Things that would surprise people if they knew. Our land isn't simply where humanity was born.' He looked over, meeting my eyes with clear conviction. 'It is the world's spiritual heart.'

~

The Harare Jazz Club evening was in a venue next to Bistro Veldemeers. We were lucky to find a place in the car park — little did we know that tonight was the club's Christmas party. On this balmy summer evening a stage had been set up at one end of the raised outdoor terrace. We heard an excited buzz coming from those gathered around candlelit tables stretching across the expansive lawn.

We arrived during a break between sets. Standing at the back and scanning for somewhere to sit, as liveried waitstaff ferried drinks and food to the tables, within moments we saw Riley hurrying towards us, radiant in a red strapless dress.

'Lobster!' she enthused, kissing Tinashe and me. 'Will you join us?'

'Haven't booked,' I explained. 'We didn't even ...'

'We've a couple of spare seats.' Grabbing me by the hand, she led us towards the stage.

'Come to support our girl?' she called over her shoulder.

'Girl?'

'Up next. Lakshmi.'

I turned to Tinashe, who shared my bemusement.

Riley led us right to the front. Luke was drinking a Zambezi. Beside him sat Simba, with Lakshmi perched on his lap. Diva and her husband Herbert were seated next to them. In the hubbub Riley introduced us to Dennis from the British Embassy, and Liesel and Sven, aid workers from Europe. I recognised the names of the latter three from the Ruwa Buddhist Society member list.

It was wonderful to find myself among friends. Of course I wanted to speak to Lakshmi in particular, not that this was the time or place. In a black dress, her hair immaculately coiffed and stunning in her make-up, she looked ready to step on stage.

As I drew closer, she rose to meet me. 'Thanks for coming!' she greeted me, dark eyes gleaming.

I wanted to tell her how much I'd been thinking about her since our last encounter, to ask about the pendant and its provenance. Instead, I said, 'Last time I saw you, you were a resplendent Maharani. This time it's sultry jazz singer!'

As she threw her head back in laughter, her earrings glittered.

'Not the pendant tonight?'

'No Aum made visible,' she confirmed merrily.

'What was that?' Amid the clamour, I couldn't be sure what I thought she'd said.

'No Aum made visible,' she repeated, gaze connecting to mine with a heart-stopping power quite unconscious on her own part. 'That's what Mum used to call it, after the person who gave it to her.'

I was so overwhelmed by this, I couldn't think of anything to say. I stood there, foolishly mute while a stage manager approached, tugging her by the elbow. 'Two minutes!' he told her. 'We need to mic you up.'

She turned to leave. 'I told Mum about you, by the way,' she said. 'She's longing to meet you!'

Then she headed towards the sound desk, waving back at our table.

~

There were a few moments' uncertainty as Tinashe and I took our seats. The chairs on both sides of Simba were empty. I sat at one, expecting Tinashe to take the one on the other side. After some dithering, he chose to sit next to Liesel and Sven further along the table. Catching his eye when our drinks arrived, I raised a glass of wine in a toast which he returned, somewhat diffidently.

The surrounding lights dimmed, and people moved back from where they'd been standing at the terrace balustrade smoking Madisons and quaffing drinks. Zimbabwe was a nation of committed smokers. And dedicated drinkers. Apart from tealights set on the white tablecloths, the only illumination was the uplighting caught by the outstretched limbs of jacaranda trees reaching towards the stars. The heady perfume of Yesterday, Today, and Tomorrow bushes rose from the gardens below. In the lull of anticipation, a Scops owl hooted from a nearby msasa, causing a ripple of glee.

A small band struck up — bass, keyboard, drums — and within moments, Lakshmi was singing "Have Yourself a Merry Little Christmas". A round of applause followed her lusciously delivered first line: she was popular, no doubting it. And as she continued, drawing us into the world of the song, it was easy to understand why.

Even without fancy staging, she commanded attention. She mesmerised. It wasn't only her voice, beautifully trained though that was. There was something else about her presence that enraptured. Something that, to me at least, felt powerfully familiar.

A single spotlight was placed on her as she performed. I was utterly absorbed in her every gesture, the cadence of each phrase. I knew this song so very well, not just because it was a jazz standard, but because it had also been one of Dad's favourites, one he'd included in Christmas concerts year after year.

Lakshmi was arching back in musical fervour, eyes closed and microphone held to her lips, when her motion caused the hem of her black dress to ride momentarily upwards. As immersed by the song as she was, I was equally transfixed by what I saw below her right knee: a small black mole. Just like the one I had in exactly the same place. The one I had inherited from Dad.

The applause that followed her first song was boisterous, accompanied by appreciative hollering. Everyone at our table was elated as we clapped. For my own part, I struggled to take in what I saw. It all made sense. Yet it felt unbelievable!

'She's brilliant!' I leaned over to Simba.

'I know!' He flashed a smile.

'How old is she?' I had to ask. I had already worked out the number. But I must have it confirmed — even if the question seemed irrelevant.

If the question was strange to Simba, he gave no sign of it. 'Thirty-eight,' he told me, 'in April.'

I nodded. The number of years since our family had moved to Scotland. The number of years since Dad gave up his lover. For almost four decades I'd had a half-sister and had never known it.

Chapter Eleven

NEXT MORNING I woke to unfamiliar darkness. When I stepped outside, the whole sky was heavy, billowing indigo. Low-level wispy veils scudded from one horizon to the other, so close it seemed that if you reached high enough, they'd stream between your fingers. Gusts of warm wind were ripe with rain.

Inside, my phone vibrated as I lifted it off charge. Mugdha Kumar had sent a message in the early hours. 'I would be grateful for the chance to meet as soon as possible about my daughter,' it read, adding unnecessarily, '(Lakshmi).' It didn't take me long to send a return message, to which she replied immediately. We agreed that she'd visit me in an hour.

I showered and dressed in chinos and a long-sleeved shirt, conscious of the most unusual encounter ahead. What was the protocol for such occasions? For a man about to meet the woman who had been his father's lover nearly forty years earlier? Since watching Lakshmi on stage last night, questions had buzzed across my mind like the white clouds scurrying across the pregnant sky.

I wondered what she'd look like — Lakshmi's mum.

Dad's sketches, sparse on detail, were striking in allure. I also wondered about her timing. Was she really 'longing' to meet me, as Lakshmi had said? Why in particular, I wondered, had Mugdha Kumar decided to message me last night?

I boiled the kettle for a plunger of coffee. I set a tray with some of Aunt Carrie's bone China cups. I exchanged messages with Ezekiel in the stables, who had the morning shift with Kadiki before I took over elephant duties in the afternoon. Then, giving Thor and Tiki their Saturday morning bones, I sat on the veranda, waiting.

Ruwa Rock was imposing as ever against the leaden sky, the atmospheric tumult lending it a permanence, an inviolability, having withstood millennia of the very worst that the elements could throw at it. Still it stood, an unchanging sentinel towering above the district.

My own visitor, no less intriguing to me, arrived before the deluge. I heard the sound of a car turning into the driveway and coming to a halt at the side of the house. I rose from my chair as she stepped onto the veranda. In the first instant I saw her, I realised what an assumption I had made. We paused, taking one another in.

'You look so like him,' she murmured in a deep voice.

I expected to meet an elderly woman of my parents' generation, but she looked only five to ten years older than me. It was as though she was Lakshmi's svelte older sister: the same combination of Maharani poise and enigmatic glint of the eye. It wasn't, I realised, only her allure and exoticism that Dad would have found so beguiling. He would have been flattered by the attentions of a woman much younger than himself.

I ushered her into the sitting room. A single orange-shaded lamp cast a glow in the dark morning. The first heavy drops were beginning to explode on the veranda roof. But sitting across the coffee table from one another, we barely noticed. It was her skin, I thought, so very different from our own Scottish pallor — a flawless, radiant gold. She wore about her neck a silk scarf, richly patterned in crimson and sapphire, that set off her high cheekbones. Eyes like deep dark pools gleamed with an inner light.

'Lakshmi doesn't know about my father?' I asked. It felt important to confirm this — the reason I thought she must have been prompted to urgent action.

She drew back in her chair. 'You do?' She didn't seem completely surprised.

I leaned over, gathering the right leg of my trousers, tugging it up until I revealed the single, dark, mole beneath my knee.

'Ah,' she understood.

'When I saw the special pendant, I began wondering,' I said. 'Then last night she used the words "Aum made visible ..."'

'Euan's phrase.'

'Which Kay told me.'

'Nyanga Kay?'

I nodded. 'When he made it for you, he couldn't help himself. You know how Dad was like a small child sometimes? He was so proud of it he had to show it to someone.'

'So, it was Kay who helped you unlock the secret,' she observed, touching back her shoulder-length hair. 'He would have liked that.'

'Yes, he would.'

'I wish I could have thanked her.'

'You still can,' I met her eyes. 'She lives in Juliasdale.'

'Still?' Mugdha was taken aback. 'She's the only person from that time that I would want to meet again.'

It was my turn for surprise. 'You knew her?'

'We were in the same yoga group. Euan and I were discreet. She didn't ... didn't know.' She observed me closely as I absorbed this. 'You and I met once too.'

I raised my eyebrows.

'After a yoga class. You wouldn't have been very interested. You were with your girlfriend.'

'Mandy.' I tried to remember a time we'd gone to fetch Dad after yoga.

'Mandy Graham,' she said.

'Ellis,' I corrected. 'Mandy Ellis.'

'Yes,' she said, darkness clouding her expression for a moment. 'Before she married.'

The heavens fully opened, and rain drummed heavily on the roof. In the soft lamplight, inhaling the breath of life gusting through the veranda doors, Mugdha told me the secrets our family had left behind.

She had discovered she was pregnant the same week our family left for Scotland. She hadn't told Dad. She herself struggled to take in the news. She suffered badly from morning sickness. When her parents found out, they'd been beside themselves. They wanted to send her away, to give birth secretly and adopt the child out to preserve her honour and the family name.

There had already been much talk of an arranged marriage to Kabir Kumar, heir to a respectable pharmacy business. The match was a good one for both families and would help to expand their combined retail chains. But Mugdha was adamant that she wasn't going to give up her baby. Somehow the truth got out. When Kabir said he still wanted to marry her and bring up her child as though it were his own, she felt she no longer had any choice. Older than her by some years, he was willing to overlook what he chose to view as the predation of an older man no longer on the scene. Mugdha made him agree that their child should learn the truth when old enough to understand.

Mugdha told Lakshmi about her past after she turned eighteen. Not the details. Lakshmi hadn't asked for them, content in the loving embrace of the only family she knew — Mum, Dad and her two younger brothers. All that Lakshmi understood about her biological father was that he had moved to Britain before she was born.

Over the years Mugdha learned of Mum's death and then Dad's from a friend who played bridge with Aunt Carrie. In time, Lakshmi befriended her yoga teacher, Riley, who sometimes shared news of 'Lobster' — her Uncle Robbie — in London. Lakshmi would pass snippets of news about me to Mugdha, without knowing of her own connection. Which is how things would have continued in that curious, Zimbabwean way of two degrees of separation. Until I arrived.

'I heard you were only here temporarily for Carrie,' said Mugdha.

'That was the plan,' I confirmed, glancing to the window to where the rain was sheeting down. 'But I haven't been able to bring myself to leave.'

'You were very upset the first time,' Mugdha was sympathetic.

'So was Dad.'

I told her about the night Mum announced we were emigrating. How Kate had stormed to her bedroom and, much later and unable to sleep, I crept to Dad's studio at the back of the garage to hear him weeping.

Transported through the years as she listened,

Mugdha's own composure was threatened. But she lifted herself more upright, determination in her eyes. 'The reason I wanted to see you so urgently,' she said, 'is for Lakshmi. I saw her last night when she came home. She told me you were at the club. You heard her sing. She was so proud that you were there.'

I raised my eyebrows.

'She thinks the world of you.'

'Really?'

'Successful but sensitive. Not like so many money markets people.'

I grimaced. It was what Nick Berkeley used to say.

'I think she needs to know who you are,' she gazed at me directly. 'But how would *you* feel if I told her?'

I was still revelling in the discovery: one that made me happier than I would have imagined. I tried to understand things from Lakshmi's perspective.

'Would it be a problem for her?'

'I'm asking you,' she persisted, eyes fixed on mine with that gleaming energy. 'Would it be a problem for you?'

Thunder sounded across the veldt in a prolonged, extensive drum-roll.

I shook my head. 'The opposite,' I said. 'But opening up the past may not be so great for your husband.'

'My dear Kabir,' emotion tugged at her lips, 'was diagnosed with dementia a year ago. It is progressing fast. I think it's for the best if we don't ...'

What she said explained his reaction on being introduced to me that day at Treasure Trees Apothecary, that look of fearful alarm.

'Okay,' I murmured.

Glancing down, she told me, 'We've had a good life

and grew to love each other — even if it was a different future from the one I dreamed of.'

She brushed her eyes.

'The fantasies of a selfish young girl,' she said. 'When I think about what I put your mother through,' her voice choked with emotion, 'I feel so ashamed.'

I followed her closely.

'I was young and reckless. I didn't have any idea about holding a family together. How important it is to have a stable marriage for the sake of the children. I was interested only in myself. My own whims and excitement. Only years later, when we had boys of our own, I realised what I'd done. How terrible it must have been for your mother.'

I remembered Mum around the time we had moved to Scotland. How I resented her for displacing me from my own exhilarating world with Mandy. Kate actively hated her. Our forlorn father was making amends. Back then, Mum seemed like a rock, determined, unassailable, seeing what needed to be done and seeing it through.

Only recently had I come to understand how it was Mum's inner strength, seldom revealed beneath her genteel exterior, that had held our family together. I remembered, also, the one time she referred to what happened.

It was in Scotland a year or so before she died. She was frail and grey and the two of us were sitting at the narrow galley kitchen table, having tea and shortbread. I told her that Justine and I were going through a difficult patch — Justine had just accepted a job in New York, and I was trying to decide whether to look for a transfer.

'Once you've decided what matters most,' she advised

me after a pause, 'don't let anything get in the way of it.'

I had spent so much time in my head trying to balance all the whys and wherefores that Mum's common sense had sounded like the deepest wisdom.

'If Landers don't come up with anything, it could be tricky,' I replied.

'You may have to move heaven and earth, as I did with your father.' She met my eyes in a way that told me she was referring to that particular time. 'But stick to it. It will work out in the end.'

For Mum, things had worked out. My dad, never again straying, made a life for himself — for them both — in Scotland. Her kumusha. She had returned to civic norms and conventions, to order and decency. She had consigned the threatening, untrammelled wildness of Africa to the past. No longer an island-hopper, she was safely back on the mainland.

I took in the contrite furrows on Mugdha's face. In front of us both were untasted cups of coffee.

'It really was a very long time ago,' I said as the rain rolled on. 'My parents have died. We've changed. At least, I hope so.'

'Not so self-obsessed as when we were young.' There was a glimmer of lightness about her.

'You were quite a lot younger than Dad?' I said.

'Big age gap,' she agreed.

'Yet, you were still drawn to him?'

'It was part of his appeal. Your father wasn't just some ... some love-interest to me,' she told me earnestly. 'He was my guru.'

I was astonished. Of all the many ways that my father had been described over the years, guru had never been among them. Teacher — yes, of course. But guru? Her use of the term, when I was still trying to settle on an understanding of it myself, seemed like remarkable synchronicity.

'You are surprised?'

I didn't have to answer.

'There is a lot of confusion about gurus in the West, but they are part of our culture, as Indians. Guru yoga, *bhakti*, devotion for the teacher, is ingrained in us.' Her gaze deepened to the point that it seemed somehow pervasive, as if able to divine what I most needed to know before she tossed her head, chuckling with merriment, 'You know, guru yoga has a lot less to do with the actual guru than you may think.'

'Really?'

'There may be things about the guru on a human level that you find difficult. That you don't like. Those things don't matter.'

'No?'

'They're coming from the same place as the good you see in the guru.'

'From your mind?'

She nodded. 'You're not practising guru yoga for the guru's benefit. When you find someone you believe has certain admirable qualities, someone with capacities you wish for yourself, you imagine them becoming part of you. Merging with you. Bringing those same qualities to your heart,' she brought a hand to her chest. 'This is what's meant by yoking one's mind to that of the guru. It is to develop the qualities we most yearn for.'

I pondered this for a while, before asking, 'What quality of Dad did you most wish for?'

'His joy,' she said immediately.

I smiled.

'He found joy in what he did, and he shared it with others. This, I think, was his greatest gift. He brought us joy. We loved him well.'

'The guru of joy,' I mused. I had never seen Dad in this light. I was pretty sure that Mum never had. But through Mugdha's eyes I could see how such a thing was possible.

'I hope he was able to find joy in Scotland afterwards?'

I knew I was the only person she had spoken to in nearly forty years who could reliably answer that question. I held her gaze. 'It was difficult in Scotland. The weather. The people. Living in a town instead of the bush. A different way of being. It took him a while. But in the end, he found contentment.'

As gently as I trod, I was confirming what she already suspected. I didn't want to tell her how diminished Dad had been. How constrained he had become moving from free-range to battery-cage hen. Some things were best left unspoken. In the absence of words, she rose from her chair and stood looking through the French doors across the veranda. I stood to be with her.

The joy of Africa has always been of a different order. Unfettered as baboons hooting among the kopjes. Unconstrained as tribal drums throbbing through the night. Elemental as the first rains breaking across parched brown landscapes. But primal exuberance isn't as free as it seems: heartbreak and devastation are never far off. Living among lions comes at a price.

We watched the rain falling — nothing half-hearted even in this — contemplating Dad in the subdued predictability of his life after Africa, calm but constrained. As we stood, Mugdha reached out, taking my hand in hers.

By mid-afternoon the storm had passed. Sometimes it happens like this, the usual afternoon thunderstorm rescheduled without notice for morning. And by the time it ended, the storm clouds had dissolved as unambiguously as they had appeared, revealing a vast sweep of limpid blue above the warm green haze.

Kadiki had spent much of the morning inside. The time was right, I decided, to take her on her first expedition to the dam. Accompanied by Thor and Tiki, we followed the path from the homestead towards Aunt Carrie's, passing the bottom of her garden before venturing into the veldt. While this was unexplored territory for Kadiki, the stretch of bush between the homestead and the dam was home to Debbie, the expectant giraffe, and her sister Kim, and to the kudu herd, to Mampara, and an assortment of impala, duiker, and other creatures. During the dry season many more animals came to live here, near to the life-giving waters captured by the dam wall.

As a teenager, when my parents brought me on family visits to Aunt Carrie and Uncle Adrian, I used to leave them at the house, going to the dam to swim or fish or do nothing in particular. Today as we made our way in the same direction, I recognised landmarks from decades before. It was strange to be in a landscape that felt so familiar, but in such unfamiliar circumstances. Last time I was here, my whole life was ahead of me. Now, with it mostly behind, I was accompanied by an elephant calf, a pair of adopted dogs, and a very different understanding of family.

Only after committing to stay here did I come to this understanding. Only after I let go of the certainties of my previous life was I available to new discovery. Would any of this have happened if I'd returned to London? Or had I needed to loosen my grip on all that felt so secure? Perhaps this was how it worked: Only after you have sufficient trust to let go of the old reality is there sufficient space for a new one to arise.

If it hadn't been for Kadiki I wouldn't have stayed. The cute little elie trotting alongside me, adventurous, frolicking, and yet so completely vulnerable, was the reason I switched tracks. Without her I would have kept doing the same thing I'd always done, because that was what I knew.

I kept a look out for Kim and Debbie on our walk. They were a curiously elusive pair, seldom there when you looked for them and appearing when you least expected, sometimes quite close. Today I caught sight of the distant pair of silhouettes as the two fed from an acacia tree.

We reached the edge of the dam, where vegetation had been eaten or trampled under hoof. A wide, beach-like curve of red sand was scattered with trees and boulders. As I scanned the area, I was glad to see one special boulder still there. In the shade of an ancient Mahobohobo tree, it was sculpted into two lichen-encrusted steps that were perfect for sitting.

Kadiki and the dogs paused, looking across the water. I wondered if she'd ever seen such an expanse before. Then I remembered she'd come from Mana Pools, the four — *mana* — pools that hold water throughout the year, only a short distance away from the great azure sweep of the Zambezi. It was this ancient river and the distant mountains on the Zambian side that cast the unique ethereal haze over the Mana flood plain, an effect so powerful that all who went there sensed the sacredness of the place.

Sinking to my knees, I put my arm around Kadiki as we shared the moment. Was anything suggested to her by the blue expanse? Any early memory triggered of her first days on earth with the herd? She turned her head into my shoulder for a cuddle. I held her to me, forehead to my chest and to the sound of my beating heart. For the longest time we stayed together. *I was home now*, I sensed the message. From whose heart it had emerged was hard to tell.

I thought it best she become familiar with the dam. I began leading her around the perimeter. The dam had been built about seventy years earlier, a modest but sturdy farm embankment. Although the reservoir no longer served its original purpose — the farmlands around here had long been abandoned — it was the centre of its own world of flora and fauna.

That afternoon, we came across clouds of African caper white butterflies. Kadiki ran towards them inquisitively, trunk aloft as they danced. Although they were nothing special to look at, I remembered learning at school that every year African caper whites migrated from Africa to India, the offspring of the original butterflies intuitively understanding migratory direction from parents and grandparents. Part of the eternal exchange between this land and the one of the Buddhas. I wondered how much Kadiki would inherit from her own parents about how to be an elephant, and how much she would have to be taught?

Today's visit was mostly about showing her water. After our leisurely amble, disturbing a few fat-tailed geckos, punch drunk in the sun, we returned to the curved sprawl of the water's edge. Taking off my shoes and rolling up my pants, I waded in.

'Come on, Kadiki! Try it!'

Thor needed little persuasion to venture in. Tiki

yapped excitedly from a boulder at the side. From the water's edge, Kadiki watched me cautiously. She knew only the small pond behind the homestead where the water barely reached her chest.

I got down onto all fours. 'Water isn't just for drinking,' I remembered Tessa telling me as part of what a baby elephant needed to learn. 'It's for life! For fun!' Even on my hands and knees, my cajoling fell on deaf ears. She was unusually still as she studied me.

I tried to shush Tiki, who was getting over-excited as Thor swam closer. When she didn't shut up, I splashed water in her direction with my hand. In an instant, Kadiki was intrigued. She raised her trunk before letting it fall to the surface.

'That's right, Kadeeks!' I encouraged. 'Harder.' I lifted my arm, slamming it to the water. She did the same. The splashing did nothing to stop Tiki's incessant barking, but I didn't care. Kadiki was excited by the new game.

After a while, she took her first few tentative steps, thrashing her head from side to side for extra leverage as she dashed her trunk to the surface. She discovered how she could suck water into her trunk before squirting wherever she chose, blasting both Tiki and me, more by luck than design — at least the first time.

'You little madam!' I splattered her in return.

Soon we had a water fight going on, Kadiki gurgling with laughter as she unleashed spray upon spray around her. The dogs, out-gunned, scrambled to the sidelines, Tiki leaping in after a while, then doggy-paddling to the side. I'd watched families of elephants play in exactly this way, lolling and squirting and romping. It didn't take Kadiki long to find the confidence to wade in deeper, to immerse herself more fully before raising her head to look around.

We played on. Even as the yapping subsided and we stopped splashing one another, and Kadiki relished the simple pleasure of being in water, that afternoon I knew that we had found Kadiki's new favourite place. After a while, drenched in muddy water, I was thinking it might be time to return home when I realised that we were no longer alone. Glancing towards the boulder seat under the Mahobohobo tree, I saw Lakshmi, a glowing intensity about her face.

I climbed out of the pond, adjusting the soaking trousers that clung to me.

'She looks happy in there,' observed Lakshmi as I approached.

I turned to see Kadiki, knee high at the edge, splashing water at the dogs. 'She's an elephant,' I said. 'She just needed to be encouraged to act like one.'

I slipped on my shoes and walked to the boulder. She edged along it, making space for me to sit to her left. When I did, she took my right leg in both hands, tugging up the leg of my soaking pants. She soon revealed the mole. She was wearing a pair of fawn Bermuda shorts. We looked down and both took in the identical moles on our legs.

'Mum told me.' Her eyes burned with incredulity. Disbelief. My feelings, too. We held one another's gaze with an openness that would have been unwelcome before but now was an unaffected shared amazement.

'I only found out last night,' I told her. 'At the jazz club.'

'Because of the mole?'

'Because of what you said about the pendant. "Aum made visible". I knew those were Dad's words. *After* that,' I nodded, 'when you were singing, I saw the mole.'

Wiping my face, I looked ruefully at my mud-smeared hands. 'Not exactly presentable.'

'I don't care,' she reached over to hug me, smudging her face and blouse. 'You got muddy for our little girl. Now I'm muddy *as* well.'

We both gazed at where Kadiki was using a root protruding from the bank as a teething stick, tugging it from side to side in her mouth.

'Our father's words?' she queried.

'He was an art teacher. I don't know if your mum told you?'

'No.' She shook her head. 'It's all pretty hectic. But I want to know everything about him.' She seized my arm, her gaze fervent. 'And you.'

Her impetuosity was so familiar it made me smile. 'You're so much like him!'

'How?'

'Like this,' I gestured toward her expression. 'Dad was always wholehearted. When he made that pendant, he wanted to give your mother the whole universe. Aum made visible. That was him. The grand gesture. The extravagant flourish. He was very musical, you know — a choirmaster. And a showman. He had a great singing voice.'

She was engrossed.

'He would have been so proud of you last night. Those jazz numbers. You performed a few of his favourites.'

'Really?' Her eyes brimmed.

'I've got video clips somewhere I can show you,' I said.

'I'd love that.' She wiped her cheeks with the back of her hands.

'The first time we met, when you brought milk for Kadiki. You were singing "When I Fall in Love" to her.'

She nodded.

'Dad often used to sing it. It reminded me immediately of him. There was this ... this familiarity.'

'Which we thought was because of Landers.'

'We never met at Landers.'

She frowned, disbelieving. I told her how I'd worked things out afterwards. How the dates didn't fit. For a long while we sat on the rock in silence, watching Kadiki and the dogs, coming to grips with the marvel that what we'd found so familiar in one another hadn't been because we'd ever met, but for an even more fundamental reason.

Then Lakshmi turned. 'What I remember about singing "When I Fall in Love" to Kadiki is that you wanted me out.'

As I remembered the afternoon, I knew what she said was true.

'Get out!' She pulled a theatrical scowl, pointing to an imaginary door. 'This is my elephant. Mine, mine, all mine. Skedaddle!'

'Was not like that!' I jabbed her with my elbow.

'Was so!' she teased.

We were both laughing.

'She'd just arrived,' I protested, 'then you come waltzing in with your love songs.'

'Well,' she nodded towards Kadiki, 'she's very lovable.'

'And she'll be getting very hungry soon,' I nodded. 'We better get her home.'

~

As we made our return walk through the bush in procession, Lakshmi spoke about Riley. How they met through yoga, years ago, and sensed an instant bond. They were soon spending time together outside of yoga, getting to know one another's families, sharing meals in each other's homes. How they often remarked on the strangeness that, despite coming from such different backgrounds, they felt so inexplicably connected.

'Even Kate sometimes comments,' said Lakshmi.

'*Even* Kate,' I responded to what she implied in her tone.

She delivered an eye-rolling expression. 'Well, you know what Kate's like.'

'No,' I returned a wry smile. 'Tell me.'

'Just because it turns out we're sisters,' Lakshmi suddenly became a satirical version of her half-sister, 'don't expect me to eat vindaloo!'

I chuckled. 'Seems like you know her as well as I do!'

'Probably do,' agreed Lakshmi.

'She doesn't enjoy a curry?'

'Indian food of any kind,' Lakshmi shook her head. 'Except for Peshwari naan. She'll tolerate that.'

We exchanged a side-long glance and laughed.

'She has a heart of gold. You can always depend on her. But so unemotional. So nuts and bolts about everything!'

'Takes after Mum,' I agreed. 'You and I are more like our father.'

'Willing to take crazy leaps into the unknown?'

I mulled this over for a while. I didn't think of Dad, much less myself, this way. I could see why it might be said, but I'd probably resent the observation unless it was made by someone I was close to. Like a newly discovered sister.

'There's so much to discover about you,' I found myself saying, still giddy from the novelty of finding a sibling so inexpressibly congenial.

I could tell it was the same for her, too.

'You saw it all last night,' she told me. 'Singing is what I do. What I want to do more of. And those people around the table, they're shamwaris.'

'Diva and Herbert,' I recollected. 'The aid workers — Liesel and Sven.'

'And Dennis. Dazzling pianist. He accompanies me sometimes.'

'I thought he was a British diplomat?'

'Spends most of his time doing 'cultural' things,' she said with a cryptic expression.

'Charmed life.'

She shot me a glance as if I wasn't getting it. 'Oh,' I realised. 'Intelligence?'

'An open door to the President, they say.'

'Not very undercover if he's talking directly to his targets,' I was puzzled.

'He isn't spying on the Zimbabwean government!' she said. '*They're* an open book. They don't even bother pretending any more. No, spying on our colonial masters: the Chinese.'

I heard how powerful China had become in Africa, offering governments loans for infrastructure that, when inevitably defaulted on, would be renegotiated to include a military presence.

Remembering our group from the night before, I said, 'I like your partner, Simba. He was such a help getting Kadiki from the plane.'

'He told me.'

The large, soft-spoken man was jovial when I'd sat next to him last night, but beneath the banter I had sensed a reserve.

'Good company,' I said. 'But it feels like he keeps

people at arm's length.'

Her eyes widened. 'You're a good judge of character.'

'A Saints guy?' I recalled her telling me he'd gone to Harare's prestigious St George's High School. 'What did he do after that?'

'Ruskin in Oxford.'

'Wow!' Just being accepted by Ruskin School of Art in Britain was extraordinary. 'His work must be amazing!'

'I told him about your family interest in Shona sculpture. How you had one by Henry Munyaradzi. He was impressed. Most Zimbabweans wouldn't even know the name.'

'Does he have a studio?'

'He's very private.' Lakshmi was hesitant.

'I know some artists don't like having strangers poking about where they work,' I backed off. 'I can wait for his next exhibition.'

'He has one in California next year.'

'Nothing local?'

'Keeps a low profile here. He doesn't want to be known.' She shot me an anguished expression before finally saying, 'The thing is, he's really ashamed of his family.'

'Oh.'

'Doesn't want people to know about them.'

I raised my eyebrows, wondering if his talent had propelled him beyond the orbit of distressingly humble origins. But wasn't that true of so many artists?

'Please don't tell anyone. His father is Hastings Dube.'

General Hastings Dube was one of the most powerful and corrupt despots in the government.

I was aghast. 'How on earth could someone like Simba ...?'

'The people at the top,' she said. 'The twenty or thirty families who run this place, they want the best for their kids. They send them to the top schools and overseas universities. Which is where the children learn the truth. For someone like Simba, whose cultural roots run so deep, it's a real conflict.'

She took in my dismay.

'He does his best to live a separate life. To keep the connection quiet.'

I remembered Tinashe's odd behaviour last night. How, instead of sitting in the empty chair beside Simba, he'd moved to take the seat next to Liesel and Sven. 'Last night, Tinashe seemed a bit nervous around Simba.'

'Exactly,' she sighed, 'Tinashe knows. Problem is, so do others.'

I shook my head. 'How does Simba cope?'

'The Dharma helps,' she said. 'And he says his work is a form of meditation. More than anything, That's what keeps him sane.'

~

We ended that most extraordinary of days sitting together against the stable wall. Kadiki, exhausted from her very first swim, made short work of dinner before settling on the straw, head nuzzled between our legs. The dogs, similarly replete, were soon dozing. Through the warm December night, marimbas thrummed tinnily from a staff cottage radio above a rhapsody of Christmas beetles.

Beside me, holding my phone, Lakshmi watched my videos of Dad, clips going back to Peterhouse days, conducting a full choir in spirited concerts. Cabaret-style performances showing Dad backed by a handful of musicians, singing jazz standards. When he began 'Have Yourself a Merry Little Christmas', she looked up, eyes wet with tears.

She didn't have to say anything. There were no words for the connection. I reached my arm around her shoulders and hugged her to me. 'You are here to connect with your family and your true purpose,' Rinpoche had told me in the garden.

I hadn't known what he meant, exactly. I had thought he was talking about a metaphorical family. Never would I have guessed at the literal truth. What I felt with Lakshmi was like nothing I'd ever experienced before, a newly discovered glittering jewel with so many facets to explore.

As for my true purpose, that was still a work in progress. Being parent to an elephant calf. Creating an orphan herd who could live independently in the wild. Setting up a bakery to pay the bills of an animal sanctuary. Of much greater importance was my understanding that, central to this all, was Rinpoche himself.

'Guru yoga is a lot less to do with the actual guru than you may think,' Mugdha had said. 'You're not practising guru yoga for the guru's benefit. When you find someone you believe has certain admirable qualities, someone with capacities you wish for yourself, you imagine them becoming part of you. Merging with you. Bringing those same qualities to your heart. This is what's meant by yoking one's mind to that of the guru. It is to develop the qualities we most yearn for.'

From the moment my eyes first met those of Yogi Tarchin, I'd sensed in him the most extraordinary capacities. More than anyone I knew, he saw the world as a place of enchantment, a place where even a cup of coffee in the morning sun felt exalted.

He was free with his wisdom: Reality arises from mind, and the more virtuous the mind, the more immaculate the reality. If I hadn't met him, I would never have believed such a stunningly simple yet challenging premise. But I had met him and had caught a glimpse of the sublimity he saw. Accepting his advice of service to others — in my own case, to the little elephant beside me — took a direction I could have never predicted.

And what a reality!

I felt a perfection sitting on the straw this summer night, with exquisite little Kadiki beside me, the tip of her trunk curled possessively about my leg and her reassuringly earthy tang in my nostrils. In my jazz singer sister and her whole world, her mandala, such an unforeseen but enlivening presence. Watching Lakshmi follow Dad on the phone, and recalling how Mugdha thought of him, revised my memories in an unexpected way. No longer the somewhat forlorn figure sitting in a thick Aran sweater in his Inverness art room, but a guru of joy, galvanising love and inspiration at this very moment.

For us, there was no other moment, nor any other place, as a breeze whispered in the flower-studded limbs of the marula tree, casting ribbons of ethereal citrus through the darkness. And as the trill of nightjars rose and fell amid a symphony of cicadas, never had the world felt more transcendent, nor our hearts more filled with wonder.

Chapter Twelve

THE DAYS THAT FOLLOWED were as ephemeral and ever shifting as the drama of the summer sky. The festive season was in full swing, everyone in a hurry to meet the looming Christmas deadline, whether to buy gifts or finish work projects. Gatherings and reunions happened spontaneously.

The lucky few of Zimbabwe's diaspora returned home. Standing in the grocery checkout line at Spar Ruwa, or watching passers-by at Café Nush, I learned to recognise the signs of dazed relief on the faces of those who had emerged from the grim northern winter where they'd been saving hard-earned pounds.

'BBC', they kept saying, was where they'd been working. Not the broadcaster, I soon discovered, but an ironic local euphemism — "British Bum Care". Like other developing nations, Zimbabwe was a fount of caregivers for the first-world elderly, willing to undertake the work their foreign peers couldn't be paid enough to do. But arriving home with their savings: *eish*! How wonderful to be back this side, in the sunlit kumusha once more!

At Ruwa Buddhist Society, the temple was fully

thatched, construction work almost complete. All that remained was for the electric cables to bring power to the site to be connected at the house. Mr Nzou attended to the landscaping around the temple, creating new garden beds filled with shrubs and colourful flowers. Gogo was readying the homestead bedrooms and the second guest rondavel for the influx of visitors coming to the refuge ceremony in early January, her domestic tasks punctuated by the occasional cry of triumph when the *New York Times*, no less, declared her to be 'Magnificent!' for cracking words like PLUMP in just three lines!

The flow of emails about the ceremony continued. The number of people from around Southern Africa wanting to join burgeoned by the day. Then there were the invoices from sub-contractors on the temple job, all demanding payment by Christmas. On the London front, there were trusts for me to exit before people left work for the year. At Aunt Carrie's, I sorted out the main bedroom in readiness for Kay; I had asked her to visit for Christmas and stay on for the refuge ceremony.

~

She arrived shortly after nine am, having left Nyanga soon after sunrise. In mid-summer, she told me, it was her favourite time of day to travel, the early morning drive from the distant mountains to Ruwa taking her through high veldt vistas of pristine light.

After we breakfasted together and she'd had time to settle in, the dogs and I led her along the path to the homestead. I knew how much she wanted to meet Rinpoche and my indigenous animal companions. I was equally intrigued to see how they would respond to her.

When we reached the lawn, I spotted Bodhi sprawled on a granite boulder between the temple and Ruwa

Rock and knew where we'd find Yogi Tarchin. The dogs raced into the bush in futile pursuit of guinea fowl as we headed towards the new building.

He was alone in the middle of the temple as we approached, using the pathway that curved past Mr Nzou's recently planted flowerbeds. At each of the four corners of the building, the thatch curved almost to the ground, creating sweeping arcs along each side, with the entrance an impressive doorway framed by a granite boulder wall. Even though there was nothing to suggest the building's purpose — not a single Buddha statue, thangka, nor meditation cushion — beneath the vaulted roof, the space was a natural sanctuary.

Rinpoche turned as we stepped inside.

'I'd like you to meet my godmother, Kay,' I said.

My words were superfluous. Already both knew about the other. As their eyes and hands met there was a palpable connection of the heart. Along with it, a sense of culmination, of inevitability, that the person who first introduced me to the Dharma was now meeting my guru here at this temple in the veldt.

Rinpoche made a sweeping gesture with his hand, an effortless curve encompassing the *gompa*, with its clean thatch aroma and undertone of creosote, and more broadly the place where we were standing. He began showing Kay how a Buddha statue would be positioned, along with other wall-hangings and emblems. Where the teaching throne would go. How mats would be arranged on the floor in rows, meditation cushions on top of them. I knew all this from the building plans, but to have it brought to life by Rinpoche felt like the fulfilment of a plan, the flowering of potentialities in play far longer than could be imagined.

'Of course, this one,' he gestured towards me, 'is organising everything.'

It's true I was in charge of the refuge ceremony, and some of the important finishes to the temple — not least of them the delivery of carpets and cushions on which our visitors were to sit.

'When the statues arrive from India in a few months, he'll be arranging the materials for consecration.'

This was the first I'd heard of it. I hadn't even been aware that 'consecration' was needed.

'My young man has always been good at managing things,' said Kay.

'Yes, yes,' nodded Rinpoche. 'The temple. Refuge for elephants and the other sem chens. Very busy around the back,' he pointed in the direction of the tobacco barn where he had taken me days before.

Rinpoche and Kay exchanged a knowing look, and it was as if the two of them had been conspirators all this time without me realising. Then Rinpoche pointed out the tracks of Bodhi and Kadiki on the polished floor leading from the entrance right to where the Buddha was to sit. 'By special appointment!' he chuckled.

'Unique!' marvelled Kay.

'Oh, yes! The fastest sem chen and the largest. Both showing the way to *moksha*, to satori.'

'To enlightenment,' chimed Kay.

'Quite so.'

~

He took her left hand and, holding it between his own, led her towards the *gompa* entrance. They gazed up the immaculate lawn to where the Tibetan prayer flags rippled under the trimmed reeds of the homestead.

'Tell me, my dear,' he looked into her eyes. 'You can live anywhere in the world: Britain, Europe, America. Why do you choose to live here?'

'It's the place,' she replied spontaneously. Her answer

felt self-evident, and at this very moment it was the only explanation required.

'You feel it here. Also at Nyanga,' she continued after a while. 'I do hope you will come to visit our sacred mountains. There you don't really have to meditate. Meditation comes to you. When you look out into pure space it's somehow easier to let go of thought. The boundlessness of Buddha nature arises right before you.'

'You live with it all the time,' nodded Rinpoche.

'I think it affects the people,' she agreed. 'When you live closer to nature. In accord with impermanence. For modern people there's something child-like about being content to live for the day. Irresponsible, even. It's the opposite of our ferocious grasping to have and to build. But in Africa we are continually reminded to live fully each day.'

Rinpoche led the way from the *gompa*. I glanced to see Bodhi watching from the boulder. Stretching so luxuriously that all four limbs quivered, she yawned, incisors flashing white in her wide pink mouth. She sensed that we were on the move, or more particularly, that Rinpoche was. Scraping her stomach towards to the round edge of the boulder, she dangled her front paws down kitten-like, before sliding from the rock into the long grass with a final shove.

As she disappeared into the bush, there was movement ahead of us. From around the side of the homestead came the distinctive silhouette of Kadiki, accompanied moments later by Lakshmi. Raising a hand to her face in the sun, my sister looked towards us, a smile appearing on her face. The simple gesture felt familial.

I had, of course, told Kay all about Lakshmi, as well as my encounter with Mughda. Now, Kadiki was raising her trunk and sniffing the air with a curious excitement, taking in the presence of a newcomer. She began to trot, then charge in our direction.

Elephants of all sizes can move surprisingly fast. Elephant calves in full flow with their flapping ears seem almost about to fly! With the length of the lawn ahead of her, Kadiki's ears waved as she made her exhilarated stampede. Thor and Tiki appeared from the flowerbeds to scamper at her side. Long before she reached us, Rinpoche, Kay, and I were laughing at her unbridled elation.

And as she rounded behind us and came in for a cuddle, I told her, 'Yes, Kadeeks! This is Kay. Who you know all about!'

Kay bent to touch the rugged grooved skin of her elephant face and the contrasting cool smooth flatness of her ears. Searching with her trunk, Kadiki opened the tip of it wide near Kay's face, inhaling her. Then exhaling. And with the exhalation, dispensing a dose of muddy wet.

'Elephant kiss,' I told Kay.

'I don't mind,' she giggled, wiping her face with the back of her arm, while stroking the criss-crossed furrows and wiry bristles of Kadiki's trunk. 'An honour!'

'None higher!' I agreed.

I wasn't just saying it; it felt true. Kadiki was tilting her face to take in Kay, while reaching behind Kay's neck with her trunk. Kadiki's curiosity was unconstrained as she tugged the new arrival closer. Such attention from an elephant felt unlike anything else.

Lakshmi walked to us and I introduced her to Kay. Both of them dishevelled from Kadiki's attentions, as they took each other in, it felt apt that they were meeting not only in the presence of Rinpoche, but also with Kadiki tugging variously at their arms and legs. Sublime and mundane drawn into a singular moment.

We walked to the homestead, Kadiki chewing on a teething stick that she found lying on the lawn as Mbudzi bounded to join us from beneath the flamboyant tree. One of the flame-coloured blossoms caught between horn and ear, he bucked about like a crazed flamenco dancer.

Kay and Lakshmi were soon talking about elephant care, and I left them to give Kadiki a feed as Rinpoche and I stepped inside — Rinpoche to his office and ceaseless calls to students and other centres, and I to mine — and the various opportunities he gave me to emulate him. 'Serve others.' His message was never far from my thoughts. 'That's the main point — the pathway to bliss!'

~

I hosted Christmas lunch. The idea started with Kay and me preparing a meal for Rinpoche. My sister Kate and husband Johan always spent Christmas with his family in Cape Town, so I was free of any obligation to spend time with them. Before I knew it, Kay had told Lakshmi, who wanted to join us, her Hindu family not observing Christmas. Mughda, whose food was excellent, offered to cook. Because Tinashe would be on his own, his mother travelling to spend the day with her eldest brother, we invited him too. Diva and Herbert Derembwe always hosted Harris at Christmas but when they heard about our plans, they suggested we have a joint celebration. When Riley and Luke got wind of what was happening, they decided that they too would rather come to us, instead of going to Luke's family at Kariba.

So in the days leading up to Christmas, along with all the other plans, we prepared for our own festivities.

Arrangements for the food courses, whether they were to be cooked in the kitchen or elsewhere. Drinks, decorations and festive treats. Which matching dining tables and chairs were to be put on the veranda. It was more than the gathering of family — with Rinpoche coming, we wanted to make sure that everything was, as Mum would have put it, "just so".

~

Two afternoons before Christmas, Harris knocked on my office door. Rinpoche had gone into town, and while he was out, Harris explained, he needed to turn off the electricity for the connection of the temple power line.

A bit later, I went outside to investigate. The homestead electrical panel was in a garage behind the homestead. With the same foresight that had seen him sell his land off well before the farm seizures, John Elliott had installed solar panels around the back of his property, together with a battery. It was as if he had known in advance that everyone would need their own power source.

Inside the garage I saw Harris with Mr Buba, the same electrician who had come to check on Aunt Carrie's solar system. Some of his men were installing a new smaller panel alongside the existing one. During the morning, a straight narrow trench had been dug all the way to the temple and a white plastic cable duct laid in it.

I was surveying the neat line of cut turf, carefully replaced after the excavation, when Harris came outside, brushing a snowy lock from his face. 'Should be back up in half an hour.'

'Reliable guy, Mr Buba,' I gestured behind him.

'Mm,' he nodded knowingly. 'A Lemba.'

The Lemba were quite different from other Zimbabwean tribes, with their own customs and traditions.

'The Lemba know about power?'

'In many forms,' he replied, enigmatically.

I gestured the line in the ground. 'Our own special meridian?'

'Indeed!'

'I had an interesting chat with Tinashe,' I said, 'about 31 degrees East. He told me the African legend of an underground river that runs all the way down the African continent. As a geologist, do you think there's any literal truth to it?'

'I wouldn't dismiss it out of hand.' Harris was contemplative. 'Even though we are such a mineral-rich part of the world, there is so much we haven't fully explored, the Chinhoyi Cave complex being one example.'

'So, the underground river myth isn't a reference to the 31 East meridian?'

'I imagine it's an intuitive response to something we're only starting to understand,' he replied. 'You see, 31 East is the centre of the landmasses. All the other continents are drifting away a couple of inches each year. Africa, we used to think, sat on its own tectonic plate. But in recent times, geologists began to realise that we have it wrong. Instead of being the stable centre, 31 East is where the final tectonic shift is happening. As became dramatically apparent in 2018.'

From my blank expression he saw that I had no idea what he was talking about.

'An enormous crack appeared in the ground in southwestern Kenya. A sudden tear in the earth's surface that swallowed a whole section of the Nairobi highway.'

'The Rift Valley,' I nodded. 'We learned about it at school.'

'The rift is coming all the way down Africa, like a zipper,' he said, eyes intense with significance. 'Where African legend talks about a river.'

'Wow!' I tried imagining the shape of the Africa I was familiar with, dividing into two.

'One day,' his eyes twinkled, 'Ruwa may be a seaside resort.'

'One day?'

'No need to panic. Millions of years from now. In the meantime, we're at the centre of some of the most exciting tectonic activity on earth. Anyone with an interest in how planets evolve is keeping an eye on it.'

I remembered that other part of my conversation with Tinashe. 'Including visitors from other parts of the universe?' I probed.

'*Especially* such visitors,' he replied with relish. 'You know, we humans are so stuck inside our own limited view of reality that we find it hard to imagine a different one. We read stories in the Dharma about humans spending a couple of hours, say, in a Buddha land, before coming home to find that fifty years have gone by. But what if they aren't just stories?'

He warmed to what was evidently a favourite theme. 'What if there are beings for whom time has a completely different meaning? Who live outside our narrow understanding of days and weeks? For whom the fastest velocity is not the speed of light, but the speed of thought? And what if they have an interest in how other planets evolve?'

'I'm open minded about it,' I shrugged. 'But some people warn that if extra-terrestrials were to visit, it would probably be to exploit us.'

'If they've made it this far,' Harris was wry, 'they probably don't need anything *we* have to offer. I'd say that if anyone's doing the exploiting, it's us. That was the warning they gave the kids at Ariel School.'

The message, he told me, recorded by a cameraman interviewing the children soon after their otherworldly visitors, had been received via powerful telepathy and was clear: 'You're destroying your own planet — stop polluting it!'

'You know,' he continued, 'when Rinpoche asked me about the full moon club on Ruwa Rock, he said something that stopped me in my tracks. According to the *Abhidharmakośa*, there are at least one hundred thousand planets in the universe with intelligent life similar to us. If we accept that possibility, then being born as an intelligent being on earth is not in any way inevitable. Statistically you might even say that it's quite unlikely.'

He fixed me with a gaze of warm conviction. 'There are many more planets and realms of existence than we can fathom. And if we've existed since beginningless time, we've possibly lived on many of them.'

'You're saying,' I caught up with him, 'that in past lives, we've all been born elsewhere. That some time or another, although we can't remember it, we may have been little green men?'

'That's the gist,' he chuckled. 'But if you accept the possibility, it makes the idea of extra-terrestrials seem a little less outlandish.'

'Because we've all of us been extra-terrestrials ourselves?'

An oracular look in his clear blue gaze, Harris nodded. Not for the first time, as I came away from a conversation with him, it was with a new, mind-spinning perspective.

~

When Christmas morning came I was in the stable with Kadiki. The day had no special significance for her, but it felt somehow right for us to wake together and venture into the dawn, and that I should give her the first feed of the day.

Heading home with the dogs, I got there to find Kay in the kitchen making pancakes for breakfast. Lakshmi arrived soon after, and it wasn't long before the three of us were sitting at a small garden table on the lawn, each of us slipping Kadiki handfuls of blueberries from the table. 'Elephant chocolates' as we came to know them.

We talked about the miracle of finding one another, of how, even a few months ago, the four of us sharing Christmas breakfast would have been an impossibility. It was Rinpoche who brought this precious reality into being.

'He is a true lama,' observed Kay. Then as Lakshmi and I both turned to her. 'Lama,' she repeated. 'In Tibetan, "la" means "high" — in this case, high wisdom or knowledge. "Ma" means "mother". In the mammalian world,' she said, stroking Kadiki's face tenderly, 'a mother feeds us milk from her own body. She nurses us and gives us love. She cleans up our mess and watches over us when we are sick. She is the one who takes care of us until we can stand on our own feet.

'In the spiritual world it is the lama who gives birth to our capacity for higher wisdom. Who nourishes our inner growth when we are helpless and can do little except make a mess of things.'

Following her intently, Lakshmi and I smiled.

'The lama mothers us until we have some inner maturity. Until we can take care of ourselves and one day, hopefully, others.'

In the blue morning a pair of fiscal shrikes frolicked among the rain-tipped poinsettia flowers.

'It's actually quite awesome,' I said after a while, 'how much the lama gives without any thought of a return.' I couldn't help contrasting this attitude with the usual calculations of my work at Landers. 'But,' I shrugged, 'how is it even possible to repay a mother?'

A glint appeared in Lakshmi's eyes. 'I tried, once. As a little girl, for Mother's Day. All the kids in our classes made lanyards for our mothers out of different-coloured plastic wires. I was about eight years old and intense about wanting to give Mum something back for all she'd done for me. The best I could do was a lanyard! I still remember presenting her with it on Mother's Day.'

As we chuckled, Kay said, 'I am sure you made her very happy?'

'Oh yes,' agreed Lakshmi. 'She really did seem to treasure it. She wore it for a long time afterwards. She still has it, I think, somewhere.'

'It's not the token itself but the state of heart it comes from,' observed Kay. 'That's what counts.'

After breakfast, there was furniture to move, a fridge to set up, and decorations to be arranged. I had long since given up on the idea of trying to manage what was about to happen. Between Diva and Mugdha, Christmas lunch was taken care of. I didn't even have the job of putting people at their ease; just about everyone coming knew the others far better than they knew me. As for our honoured guest, Rinpoche, the only thing you could expect around him was the unexpected.

Riley and Luke were the first to arrive, which I was glad about. I had already called Kate, as was our custom, to wish her "Happy Christmas". During the conversation I told her about Dad, Mugdha Kumar, and Lakshmi. She was every bit as unexcited as I thought she would be, regarding it as a curiosity from the past and of little current relevance. When I asked if she'd mind me telling Riley, she told me to go ahead. I knew that Lakshmi was impatient for me to do so.

Guiding Riley and Luke to the lawn, I told them everything. I had wondered if Riley would be overcome with emotion, perhaps, or too shocked to respond. In the event, she was neither.

'So, Lobster, you're saying that Granddad Euan and Mrs. Kumar ...' her eyes gleamed, trying to make sense of the coupling.

'*Before* she was Mrs. Kumar,' I noted.

'She must have been very young?'

I nodded.

'So that makes Lakshmi to me ...'

Beside her, Luke watched with wry amusement. 'Your old lady's step-sister, hey,' he said, drolly. 'Your aunty.'

'But there's only three years between us!'

~

At that moment, Lakshmi stepped onto the veranda. Seeing the three of us huddled, she hurried over.

'I knew it!' Riley threw her arms about her.

'We've always said,' agreed Lakshmi, at her shoulder.

The two of them looked rapturous.

I met Luke's eyes happily as we watched them hugging.

Riley said in an exaggerated tone, '*Aunty* Lakshmi.'

'You!' Lakshmi pulled away from her, with an expression of *faux* indignation. 'I knew you'd use it against me!'

~

The others came, bountiful with food. Diva and Herbert, laden with goodies for the kitchen — we had a strict 'no gifts' policy, but that didn't include culinary delights. Mugdha Kumar next, equally laden. Out the corner of my eye, I noticed how she and Kay stood close together on the veranda, their first conversation — could this really be? — since they'd last rested in Shavasana together, forty years before.

Tinashe walked down the driveway, his typically still self, but looking somehow more relaxed than usual. As I helped him to a drink, I realised I hadn't spoken to him since the night of the jazz club.

'Did you give your mum those flame lilies?' I asked.

'Oh yes!' he flashed the widest smile.

'And?'

The ceramic pot of flame lilies turned out not to be the random gift it seemed. When he gave it to his mum, her gratitude was mixed with another more powerful emotion. Eyes filling with tears, she told him to sit before announcing she had something to confess. Something that had been in her thoughts for months, years, but the right moment to speak of it never came.

She told him about his father's father, the *n'anga*. That she had lied about him being dead because she'd never wanted to lose Tinashe to that side of the family. How remorseful she felt because Mufudzi Jamba — for that was his grandfather's name — was not a bad man.

His son was filled with chicanery and deceit, but the *n'anga* himself had never done wrong.

He even visited to commiserate after her son had abandoned her and little Tinashe, leaving them destitute. Despite being poor himself, Mr Jamba gave her some money. He also brought her a gift he had grown for her especially: a pot of flame lilies in full bloom. They were a symbol of resilience, he said. Just as the flame lily survived the harsh dry conditions of winter before coming back into full bloom, she would too.

After she finished, lips quivering, hardly able to face her son, Tinashe took her hands in his and shared his story about being caught in a downpour and having to jump-start the car of an elderly man who spoke to him about his friend, the elderly n'anga. How Tinashe realised it must be his own grandfather of whom he spoke. How Rinpoche told him to buy flame lilies for his mother.

As he finished his own, astonishing story, she turned to face him. 'It is a sign!' she exclaimed.

'So you see,' said Tinashe, expression bright. 'Very soon I will soon be meeting grandfather Mafudzi — with mother's blessing!'

Gathering with the others on the veranda and waiting for our guest of honour to arrive, I reflected that what had started out as an idea for a neighbourly lunch, a way of sharing a traditional Christmas meal with Rinpoche, had evolved into something bigger. As Lakshmi set up background music on a speaker, as Harris arrived with books on Shona culture for Rinpoche to read, as Diva and Kay handed round tasty canapes and I poured drinks, we were all acting from the same impulse. Each one of us owed Yogi Tarchin the most profound gratitude. We wanted to thank him.

When he came to us soon after, he was alone.

Seeing him in the garden, I wondered where Bodhi was before realising that the noise and people around the house would have caused her to avoid us. No doubt she was watching from afar.

Rinpoche was serene as ever, subtly shifting the mood to one of playful awareness and light. He spent time with Kadiki in the garden, before greeting each of the human guests. He took the seat allocated to him at the head of the table and accepted his role as principal guest with equanimity. We agreed that today was to be a casual occasion, but after Herbert and I helped Diva and Mugdha serve the starters, in the pause that followed, I said, 'Rinpoche, on behalf of everyone, thank you so much for all that you've done for us. The last few months have been ... have been life-changing.'

Amid the murmurs of agreement, Yogi Tarchin raised his glass with a smile. 'Thank you, Robbie, and everyone. We are interdependent, yes? We are all changing. The important thing is to change in the optimal way,' he chuckled. 'Now is not the time for speeches, so let me just say: "Do good. Be happy. We're not here for long"!'

'Do good,' we repeated, spontaneously. 'Be happy! We're not here for long!'

We began eating, and talk resumed. I glanced up and down the table to make sure that everyone had what they needed. As I did, I caught Mugdha's eye doing the same thing. We exchanged a smile. My gaze moved from her to Lakshmi, taking in everyone around the table and further, to the garden where Kadiki and Mbudzi were mock-stampeding the dogs. I thought how extraordinarily different this was to where I would have been sitting, and what I would have been doing at this very moment, had I returned to London.

~

It was an impromptu event that turned out to be the most poignant. We had finished our starters and cleared away the plates. Diva and Mugdha were in the kitchen putting their finishing touches to the main course when, from behind the house, Mr Nzou appeared, more formally attired than most of us in that suit and tie.

I had invited him to lunch earlier in the week, but he told me that he, Ezekiel, and Gogo were returning to the village for their traditional family meals. He also turned down the offer of a lift there. They would rather walk on Christmas day, as was their custom. I went to greet him and he explained that they were setting off together. But first he wanted to see Rinpoche.

Chatter around the table subsided as he stepped up to the veranda, people greeting him and wishing him a happy Christmas. For his part, Mr Nzou walked to the end of the table with the unhurried deliberation of his clan totem. Approaching Rinpoche, he bowed, palms together at his heart in the Buddhist manner.

'Happy Christmas, Rinpoche,' he said. 'I want to thank you for all that you have done for me and for our community. Thank you for giving us rain!'

His words were heartfelt and by now everyone was listening. It was as if, in both style and substance, Mr Nzou spoke for us all. Conveying exactly what we wished, and in the way we most wished to say it.

'I am not rich,' he told Rinpoche. 'But there is something small I made for you.'

He reached into his pocket, and I saw a flash of red as he handed something to the lama. Rinpoche looked into the palm of his hand with an expression of rapture so great it seemed immediately to envelop everyone around the table.

'Lucky beans?' he confirmed, eyes alight.

'Yes, sir.'

Rinpoche held up a wrist mala that Mr Nzou had fashioned from only the reddest, roundest beads, polished to perfection, complete with guru bead and tassel. Folding his hands and blowing blessings onto it, the lama held the mala to Mr Nzou's forehead and recited mantras, blessing him too. Eyes closed, Mr Nzou's expression was one of the most profound devotion.

Then Rinpoche slipped the mala onto his left wrist, before holding it up for Mr Nzou and all of us to admire.

'Now I have an African mala!' he beamed.

'Africa mala for the Africa Buddha!' confirmed Mr Nzou.

My eyes were drawn to Lakshmi's, and then both of us looked to Kay as we recalled the story of the lanyard that she shared earlier. The lanyard had been her gift, as an eight-year-old, wanting to repay her mother for her kindness. 'It's not the token itself so much as the state of heart it comes from,' Kay had said. 'That's what counts.'

That was what counted now, not only for Mr Nzou and Rinpoche, but for us all. It had taken an elder of Clan Elephant, the rainmaker, to remind us that we weren't repaying the kindness of any ordinary being, but that of a Buddha.

As we sat around the table that afternoon, Rinpoche's radiance with Mr Nzou's gift pervaded us all with a palpable energy. Standing tall before us, eyes shut and palms held at his heart, Mr Nzou was no longer John Elliott's bent and scraggy groundsman, but a figure of more blissful stature and radiance than would ever have seemed possible.

~

A short while later, I walked up the driveway with Rinpoche and Mr Nzou to bid farewell to the rainmaker. Ezekiel and Gogo were waiting where the driveway joined the dirt road. I brought Christmas fruit pies and other goodies from our now over-stocked kitchen for them to share with the village. We waved them goodbye.

The afternoon was vibrant with chirring insects and bird calls. Carried on the breeze from beneath the lone winter thorn tree, loudest of all were the raised voices of the white-clad church goers, the largest crowd I'd ever seen, singing and dancing as they performed 'Jerusalema' on the most joyful of holy days.

'These ones are called?' Rinpoche wanted to know.

'Apostolics.' I told him the little I knew about the church.

'And this 'Jerusalema' song. Very popular. What is its meaning?'

'The lyrics are quite simple,' I said. 'It's about how their place is not here, it is in Jerusalem. They ask God to walk with them there.'

I always found the meaning to be sorrowful, an expression of disillusionment with the world, and the idea that all that could be hoped for was some future paradise. But as Rinpoche paused, he seemed more focused on the elated voices, the soaring spirits.

'Like us,' he smiled after a while. 'Same, same. When the heart is filled with virtue,' his eyes met mine with that all-embracing benevolence, 'reality is divine.'

Epilogue

RUWA BUDDHIST SOCIETY was glorious in its summer finery as we prepared for the refuge ceremony. Mr Nzou had trimmed the lawn to billiard-table perfection. The flower beds teemed pink with hibiscus and half a dozen vivid shades of impatiens. Mampara and his kudu mates had munched through the row of sunflowers we'd been doing our utmost to prevent Kadiki from demolishing. Nevertheless, the overall effect of the combination of established garden beds and new ones was one of verdant elegance.

After much cleaning, repairing, painting, and resealing, the homestead, according to Diva, was in a better state than even when John Elliott had lived here. In preparing the catering and bedrooms, we were readying ourselves for our visitors. We wanted them to be happy and comfortable, of course. More than that, we wanted to please Rinpoche.

On the day of the ceremony, visitors began arriving from across sub-Sahara Africa. From South Africa and Congo, from Mozambique and Zambia and the remotest pockets of our own country, they converged.

I saw to it that guests staying overnight were shown to their bedrooms. Liesel and Sven, the aid workers, were on hand to help. In the kitchen, Gogo was in her element cooking, chatting, 'Swing Low Sweet Chariot'-ing, quickly putting a pair of early-arriving Congolese in aprons when she discovered they'd worked in a Marseilles restaurant. Harris, in a white Panama hat, bustled about the place checking on power across the broader Ruwa Buddhist Society campus, while Mr Nzou's constant surveillance of the car park was rewarded when a shiny Pajero pulled up and from behind the driving seat emerged Success Domba, the fabled rainmaker of Manicaland, resplendent in Raybans.

Watching people step onto the lawn for the first time, wide-eyed, was like seeing anew the homestead, on which Sonny and Cher maintained their stately vigil and, in the other direction, the ancient sentinel of Ruwa Rock, the temple nestling under its protection.

I had arranged for Ezekiel, a devout Apostolic, to take Kadiki and the dogs to the dam that day, so she wouldn't be disturbed by the crowd. I had also asked Diva and Riley to be greeters near the car park, while Tinashe, Lakshmi, and Kay settled people once they got to the *gompa*.

As the time to begin drew closer, with more and more people arriving, it was evident just how unprecedented today's event really was. Never had the Congo Buddhists met the South Africans, or the Mozambiquans left their own country. Visitors from across the continent, drawn by Rinpoche, were meeting one another for the first time. We'd started with fewer than thirty people — the Ruwa Buddhist Society members — but our list of attendees had grown to four times that number.

It was equally apparent that there was no Buddhist 'type' in Africa. There were men, women, old, young, and all ethnicities. But whether they wore crystals and nose rings, bush khakis or more regular clothes, there was a deference about them, and an anticipation. This was no ordinary meeting.

Shortly before eleven, Diva walked to Rinpoche's rondavel to collect him. With Kay on one side of me and Lakshmi on the other, we found ourselves cushions in the *gompa* several rows from the front. Inside the temple, the only decoration was a single thangka of Shakyamuni Buddha. The only furniture was a raised wooden platform at the front designed to serve as a teaching throne. Even so, beneath the soaring lines and fresh gold thatch, the space had a sacredness that shushed conversation. There was an unspoken but shared sense that our time together was rare.

We stood as he arrived. Walking up the aisle in the centre, the one on which both Kadiki and Bodhi had left their permanent impressions, he met the gazes of those on both sides, eyes bright and palms at his heart. At the front he prostrated before the thangka of Shakyamuni.

Sitting in meditation posture, gaze lowered, he invited us into a state of relaxed presence. Even though we were mostly strangers, in that stillness I felt a merging of minds, a meeting of hearts, all of us coming together with a shared purpose beyond expression.

Rinpoche recited the lines of refuge and *bodhichitta* that had been chanted in Himalayan temples through the centuries. He invited us to imagine Shakyamuni Buddha not as a mere painting in front of us, but vividly real, like a hologram in the nature of light. He was floating in space at about the height of our foreheads a short distance ahead and gazing at us with as much love as a mother for her child. As we took refuge, said Rinpoche, we were doing so in the presence of innumerable bodhisattvas. In becoming children of the Buddhas, we were welcomed into the family of those on the path to enlightenment, as "noble sons" and "noble daughters".

'Today, we are here to take refuge,' he said. 'Why? Because we wish to end dissatisfaction — dukkha — our own and others.' We take refuge in the Buddha and his teachings which reveal how to do this, and we also take refuge in our own Buddha nature. Because like Shakyamuni,' he gestured toward the thangka, stirring slowly in the breeze behind him, 'our primordial nature is boundless and pristine. The basis of enduring bliss.'

He explained how the start of our inner journey often begins with the wish to bring an end to personal pain. While that can have so many different causes, the main one is consistent. It is an assumption to be found in every experience of hurt: the belief that what we are experiencing is completely separate from our mind, that the source of our dukkha lies in an objective reality that has nothing to do with us. In truth, reality, more than anything, is our own creation. If we wish to experience happiness, we first must create its causes.

It was the same understanding he'd conveyed on the first day I'd sat with him and Bodhi in the morning sun. The same understanding he'd referred to while listening to the white-clad Apostolics singing 'Jerusalema': A happy mind arises from benevolence, from an outward gaze, from the recognition that whatever 'I' am has little to do with this modest bag of bones with its attached biography. More accurately, we may regard the 'I' as unbounded consciousness.

As he spoke, I could see in Lakshmi's eyes a yearning for all he said, and in Kay's radiant expression, how utterly his words resonated. More widely, in our temple there was a dynamic dance of coherence as profound in depth as it was sweeping in breadth.

Rinpoche guided us to refuge, noting that what mattered wasn't so much sitting through a ritual but what took place in our hearts. True refuge happens when we have had enough of dukkha — our own and others' — and we commit ourselves to doing whatever it takes to end it. Today was only a formality, albeit a sacred one.

It required only a few minutes to repeat the lines of refuge after Rinpoche. To accept for ourselves those of the five vows we wished to take, only the first — to abandon killing — being a requirement. It wasn't a moment of drama so much as reflective confirmation. Or reconfirmation, in the case of people like Kay. 'If the merit from taking refuge had form, the three realms would be too small to accommodate it.'

After we had made our own silent commitment, Rinpoche asked us to recollect the Buddha, whom we had visualised poised in space a short distance in front of each one of us. He was drawing closer, said Rinpoche, and as he did, he was shrinking in size, and rotating, to face the same way as us. He wasn't losing any of his golden brilliance, but becoming a more condensed version, moving ever closer until he was the size merely of a thumbnail poised directly above our head, intensely radiant.

We visualised the Buddha of light descending into us, specifically into the crown. In that same instant, golden light burst within, flooding our physical form with a healing shower of blissful radiance. Continuing to glide gently downwards, the visualised Buddha arrived at our throats, where the light once again pervaded the whole of our being, especially our speech and capacity to communicate, with uplifting energy.

When Buddha descended to rest in our heart, the extraordinary surge of transformative light touched every aspect of mind. And because we were being guided by Rinpoche, it felt as if his mind also merged with ours, and he was beckoning us to experience reality as he did. Not only in this moment — one summer morning in Africa — but all moments, including unreservedly everything that had ever happened, all joys and woes including even the most profound miseries. But they were being experienced from a place of effortless equanimity. Could this be the 'result refuge' Kay had spoken of, where we took refuge in the Buddha nature that we already possessed? The *tathagatagarbha* that is our own primordial state?

It was a reality-widening sensation, a panoramic stepping back to sense the whole of time touched by wisdom. All darkness of the past illuminated ... from this exalted vantage there was no pain, grief, or hatred. If reality had no inherent qualities, all depended on mind's participation, and if that mind was transcendent, then everything in the past was revised too.

'Serve others!' Rinpoche always emphasized. 'Only if we give happiness can we experience it.' In such a state as this, the truth of his advice was self-evident. What I hadn't understood, it dawned on me, was that the path to enlightenment not only held the promise of a completely different future, it changed the past too. Time itself was transfigured.

'"The mind's original nature is like space",' Rinpoche ended our session together, quoting the famous Tibetan guru Tilopa.

'"It pervades and embraces all things under the sun.

Be still and stay relaxed in genuine ease,

Be quiet and let sound reverberate as an echo,

Keep your mind silent and watch the ending of all worlds".'

After the meditation session ended, there was a period of silence before our lama left. We emerged from the *gompa* and walked to the homestead. It felt as if something miraculous had happened.

~

It was a full moon only a few nights later. Leaving Kadiki in the care of Mr Nzou, I walked through the twilight to Ruwa Rock. I expected to find others there, but the granite dome of the looming boulder was deserted when I clambered to the top.

Sunsets during rainy season were much clearer with the air purged of dust. I inhaled the moist warm breeze and followed the dwindling sun where it left only the faintest, gold mist after sinking from the horizon. Hearing a movement behind, I turned to find Tinashe. As he joined me, we caught sight of Diva with Rinpoche walking in our direction.

They too came to the top, Diva explaining that Harris had phoned a short while ago to say he was needed by a friend in Dandaro Village. No one else, it seemed, would be joining us. Sitting under the darkening sky, I recalled how the last time here it felt like Rinpoche himself had determined who would be present. Was it the same tonight?

From the direction of the homestead came the sound of a small elephant trumpeting. Light and high pitched, like a beginner on a wheezy brass instrument, this was Kadiki's latest sport. Instinctively, she'd squeak when excited — it sounded quite comical. Moments later came the distinctive cry of a fish eagle, so loud it sounded only the shortest distance away.

Rinpoche chuckled in the twilight. I sat facing him, Tinashe to my left, Diva on the right.

'Africa!' he murmured with a smile.

We knew what he meant. We felt the same. The great lunar rim began looming over the horizon, moonlight flooding the landscape with magic, so that boulders gleamed and spear grass foamed in the breeze, and on the lawn, the kudus' spiral horns rippled in silver arcs as they strode. Africa is a state of being as much as a place. To be in Africa is to awaken to the senses. Africa is always tugging us away from our thoughts — *Look here! Listen now! Breathe in the aroma of this!*

'At the time of the Buddha,' said Rinpoche, 'India was the same. Vast open spaces,' he curved his arm gesturing limitless distance. 'Few people scattered across the land. Yet not separate from one another. Travelling. Trading. Coming into contact.'

As so often, Rinpoche communicated with more than words alone. India and Africa were connected in ways beyond those usually understood, not merely because of their shared vast wildernesses of flora and fauna, but in a deeper sense. Just as Harris had told me about coins from pre-Christian times unearthed near gold workings in Nyanga, of buried Indian glass treasures dating from times of antiquity — what if esoteric wisdom was also buried here?

I was humbled by how little I knew about the sacred history of this land. How Great Zimbabwe was constructed at 31 East, just like the Great Pyramid of Giza. How legends of an underground river running the length of the continent had a reality more fundamental than had ever been supposed. Was this only a coincidence? Or was there more to it, perhaps as understood through the ages by observers from afar?

If an unseen meridian ran north from here, what of the metaphorical one extending east, the one implied by Rinpoche evidenced the same symbols found in Himalayan monasteries. The spiralling ndoro or conch, as a means of embodying the divine. The subtle energy indicated by dual chevrons, and consciousness shown by two circles. More than anything, the fact that the preeminent symbol of this country, deferred to by political leaders for the last millennium, was nothing less than a symbol of enlightenment — the omniscience of the eagle arising from subtle energy and subtle mind?

What if more than moringa trees had taken root here from the slopes of the Himalayas? If ancient beliefs had also become indigenous? Beliefs like those of the East holding that reality could not be contained within the measure of a single lifetime, making sacred the animals and the lands they lived in? That medicine men, the magicians of the tribe, had power to invoke voices of the unseen and ever-present realm of spirit?

Our own refuge ceremony had been momentous, no doubt. But maybe it was not the first time that the great wheel of the Dharma had been turned in Africa. Perhaps, along with traders, gurus had visited these lands in the timeless past. Sandalled visitors who explained that the real work of this life was not worldly self-enrichment so much as the cultivation of inner qualities: patience, gratitude, ubuntu. What if the Buddha had visited this place — if not literally, then figuratively? If his feet, in ancient time, had walked upon Africa's golden veldt? If he too had breathed in the vitalizing air of this continent of light? It seemed no more improbable than Rinpoche's presence on Ruwa Rock right now.

A Scops owl hooted softly in the shimmering pearl canopy. The wind was sweet with frangipani. Rinpoche leaned forward, taking Diva's hand in his left and Tinashe's in his right. Nodding to me, he indicated that I should also take their hands, so that we formed a circle with the ever-still Tinashe on one side and Diva's vortex of verve on the other. Yin and yang.

'You are the ones to take our work forward,' he said, in that instant explaining why we were here. 'There are many beings to be helped. Much work to be done.'

'Please don't say you're leaving, Rinpoche!' Diva protested. 'You're our guru! Our Spiritual Director!'

'I am not abandoning you,' he replied. 'It is my privilege to serve. But there are others who need me.' He looked towards me. I was the one who, more than anyone, overheard his many phone conversations each day. 'I will return. In the meantime, there are things you can do without me.'

What he said was true. Whether personally or on behalf of the Ruwa Buddhist Society, I had the inescapable feeling that the refuge ceremony was only the beginning of a much wider story. Tinashe had already told me that Zimbabwe was the spiritual heart of the world. What secrets might flow when he reconnected with his n'anga grandfather? Could there be significant revelations to come? As for Diva, I had only recently begun to understand how deep her connection truly was to the trees and their untold stories.

Tinashe, Diva, and I exchanged sombre expressions. The two of them were still clinging to Rinpoche's hands for dear life. For my own part, I had been wondering when

Rinpoche would make this announcement. He couldn't stay with us forever.

'We will remain in touch,' he assured us, still holding hands. Glancing behind where we were sitting, he raised his chin with a smile. 'I will be keeping an eye on you all the time with the help of my special representative.'

We turned, following his gaze to where he took in the long straight branch of the umbrella tree. Bodhi was sprawled along it. During our time on the rock she had climbed to her special vantage place, once again in complete silence.

I looked back. 'Who will look after her when you're away?' I asked.

From behind came a light thud. Diva and Tinashe dropped my hands quickly. Moments later I felt the firm but supple weight of a muscular body pressing against my right shoulder. I wasn't going to turn. I didn't dare. Her head was so close that the tips of her whiskers were brushing my cheek.

Often at sunset I climb Ruwa Rock and have the whole country to myself. 'From the vast spaciousness of mind,' Rinpoche had told us at this extraordinary place, 'all arises.' Here I recall Kadiki's rapturous connection. Curious about the mole on my leg from her very first day, she discovered Lakshmi's one afternoon when we were sitting together, both in shorts. She'd broken into a jig of such excitement, moving the tip of her trunk from one knee to the other, that Lakshmi and I burst out laughing, my sister's eyes ablaze with joy. Kadiki wrapped her trunk about both our heads — something she'd never done — drawing our faces to her own. There was no mistaking the recognition in her gesture. The unutterable understanding of kinship.

Here I feel closer to Rinpoche, the Africa Buddha, better able to let go of life's passing cavalcade. How easy he makes it to invoke a state of heart embodying his wisdom! One that is free from needs and constraints, free from thought itself.

Occasionally I am joined on my twilight vigils by Harris, Tinashe, or Mr Nzou. Mostly I sit by myself — but never alone. Thor and Tiki are always nearby. Never far away either is the presence of unknown predecessors, on this same rock since the beginning of time, awed to silence by this same twilight vista. And I have come to revel in watching the sun's final salutation as it slips beneath the horizon, the amber-streaked sky softening and deepening moment by passing moment, all the while feeling the warm breath on my neck of Rinpoche's watchful special representative.

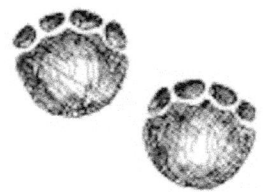

About the Author

DAVID MICHIE was born and raised in Zimbabwe by Scottish parents who returned to their homeland in 1983.

After living in London for ten years, he and his Australian wife moved to Perth. There he met his Dharma teachers as well as a sumptuous Himalayan who became the muse for the Dalai Lama's Cat.

Since 2015 he has been leading groups home on Mindful Safaris at Victoria Falls, combining wildlife viewing and meditation sessions. He regularly shares stories and articles at:

https://davidmichie.substack.com

Book Club Discussion Points

1. What particular passages, themes, or characters engaged you in a way that was enjoyably unusual?

2. We see Zimbabwe/Africa through the eyes of different people: Bruno experiences it as a space where he can breathe, a "continent of light". For Tinashe it is a place of grinding poverty and hardship. Rob feels profoundly drawn to the land, the animals, and the sense of ubuntu — "I am because we are". How do these contrasting perspectives chime with your own perceptions of Zimbabwe/Africa?

3. Bruno refers directly to the "Dark Continent", suggesting that the real darkness was to be found in hearts of those who wished to enslave and hunt for trophies. Is this perspective one that resonates with you?

4. Rob finds himself at a crossroads in his life and makes a decision that, only a short time before, he wouldn't have believed possible. Have you ever been in a similar situation? What were the consequences of the choice you made?

5. Some of the many ancient connections between southern Africa, India, and the Arab world are explored,

including animals and plants, symbols and ideas. Were you surprised or particularly struck by any of these parallels?

6. What do you think of the idea of animal totems? Which animal would you choose as your own personal totem and why?

7. One of the main themes is the importance of the guru. From Kay, we hear how the guru is the foundation of all realisations. From Pema, that he is our companion of the heart, someone whose example we learn to imitate by spending time in his presence. Mugdha Kumar talks about guru-yoga being more about us than the guru — it is seeking to embody inspiring qualities for ourselves. Do any of these ideas seem helpful to you? Do they pattern ideas you are familiar with? How does a Western conditioning help or hinder such a relationship?

8. Rob wishes he was close to his sister, Kate, the way he sees in other families but that 'an invisible ocean' lies between them. How typical are sibling relationships like this? Given shared nature and nurture, why may siblings sometimes simply not 'click'?

9. In Chapter 10 the subject of politics comes up. Rinpoche stresses the importance of guarding one's own state of mind and heart, and the dangers of allowing negativity and anger to become ingrained. How valid does this view seem to you? Is it possible to take effective action against political opponents without being motivated by anger?

10. Rinpoche explains that the way we perceive reality is affected by our state of mind and heart, and that the optimal state arises from giving happiness to others. Do you know people for whom this explanation

seems true? How does it compare with other recipes for happiness?

11.   Rob finds that being in Africa makes it easier to live in the present moment. Why is this, and might it be possible to replicate mindfulness cues elsewhere?

12.   In the last chapter, during the refuge ceremony, Rob catches a glimpse of his 'Buddha nature' — a sense of lucid, panoramic consciousness. This contrasts with our normal sense of a physical self with certain attributes and a biography. How does Buddha nature contrast with other models of our self, and why might it offer an effective way to help navigate life?

May all beings have happiness
and the true causes of happiness.

May all beings be free from suffering
and the true causes of suffering.

May all beings never be parted
from the happiness that is beyond suffering.

May all beings abide in peace and equanimity,
their minds free from
attachment, aversion and ignorance.

Watch a short video from the author about this book:
https://davidmichie.substack.com/p/the-good-karma-refuge-for-elephants